A THOUSAND CUTS

A Max Starkey Thriller

GREGORY POIRIER

DIVERSION
BOOKS

For My Boys

Diversion Books
A division of Diversion Publishing Corp.
www.diversionbooks.com

For more information, email info@diversionbooks.com

First Diversion Books Edition: April 2026
Trade Paperback ISBN: 9798895150900
e-ISBN: 9798895150917

Design by Westchester Publishing Services
Cover design by Jonathan Sainsbury // 6x9 design

Printed in the United States of America
1 3 5 7 9 10 8 6 4 2

Diversion books are available at special discounts for bulk purchases in the US by corporations, institutions, and other organizations. For more information, please contact admin@diversionbooks.com.

PROLOGUE

SEVEN YEARS AGO

THE RAID

The villa was on fire, the woman was nowhere to be seen, and Max was bleeding profusely from the head. The bullet had only grazed his skull, he knew; otherwise, he'd be dead, but even shallow head wounds bleed. He could barely see through the smoke and the blood running into his eyes, but he could hear gunshots and shouting all around him. He pulled his shirt up over his mouth and nose and slid across the cool marble floor on his belly to stay below the smoke, while he tried to figure out where it all went to shit. They had received a coded message sending them to Laos, and the codes were the authentic ones the agency used to send them on actions, down to his individual operative ID. But clearly this raid was not officially sanctioned, and it had gone all to hell the moment they breached the house. They were outnumbered twenty to one, and some of the men trying to kill them were American soldiers.

He found the stairs and slipped down one at a time, his .45-caliber pistol ready in his hand. Halfway down he heard her calling his name.

"Kelly!"

"Here," she called out, "Max! I'm here!"

"Keep talking!"

He made his way toward her voice, staying low, and he saw her boots first, a comforting, familiar sight. She always wore high-end RAT (rugged all-terrain) boots, when they went on an op. He followed the boots until he had her in his arms. He wanted to hold her, to tell her how relieved he was to find her, but there was no time. They helped each other move in the general direction where they figured the door should be.

"I checked and double-checked everything," he said, "This seemed like a legit op." The mission had been simple: find and exfiltrate an American spy working in General Vong's household. But it had been a setup, and by coming to retrieve the spy, they had exposed him. Now he was dead, and they were doing whatever they could not to join him.

"I see the door!" Kelly said, coughing.

She was struggling, but Max kept her on her feet and moving toward the rectangle of light barely visible through the haze.

"Where's Moss?"

She just shook her head. "Killed maybe. We got separated too."

As he pulled her through the door, Kelly was sagging in his arms. They both yanked their shirts down from over their faces and gulped the sweet oxygen, still coughing. Gunfire erupted, and bullets rained down around them as Max and Kelly scrambled for cover. He was splashed with blood as Kelly was hit. Blazing fire behind them, an angry army in front of them, they were in hell. Kelly asked Max two questions as he dragged her to safety:

"Who sent us here?"

And "Are we traitors now?"

CHAPTER ONE

NOW

He'd rather stab himself in the eye than go back to Bangkok. Max Starkey had loved Southeast Asia once, but when he recalled the physical torture he had endured there, he swore the long-healed scars on his back throbbed. He didn't think about the other kind of pain he suffered there. He stuffed that down into the dark places that give men ulcers. Unfortunately, despite his vow not to return, Thailand is where Rocket's bag of cash had ended up, so here he was crossing the Pacific in a first-class seat Rocket had paid for. Max knew approximately how much money was supposedly in that bag, and the amount Rocket was laying out to provide the flight, the hotel room, and the large per diem on top of his fee hardly seemed worth it. He figured the job was more about finding the person who took the bag than the money itself. That meant violence was expected of him, and, as usual, he would do his best to avoid it.

Max Starkey was capable of violence and had relied on it often enough, but only when every other option was exhausted. The criminals he was working with these days all thought they were tough guys, but most of them had never been in a real firefight or had to use a blade in a life-or-death situation. Max gave them the courtesy of pretending he thought they were hard.

He glanced across the aisle at a businessman one row ahead of him reading an article on his tablet about the wave of layoffs at the intelligence services. The CIA, the NSA, and even the FBI were undergoing massive firings. The administration called it a budgetary adjustment, but everyone knew it was a purge, and anyone not loyal to the current administration was on their way out. Hundreds of good men and women who had risked their lives for their country were training to become baristas. Max had avoided all that, leaving the agency voluntarily shortly after the disastrous raid at General Vong's villa in Laos. Seven years on, he was working as a recovery man, which is exactly what it sounds like. Someone stole something from you—the cash from your safe, or your share of the take from a robbery, or even a sentimental keepsake—you hired Max, and he'd get it back for you, for a percentage or a pre-negotiated fee. Forget that old saying; crime paid pretty damn well for Max. Other people's crimes, anyway.

It was an absurd and mostly illegal way to make a living, but he was taking things back from other criminals, so no civilians were involved, and his skill set was pretty useless in the real world. He could sympathize with the agents and officers being cut loose now because, short of making lattes, he was satisfied that he had tried all the legitimate jobs available to a then twenty-eight-year-old man who left the Company midcareer.

His first civilian gig was as a driver-slash-bodyguard for a Fortune 500 CEO. The man had serious addiction issues, not to any one thing, just addiction in general. Max was there to drive him, as discreetly as possible, to casinos, brothels, drug deals, and bars. Two weeks in he was expected to clean vomit out of the back seat of the Escalade. Max tossed the CEO his keys and walked off, leaving him on the shoulder of the 60 Freeway to fend for himself. His bodyguard days were over before they began.

Next, he tried corporate risk assessment, a career in which a lot of ex-Company guys thrive. Max walked in his first day, sat down at his desk, and looked at graphs and spreadsheets for five minutes, then got up and walked out. He forgot to drop his laminated key card at the front desk and had to mail it back a few days later from a post office in Oaxaca, Mexico, where he had gone to clear his head with a guided ayahuasca journey, which didn't clear up much.

His last attempt at a straight job was running security at a hotel in Laguna Beach. It was gaudy and mostly pink, popular with both newlyweds and the newly divorced. That quirk made him think of when he was a little kid, before his dad took off, and on the rare occasions that Max Sr. wasn't on a long-haul run he'd day drink and watch *The Dating Game*, *The Newlywed Game*, and *Divorce Court*, in that order. "That sums the whole thing up, right there, Maxie," the old man would say every time, without variation. Max was let go from the hotel security job for not being personable enough. After a career in the shadows, he wasn't much of a schmoozer.

He was desperate and about to take a job as a bouncer at a strip club when an old friend asked him to locate and retrieve his runaway teenage daughter. Max found her quickly and just in time, catching up to her as she was about to shoot her first porn scene. She tried to act defiant, but she was scared and in over her head, and he could tell she secretly enjoyed it when Max sent the producer, the director, and the two guys playing the pizza man and the plumber to the hospital. When she told him why she had run away from home, Max put his old friend in the hospital too. The kid went into the system, and Max figured, wrongly, that she was better off.

It turned out her father was loosely connected to a network of low-life criminals, which could have been trouble, except there are some things even assholes won't condone. That's how he met Rocket, who said, "If you can find that sick prick's kid, I bet you can find this suitcase that went missing." That was six years and twenty jobs ago.

In a lot of ways, it was the flip side of his old job. In the CIA, he covered money trails, hid gun shipments, and helped people disappear. Now, instead of setting those things up, he unraveled them. He liked the work, and to be honest, the people fascinated him. They were the unapologetic fringe—thieves, dealers, hookers, hired killers, card sharks, con men, and pimps. The cast of characters was different, but the greed was the same.

He had an exit plan and figured he was about halfway to what he would need to go to an island somewhere, open a bar, and find a woman to share his early retirement with. He was only thirty-five; he could still start a family and be a dad, which he had never wanted until a few years ago, but now thought about every day. He had hoped to have it with Kelly, but if you want to make God laugh, tell him your plans.

The tall, stunning Black woman sitting next to Max finally checkmated him on the magnetic chessboard on her tray table after a long battle between her rooks and his queen in which she had somehow tricked him into exposing his king and ordered a third glass of champagne to celebrate her victory. Her name was Jules, short for Julie or Julia, he supposed.

"Take a break after this," he said. "Three glasses is enough."

She gave him an amused glance. "You counting my drinks?"

"Liquor hits harder at altitude is all. I don't want to have to carry you off the plane."

She laughed and said, "Okay, boss." The flight attendant handed her the glass, and she raised it in salute before drinking. Max liked her a lot, and thought he ought to tell her, so he did.

"Is that so?"

"You're good company. Friendly, funny. Easy on the eyes. Not to mention one hell of a chess player."

"No kidding, I beat you more than half the time up at the cabin."

"I wasn't keeping track."

"That's 'cause you were losing."

He smiled but didn't laugh. She sipped her champagne, then said, "I like you too."

From what he could tell, she was the real deal, what his mother back in Texas would have called a blue ribbon. She was the kind of woman he could fall in love with, have that bar and those kids with, except for how they met; she had been provided by Rocket too.

Max had spent the last six weeks hiding out in a cabin in Big Bear, lying low after the last job, which had gone a little bit sideways.

Knowing he was alone at the cabin, Rocket had sent Jules up to him for "companionship." She had been more than a little surprised when that was all he wanted. Max had only three rules in life: never kill anyone that wouldn't kill you first, never keep the money unless you'd earned it, and never take a woman to bed who didn't have a say in the matter. He'd broken the first two more than once, but never the last one. She was gorgeous and on the clock. He hadn't touched her.

Four rules, he supposed, if you include *stay the hell out of Southeast Asia*, because for Max, anything east of India would always be Kelly. He saw the irony—big tough Max Starkey, avoiding an entire part of the world because of a heartbreak. But Kelly Riggs didn't break his heart that day in Chiang Mai—she ripped it out of his chest and stomped it into pulp. Now she was married to his old agency rival, Derek Moss, and living somewhere in the region.

The captain announced their final approach, and Jules took that as a cue to start painting her toenails yellow. She did a remarkably good job considering the turbulence and the champagne. She had come to him with an expensive mani-pedi, but she had been stuck at the cabin with him for weeks, so he supposed it was his fault she had to do it herself this time. The contrast between the bright yellow polish and her coal-black skin was definitely working. Looking at her feet, he guessed her age to be right around thirty. She had told him twenty-four when she first arrived, but they both knew that was bullshit. They're all twenty-four, unless they are actually twenty-four, in which case they're nineteen.

Even though they hadn't gone to bed, six weeks alone together in a small cabin had sparked something between them. Max didn't know what it was yet, but he'd like the chance to find out. He had brought her with him when Rocket called him down the mountain for this assignment, and when Max said he'd like to bring her along to Bangkok, Rocket had surprised them both by saying yes.

CHAPTER TWO

The meeting took place in Rocket's opulent office in a deceptively run-down warehouse half a mile east of downtown Los Angeles, where they were greeted by Midge, Rocket's eighty-year-old receptionist, who was also his mother.

"I'll need you to check your hardware, hon."

"I know the drill, Midge," he said, opening his coat to show her. "I'm not packing."

"How about you, sweetheart?"

Jules surprised him by pulling a Luger .22 out of her clothing somewhere and checking it with Midge, who quickly and expertly unloaded it. Max had no idea she had been armed all this time, and she seemed pleased to have surprised him.

Once buzzed in, they found Rocket behind his big mahogany desk wearing his trademark gold-mirrored sunglasses and leering grin that always made Max wonder if there was a girl under the desk. Rocket was the kind of guy who found his style in his twenties and never updated it over the next forty years. His hair was slicked back in half a mullet, and he wore a pastel-blue T-shirt under a white cotton sport coat. The requisite giant ape-man stood in the corner, also unarmed. Rocket liked being the only person in the room with firepower.

"Good to see you, Max," Rocket said. "How'd that cabin work out?"

"It was fine."

With a nod at Jules, he asked, "And the company?"

"Five stars."

Rocket nodded. Then, with a little more gravitas, "What happened in Sausalito?"

Max took a beat. He knew he'd have to tell the tale, but he wanted to frame it so he didn't come off sounding incompetent or unprepared. He said, "First off, the family came back two days early, which meant more bodyguards. I knew from my recon that the money Perkins stole was in the bedroom safe, so I waited until he and the wife were in the shower, fooling around. Turns out he had a .44 Magnum in there, and he came out blasting."

"Wait," Rocket said. "He had a gun with him in the shower whilst banging his old lady?"

Max raised an eyebrow. "Whilst?"

"It means while he was."

"I know what it means."

"I'm trying to build my vocabulary. A new word every day."

"Good idea." Max wasn't pandering; he wished more people would take the same initiative.

He continued, "The Magnum was too much gun for him; he kept knocking himself backward with the recoil. Together with the wet floor, his feet came out from under him. Last thing I saw was his scrotum as he flipped over backward, cannon still blasting. The dumb bastard almost shot his wife in the face."

Rocket laughed. "The great scrotum caper. Priceless."

It was a mental image Max had been trying to shake without much success. "The guards came running, of course. I had to take out a couple of kneecaps, but there were no fatalities."

"Good," Rocket said. "So, this next thing. One of my runners got hit, lost the weekend bag. It's a simple job; I know exactly who took it and exactly where he went."

"How much was in the bag?" Max asked.

"A little over sixty K. Under your percentage threshold, so I'll pay your day rate."

"Who took it?"

"That little fuckhead they call Rabbit."

Max nodded. He knew the man. "Rodney O'Hare. Where'd he go?"

"Bangkok."

So that's how they'd get him back there. Rocket knew he had a no-Asia policy, and he stared at him with that ugly grin, daring Max to object. Max knew better and nodded.

"Well, don't stand there procrastinating," Rocket said. "Get to ambulating." Maybe the vocabulary building wasn't such a good idea after all.

Now, as the plane descended over Thailand, Max found himself hypnotized by the strokes of Jules's toenail polish brush. As his mind drifted, he wondered about her story before she knocked on his cabin door in Big Bear. Was her journey tragic—or empowering? He doubted she had ever been trafficked; her energy was too positive, and it wasn't an act. But he had learned from his mother at a young age that no child dreams of growing up to be a prostitute. Maybe Jules was just sex-positive and chose sex work. Maybe she once had money or drug problems, or a bad old man like that kid he saved. He hoped to get her story at some point.

But he had better hurry, because he was fairly certain that after he found Rocket's money, she was there to kill him.

CHAPTER THREE

As the wave approached, Kelly Riggs tightened her legs around her husband's back. Her fingers searched out the scarred-over bullet holes on his shoulder, the tangible echoes of violence that always pushed her over the top. She tried not to think about the state of her marriage as her orgasm hit; this was the one part of their relationship that still worked. She let herself get lost in the crescendo, then felt him let loose inside her as she came down the other side.

She hid her irritation as he kissed her on the forehead and rolled off her. When they first married, there was genuine passion. Six years on, he was still diligent about making sure she got off first, but it had begun to feel like something he had to get out of the way so he could finish. Shave, brush your teeth, help Kelly climax, clean your pipes. Safe to say, the romance was dead.

She watched him lumber off to the bathroom. Some men soften as they age, while others solidify into oak. Derek Moss was the latter. At forty-two, he wasn't what you would call conventionally handsome; in fact, if you looked too closely, he could be described as ugly. He was built like a fireplug, and his square face was marred by a scar that ran from his right ear to his chin. But he had a raw, animal magnetism and moved through the world like he was the handsomest man on earth. He was strong and confident and had his own gravity, attracting women who shouldn't have given him a second look. Including, she supposed, Kelly herself. His eyes were dusty gray, and she couldn't remember the last time they had really looked at her. He was also quick to anger and as lethal as a krait. Occasionally she thought about leaving him, but it was pointless. He'd shoot her before she reached the gate.

Kelly got out of bed and stood in the open window, nude, looking out over the compound. The thick jungle humidity weighed on her skin like a blanket. She knew that some of the young soldiers patrolling the fence line would see her if they looked up at the palace window, but she didn't mind. She'd been working out for two hours, twice a day; someone should appreciate her hard work.

She opened a bottle of water, sat on the windowsill, and drank half of it in one draft. She rolled the cool bottle across her forehead, then her chest, and looked across the courtyard at the northern wing of the palace, to the little balcony where President Vinthu used to make his speeches. He hadn't been out on that balcony in weeks, maybe months. Kudzu vines were claiming it, tendrils slipping through the cracks.

Eight years ago, she and Max Starkey had toppled the previous regime and placed Vinthu in power. He proceeded to raid the treasury, siphon off foreign aid, and murder his opposition by the thousands. Now here she was, with Derek, scheming to get him out of the country and into exile before the coup that was coming any day. The only difference was, back then she worked for the United States government. Now she was a mercenary, and the pay was much better.

She watched a brown shrike—which locals called the butcherbird—take off from the presidential balcony and idly wondered how many miles she had flown in her own life. She once saw a *NOVA* episode about an Arctic tern believed to have flown over three million miles, which was a lot even by Arctic tern standards. Kelly's father flew Bell Hueys in Vietnam, then ran a helicopter sightseeing charter on Kauai until he died of cancer at fifty. Her mother was a commercial pilot, mostly on long-haul flights between Honolulu and Tokyo. Kelly started flying when she was eight and definitely had that Arctic tern beat, but she had no idea by how much.

She wished she could fly away with the butcherbird. Her life with Derek was a prison, but she knew it was a prison that she herself had built, brick by brick. She had made every decision that had led her here, sitting in this window in the largest dwelling in the smallest country in Southeast Asia, married to a man she had never loved, and helping an unrepentant perpetrator of genocide escape with his money.

In spite of everything that happened between them, Max had asked her to return to the States with him. She hadn't been ready to give up her life in the agency, not even for love. And it had been love; she knew it now only because it was something she had never felt previously or since. But she liked the thrill of being at the center of these things, getting shit done, and kicking ass every once in a while. At least, that's the story she told herself then. After Max left, it became empty without him, which she realized just when it was too late. Maybe marrying Derek was an attempt to recapture the thrill. If so, it hadn't worked.

A soldier had stopped at the gate and was staring up at her, not even trying to be subtle. Maybe he was trying to decide if she was Suryakan herself. She wasn't. She was half Hawaiian, a quarter Chinese, and a quarter Irish, with just a dash of Japanese, which her grandmother explained by telling her that back in their family tree "someone climbed in a window somewhere." Kelly arched her back, stretching, pretending not to notice him there.

Derek came in from the bathroom wrapped in a towel and saw her preening naked in the window. He said, "Really?" She shrugged and watched him as he dressed.

"What harm does it do?"

"You might incite them to storm the palace."

"Sure, my tits start the revolution."

He laughed.

"Anyway, you'll protect me if they do."

"Yeah, I don't think so."

"Are you saying you wouldn't?"

He glanced at her. "No, dear wife, I'm saying I wouldn't need to. You could take any six of these mutts in hand-to-hand combat."

"Aw, you sure know how to sweet-talk a girl."

She meant it. No matter what else had faded in their marriage, he could still see her. Really see her. A year after Max left the agency and their relationship ended, she had been paired with Derek on a mission in South America and had fallen for him hard. It wasn't love exactly; more like an intense infatuation and almost palpable sexual attraction that she had acted on once before, much sooner than she should have. But she mistook it for love and married him six weeks later, unaware of the long history of animosity between him and Max. Over the years she wondered if he had married her out of some kind of perverted revenge plot, but he swore to her that it never entered his mind. Sometimes she believed him.

He was fully dressed and fumbling with his tie. She walked over and he turned to face her so she could do it for him. He didn't even look down at her bronze nakedness as she made the loops. As she tightened it against his collar, she looked up and saw him gazing into her eyes—a deep, penetrating stare. It almost made her stumble backward.

"What?" she asked.

He took a beat before he answered. "Max's plane is an hour out of Suvarnabhumi," he said. "You should get dressed."

CHAPTER FOUR

Giuliana Abara should have painted her toenails earlier in the flight to give them time to dry. Then she wouldn't have to waddle through the airport like a duck, trying to keep her toes from touching as she followed Max Starkey to baggage claim in rubber flip-flops. People were staring, but hell, people were always staring. She was thirty-two, five-foot-ten, with skin as dark as onyx and icy blue eyes. Men had started eyeballing her when she was eleven, and women shortly after. Only difference was, the men wanted to fuck her and the women wanted to be her.

Sticking out like she did, she was an unlikely candidate for undercover work. With her two degrees—criminal justice and psychology—she assumed her time at the FBI would be spent in financial investigation or some other area out of the public eye. For the first few years, she moved around a little bit, including a stint in cybercrimes, but most of her career was spent doing deep background for other agents' cases. She was a natural at research, and the field operatives came to rely on her.

She settled into a routine, unexciting life that led to a series of merit promotions. With her advancement within the bureau, she was able to put a down payment on a town house in Fairfax County. The truth was that she could have done it without the job since she came from serious money. Her father was a Chicago ward boss, and her mother had been a well-known supermodel in the 1980s. Her dad said they were a perfect match; he came up breaking legs, and she came up breaking hearts. Together they broke the bank.

Giuliana inevitably grew bored pulling research and lobbied her superiors to put her in the field. They told her not to hold her breath, that she had been behind a desk for a long time and making the transition now would be challenging. But she was determined and kept at it, telling them that she would accept any field assignment, no matter how crappy.

Two months later, they called her bluff.

She had to sign a nondisclosure agreement before she went into the meeting, which took place in a suite at the Waldorf Astoria on Pennsylvania Avenue, with a stern, older Black woman who didn't offer her name. She asked Giuliana, "Why did you join the FBI?"

"To serve and protect the people and ideals of the United States of America."

"Blah blah bullshit," the woman said, to Giuliana's surprise. "Real answer."

Giuliana hesitated, then said, "I was horribly bullied and teased as a child. I cried myself to sleep most nights. I made a vow then to protect those who couldn't stand up for themselves, so it was either law enforcement or hope I got bit by a radioactive spider."

"What were you teased about?"

"I'd rather not get into that."

"That's okay. I have a pretty good idea." She took a breath. "How did you survive it? The bullying."

"Believe it or not, my parents."

"Why wouldn't I believe it?" the woman asked.

"Because of their Olympic-level self-absorption. But they did notice, and they came to my rescue. My dad enrolled me in martial arts and self-defense classes to build my confidence and brought me along to Sloppy Joe's boxing gym, where he worked out. Some of the older men there took me under their wing, taught me how to work the heavy bag."

"And your mother?"

"She taught me self-defense of a different kind. We spent hours at her makeup table, and in salons and spas. Mom taught me how to optimize my looks, but more importantly how to care for and nurture my skin, which she called my special gift."

The woman nodded. "She taught you to love the blackness you had spent years being ashamed of."

"What the hell kind of interview is this?" She hadn't meant to say it; it just popped out.

The woman smiled. "We'll get there, I promise. Go on, please, about your mother."

"At the same time, she took me on a deep dive into my heritage, tracing back where each side of my family had come from and how they got to America. Those two stories were, of course, heartbreakingly similar. My mother's ancestors were stolen from what is now Nigeria, my father's from Ghana. It actually helped a lot."

"For the first time, you had a context for your existence."

Giuliana nodded. "I had footing."

The older woman continued, "Your father was powerful, your mother was famous. Why didn't that protect you from bullying by the other Black kids?"

Giuliana protested. "I never said it was the other Black kids."

"No, you didn't." The woman waited. Giuliana didn't know exactly what was happening, but she knew the woman was after something, so she decided to tell the truth.

"I was the darkest child in any of my classes. In all of St. Benedict, really, including my sister and two brothers. In fifth grade, during a lesson on the Civil War, the teacher discussed how the lighter-skinned slaves had often worked in the house while the darker-skinned slaves worked the fields."

"I bet she left out the part about the lights being the master's own children, produced by the violent rape of their mothers."

"Well, yes, obviously. After that day, the other Black kids teased me, calling me all sorts of horrible names. Charcoal was the one that stuck. At the same time, my blue eyes led to accusations that I was half white, that my real dad was the blue-eyed mailman or some other nonsense. The fact that the two reasons they picked on me, my dark skin and my secret whiteness, would seem to cancel each other out never occurred to them."

"They were kids," the woman said. "Kids are assholes. Why do you think you were never assigned to the field?"

"I tend to stand out in a crowd."

"Suppose I told you there was a way to work undercover where your looks would be an asset, not a hindrance. How deep would you be willing to go in answering my questions?"

Giuliana took a moment before replying.

"Try me."

"How old were you when you lost your virginity?"

"Okay, what the actual fuck?" Giuliana blurted out. "This is really weird. And intrusive."

"The door isn't locked, you can walk out any time."

She almost did. But she had lobbied her bosses for months to get her shot at moving to the field, and if she walked out now, she might not get another. She told herself, it's just an interview, might as well play it out.

"Twenty-one. Junior year of college. I held my card a long time."

"On your intake form for this interview, you said you've never once been in a serious relationship. Why is that?"

"It's the same old shit, isn't it? Brothers will date dark, but they're only gonna marry girls lighter than them. I had one jackass actually say to me, 'I like you, but I want light kids.'"

"His loss. What about white men?"

"They always turn out to be tourists, checking that box."

"And fetishists." A statement, not a question.

Giuliana nodded. "So to hell with men, I focus on my career."

"And on the apps."

"The apps?"

"You swipe right at least twice a week."

Giuliana felt warm, the blood rising to her neck. "You calling me a 3-0-4?"

"Not at all, I don't slut shame. If the apps had been available when I was coming up, I would have used them too. Get your needs met, no drama, and it doesn't interfere with work."

"But you track my app activity?"

"We do."

"Jesus. Is that legal?"

The woman shrugged. Over the next hour she asked Giuliana a series of increasingly personal questions about her sex life and her attitudes about the physical act itself. She answered them truthfully, in great detail, and it gradually dawned on her what this interview was about.

"You're recruiting me for honey-trapping."

"We prefer to say, engaging subjects in intimate relationships for the purpose of intelligence gathering. But yes."

"Why me?"

"You're intelligent, strong, beautiful, and with no romantic attachments, that's key. Most of all you're sexually confident, in a healthy way. The fact is your life won't change all that much, except that we will be doing the swiping right for you."

She wanted to protest, but the woman was right. She was the perfect candidate.

She had spent months working her way into Rocket's inner circle. Her assignment was Rocket himself, the idea of which turned her stomach, but for love of country. There had been a couple of dalliances along the way as she infiltrated his ecosystem, but nothing she couldn't handle. When Rocket ordered her to go up to Big Bear and keep Max Starkey company, she initially saw it as a setback but decided to work the opportunity. Starkey was close to Rocket and could get her closer.

When she arrived at the cabin and realized he had no intention of bedding her, she panicked, worried that he somehow knew she was FBI, and that was why he wouldn't cross the line. She realized soon enough that he was just a guy with no interest in sleeping with a woman who had been ordered to fuck him.

If he only knew.

Now, somehow, she had wound up in Thailand. As they waited for their luggage to spill onto the carousel, Giuliana looked Starkey over. There was no denying that she had grown fond of him over the last few weeks, just as there was no denying he had walked a hard path. His muscular body was a road map of scars, burn marks, and bullet holes, and what she was almost certain were healed whip slashes on his back. He had no tan; the man was ghostly pale, which gave the illusion that his large muscles were sculpted out of marble. If they ever did wind up in bed together, they'd look like the yin-yang symbol.

Starkey was a criminal, but he was also funny, intelligent, and objectively handsome. The only odd thing was that he never laughed. He'd crack a smile, but she had never seen him break out into honest-to-God laughter, even when she knew he thought something was funny. Also, movies were her passion, but he had hardly seen any, so that was one thing they couldn't share. Once she quoted *Caddyshack*, imitating Bill Murray's voice, and he looked at her like she was having a stroke.

He was three years older than she was, thirty-five, and intuitive. She was certain that he knew she wasn't what she pretended to be, although she was confident he hadn't figured out who she really was, mainly because she was still breathing. He made her laugh, and he made her horny. There was something of the wounded little boy about him too. He'd been hurt, but she knew he would never share how, or by whom.

Fuck me, she thought, as she watched him pull her pink Louboutin suitcase from the carousel. *Fond hell, I'm half falling for this asshole.*

CHAPTER FIVE

Max was expecting a nicer hotel. Something near the river, maybe, not this dive smack in the middle of the Patpong red-light district. To reach the place, they had to walk from the train down the main drag, a garish man-made canyon of neon signs advertising brothels with names like King's Castle and Super Pussy, with Thai girls in short skirts ignoring him and eyeballing Jules as if she might be some kind of threat, having whole conversations about the two of them with looks and subtle gestures. Max knew the jealous desperation in their eyes well, and it made him both sad and oddly homesick.

He didn't have luggage, but there was no elevator, so he and Jules had to carry her bags upstairs. As they climbed, she said, "Pretty sure most of these rooms are renting by the hour."

"Yeah," he answered. "I wasn't expecting the Four Seasons, but Rocket isn't usually this cheap."

When they located their room she said, "It's near the ice machine anyway."

"I strongly recommend you do not touch the ice."

He unlocked the door and pushed it open. When they stepped in, they were nearly blinded by the neon Super Pussy sign, which was right outside the window, and the room itself was even seedier than the hallway. It turned out not to matter, though, because they wouldn't be there long. Rodney O'Hare, aka the Rabbit, the man he was sent here to find, was sitting in a chair in the corner by the window.

"Well, that was easy."

"Hey there, Max."

They had come straight from the airport, so Max hadn't picked up a gun yet. He had intended to stop by Iron Sam's on the way, but Jules insisted they check in first so that she could take a shower. For a moment when he found O'Hare there, he thought maybe she was in on the setup, but she looked just as surprised as he was. He hoped O'Hare didn't have a gun either, because he'd rather not die in this crappy hotel room. He was also irritated to realize that his dominant fear was that Rabbit might kill Jules.

"I'm sorry about this," Rabbit said. "I had no choice."

Max looked the man over while he considered his next move. Rabbit fit his nickname. He was forty or so, short, wiry, and jumpy, with big ears, making him look a little like a cartoon character. Max outweighed him by fifty pounds of muscle, but he knew Rabbit had at least three bodies on him. Best to keep him talking, so Max asked, "Where is Rocket's bag?"

"There is no bag, Max. There never was a bag."

Max took a beat. No bag meant one of two things: Either Rabbit was lying in an attempt to keep the money, or this trip was about something else entirely. Thinking back on the cost of the flight and how readily Rocket agreed to let him bring Jules along, he knew it was the latter. Rocket wasn't expecting him to make his flight home.

He noticed Jules inching closer to a heavy lamp on the dresser, seeking a weapon.

"Don't," he said. "I've got this." She nodded and stayed put. "Quit fucking around, Rabbit, and tell me where the money is."

"I'm telling you, Max, there's no bag of money."

"You're saying Rocket sent me over here for a paid vacation?"

Rabbit shook his head. "I'm telling you that he and I were paid to get you here. I don't know what he got, but my end was twenty grand, so it had to be a pile. That's it. The whole thing was a play, to get you to Bangkok."

"Rocket wouldn't pay you more than twenty percent, so if you're telling the truth, then his end had to be at least a brick."

"That's how I figured it too."

"Who the hell would pay a hundred grand to get me to Bangkok?"

Rabbit shook his head. "I have no idea. But they'll be here any minute." Max looked to Jules. "What do you think?"

"Same as you, I assume," she answered. "We should go down the fire escape right now, but I'm also curious enough to stick around."

Rabbit chimed in, "You really think this dump has a fire escape?"

She ignored him. "I'm sorry we didn't stop for that gun."

"Me too," Max answered. "Grab some glasses."

There was an unopened bottle of bourbon on the dresser, and while she went to the bathroom for glasses, he inspected the seal for tampering. Rabbit noticed, and offered, "I didn't bring you all this way to poison you. That would be a monumental waste of time and energy."

Jules came back with some paper cups. "Sorry, these were all I could find." Max poured two fingers each into three cups. Jules took two, handed one to Rabbit, and they all drank.

"That's one, boss." Max tried to smile at her mild jest, but his mind was on the door. He stood over Rabbit, to emphasize his size advantage. "When the knock comes, you answer."

"Why?"

"If bullets fly, you're catching them."

"Right. How about another drink?"

Max poured three more and they all sipped this time. The atmosphere in the room was tense. When the knock came, Max nodded to Jules to go into the corner. He took up position against the wall so the door would hide him and nodded to Rabbit. O'Hare took a deep breath, opened the door, and stood aside so the newcomers could enter.

Max was expecting anyone but her.

CHAPTER SIX

Max Starkey and Kelly Riggs fell in love fast, and hard, and with the reckless abandon of youth. They were both green CIA officers on their first field assignments, although neither knew that about the other at the time. The legend the Company had built for Max was that he was a grad student in the Czech Republic to write a dissertation on the Prague Spring of 1968, when the Soviets sent troops into the city to smash down a growing freedom movement, as the Soviets were prone to do. His real task was to get close to a Czech historian, an expert on the era, whom the US suspected of passing documents between Chinese spies and their counterparts in the American embassy in Prague. Kelly was already in place as the professor's teaching aid, the latest in a long line of attractive young female assistants that the older man never touched but liked having around.

Max was smitten with her right away. For one thing, he was pretty sure she was the smartest person he had ever met, certainly smarter than him. She would bring him the stack of books the professor had picked for him, then sit on the edge of the reading table and tell him why each book was worthless, meticulously dissecting the poorly constructed worldview of its author. They started meeting at Na Palmě, their local beer bar, to discuss art, history, geopolitics, everything but movies, since he had hardly seen any. He was drawn to her intellect. She knew she was smart, but she wasn't condescending or arrogant, and in fact, she was damn funny, in spite of the fact that most of her jokes sounded like they came off a Bazooka Joe bubblegum wrapper. "What do you call someone with no nose and no body?"

"What?"

"Nobody knows!" He hated himself for laughing.

Before long they were sharing morning jogs along the Vltava, at the foot of the Prague Castle. Kelly said it was the castle from *Beauty and the Beast*, and they were like lovers in a fairy tale. They challenged each other physically. She kickboxed, she rowed, and he loved that she could almost beat him to the top of Vítkov Hill. They walked the cobblestone streets at night, and she showed him the most beautiful spots in the city, while he pointed out the chock marks in the ancient stone walls which were still visible from the Soviet tank shells, five decades later. They bonded over their difficult childhoods, and believed, like all young lovers do, that no one in the world could understand them the way they understood each other.

He was so taken with her intelligence and her physicality that it took him a while to fully realize how beautiful she was. When he did, he was thunderstruck. He began to suspect that God was playing a trick on him, that He had specifically constructed a woman perfectly tuned to all his senses. The feel of her skin, the scent of her, the taste of her lips (all of them), seemed to exist on a frequency precisely tuned to provoke need in him. Instead of pheromones, he called them Kellymones. The first time they made love, he felt like he had been drowning and didn't know it, and now he was safely on shore.

It was all built on a foundation of lies. They maintained their cover from one another for months, and when it finally fell it was purely by accident. They were in a coffee shop on Dlouhá Street, just off the Old Town Square. She was arguing that the current party in power in neighboring Slovakia would be swept out in the next elections by a wide margin, and he had asked, "What are your inferences?" It was a phrase they were taught to use at The Farm and was a dead giveaway to anyone that had been through the CIA training program. They stared at each other in silence for a few seconds, then they both burst out laughing. Somehow, finding out that they were both Company assets wasn't the big surprise it might have been. By then they were so deeply in love they could have found out they were both Martians and it wouldn't have mattered.

They would learn that putting both of them on the same target was not unusual. It was called a double blind, a redundancy in which two officers are assigned to the same case, neither of them knowing about the other, so that if one was exposed or killed the other was still in place. But they had figured it out, and working together they had the professor and his contacts at the embassy behind bars within a month. They reported their romance to HR at Langley and requested to be assigned to cases together.

From that point on, their relationship was forged in fire. They traveled through deserts and jungles. They made love in bunkers and in Humvees, and more than once, in the presence of camels. Their private joke was that for two years they never had sex more than three feet away from a loaded gun. They shared weapons and intel and dreams. They patched each other's wounds and carried each other's pain. They were young and alive and in love, and if it wasn't perfect, it was damn close.

Max's mother once told him that everyone you meet is half a person. They show you the half they want you to see, but there's another half, the side she sometimes saw in her work. Max noticed the cracks in Kelly's facade fairly early. She had a violent temper which she could lose over something trivial. She could fall into bouts of despair or petty name-calling. Her selfishness would manifest in small ways that made him uncomfortable but weren't a big deal. He could tell there was a part of her that he couldn't access, some darkness that she either needed to, or believed she needed to, keep to herself and deal with on her own. Some of her mood swings were so intense that he found himself looking up "bipolar" on the internet. But 95 percent of the time, she was the smart, funny, self-confident woman he had made love to in the stacks of the central library at Charles University in Prague. And she grew stronger, and more confident, every day. He felt lucky to be with her, and then there was that pesky thing about her scents and tastes being perfectly calibrated to his senses. So, he willfully ignored the danger signs. Denied them, even. And when he found out the source of her pain, he told himself the simple lie that he could help her heal.

The thing is, he loved her. They almost died together more than once, pulled each other from the fire, and killed together. You don't walk away from a relationship like that over a few dark moments. She was damaged, and defensive, and in minor ways, even treacherous. But Max knew that despite her increasing criticism of him, and her bouts of depression, she truly loved him, and he was still naive enough to believe in soulmates.

Some relationships end with a bang. This one died from a thousand cuts, and when she walked into his filthy hotel room in Patpong, they all came back to him. The love and the hate, the joy and the anguish, the sex and the lies.

But most of all, the betrayal.

CHAPTER SEVEN

Kelly was used to being the most formidable woman in any room she walked into, but as soon as she saw the woman Max had brought with him, she knew the position was filled. She was tall and bore a passing resemblance to a supermodel Kelly remembered from the eighties, but it wasn't her stature that caught Kelly's attention, and it wasn't something she sensed. In fact it was what she didn't sense—fear. The woman had walked into an unknown, dangerous situation in a skeevy hotel room in Bangkok, surrounded by strangers, and she was as calm as a frozen pond. It made Kelly uneasy, which wasn't a feeling she liked, especially since the plan depended on manipulating Max's residual feelings for her. Max was good at hiding his emotions, but she could read him in a way other people couldn't, and she saw him freeze on the inside when she walked into the room. That was a good sign. He didn't thaw until Derek followed her in. Then his eyes filled with a different kind of cold.

Kelly noticed something else too. When her husband walked into the room, Max's new girl recognized him. It was almost imperceptible, and if she hadn't been looking directly at her she would have missed it. But it was there; for a fleeting moment, she knew who Derek was.

Whoever this pageant queen turned out to be, there was more to her than exquisite beauty. She'd need to keep an eye on this one.

Kelly turned to Max and managed to fake a sincere smile.

"Max."

Before he could answer, Derek chimed in. "Starkey, old friend, how the hell are you? It's been a minute." He thrust his hand out, but Max ignored it.

"What the hell is this?" Max growled.

"Straight to business. Okay, fine, but I like to know all the players. Who's the sāw?"

She answered for herself, "Her name is Giuliana. She's a woman, not a girl, and she's capable of speech." Derek laughed. In spite of herself, Kelly liked her already.

Giuliana, Max thought. *Huh, okay, it fit her, actually.*

"Mea culpa," Derek said. "My name is Derek Moss, and this thoroughbred is the love of my life, my wife, Kelly."

Kelly snuck a glance at Max, but as usual his face betrayed nothing. He said, "Stop wasting my time and tell me what the fuck this is about."

A flash of anger passed over Derek's face, but Kelly touched his arm.

"Let me, baby." His megawatt smile returned. The smile that captured her heart, gutted it like a deer and hung it on his wall.

"We need your help," she said to Max. "We have a shot at something big, the biggest, but we can't do it without you."

"For Christ's sake." Max turned to the woman, Giuliana. "There's a flight out in two hours; we can just make it."

Kelly pleaded, "Max, please . . ."

"You dragged me halfway around the world to try to pull me into a job? On what planet would I do anything with the two of you?"

Derek said, "Planet tax-free millions."

Max just jerked his head at Giuliana, as if to say, "Let's go." Kelly had to stop him.

"Please Max, just listen. For me, for old times' sake, sit and listen." He met her eyes and that's all it took. He closed the door.

CHAPTER EIGHT

Max listened, but the way they told it, the whole thing sounded like bullshit.

Kelly and Derek laid it out for him, talking in turns, finishing each other's sentences the way married people do.

Derek started, "President Vinthu, up north in Suryaka, who up until recently was America's puppet in the region . . ."

"You and I helped put him in power, Max."

"You think I don't remember?"

They went on with their double act. "He's facing a coup," Derek said. "And has been abandoned by the US, of course."

"The man ripped off billions. Our government traced most of it, and they've frozen all his offshore accounts. He's got no cash left."

So far so good, all believable. It went off the rails when they talked about the gold. Derek continued, "Vinthu has four thousand gold bars sitting in his fucking basement."

"Each one weighs one pound," Kelly added. "Figuring that each ounce is worth roughly two grand, that makes his stash worth a couple bumps north of a hundred and thirty million dollars."

"He's hired us to physically get it out of the country for him before his regime collapses. The deal we made is for twenty percent. But we're not in this for twenty-six mil."

"You're gonna rip him off," Max said. "Steal the gold. Of course you are."

"The guy's a prick, Max," Kelly said. "You know that. He's a mass murderer. There's no moral gray area here, we're just gonna straight-up rob the son of a bitch."

They were right about one thing, Vinthu was a greedy, homicidal narcissist. The idea of him living out Max's dream life on a private island somewhere didn't sit right.

He asked, "How do I figure into this bullshit?"

"You know the terrain. You operated in that jungle for nearly three years, you have a better chance of getting the gold to the border than anyone."

"You also know the rebel territory and where they tend to operate," Derek added.

"Most importantly," Kelly continued. "Vinthu trusts you. In fact, he said he won't hire us for the job unless you come along. He asked for you by name; it's the three of us or none of us."

"So you see," Derek said. "You're indispensable, Max. We need you on this."

Max sighed. "How do you know the gold is even real?"

"We've been in the room with it," Kelly said. "I've stroked it with my own hands. It's the most beautiful thing I've ever seen."

Once again, he found himself looking to Jules for her take. She had an excited look in her eye. Gold does that to people.

"Might as well see if it's real," she said. Then, to Kelly, "What's the split?"

Derek looked at her with an expression that clearly said, who the fuck are you? But Kelly answered the question.

"A hundred and thirty-two million, give or take. Easily divided into three equal shares."

Jules whistled. "Forty-four million bucks. I'd say that's worth a look, at least."

"There will be expenses," Max said. "We'll need trucks, weapons, some men you can trust." Kelly smiled but didn't comment. He was already saying "we."

"That is the beauty of it," Derek said, "Vinthu is fronting the cash for whatever we need, and giving us old US-built M809 trucks to haul it in. He's financing his own robbery." He laughed. "I'm telling you, Max—with you aboard, there's no way this thing goes sideways."

He looked at Kelly. She was the danger. Rebels he could handle. Tigers, soldiers, even Derek, who he was certain planned to double-cross him and leave him dead in the jungle when he didn't need him anymore, these things he could deal with. But she just might be his end.

"I'll take a look, that's all," he said. "No commitment until I see the gold for myself."

"Good!" Derek said. "We'll head out tomorrow at noon, from Don Mueang."

Then he stood up, took out a silenced pistol, and double-tapped Rabbit in the chest and the head, right there in his chair.

"What the fuck?" Max asked.

"We don't need him anymore."

He turned his gun on Jules. Max quickly stood between them, shielding her. "No, Derek."

"Loose ends, Max."

"She's not a loose end."

"Really. Just what the fuck is she then?"

Max told the first lie he thought of to save her life.

"She's my wife."

CHAPTER NINE

Giuliana was rapidly realizing she was in over her head. Derek and Kelly had left an hour ago, and she and Max had moved to another room without giving their reason, which was that there was a dead body in the first one. They kept that room, too, and put a "Do Not Disturb" sign on the door handle so Rabbit could rest in peace until they were far away. She tried to use the time while Starkey was in the shower to think things through.

She had recognized Derek Moss right away. He was on the top-ten list, a former CIA officer turned thief and terrorist. She had willed herself not to react when he came in and was pretty sure she had covered okay. Now she was privy to his plans for an international crime, making her an accomplice if she didn't take some action to stop it.

And apparently Max Starkey, the two-bit recovery man she had aligned herself with to get closer to Rocket, was a former Company man himself, which came completely out of the blue and made her angry at herself for not figuring out sooner. There was some nasty history between him and the Riggs woman; that was obvious. He reacted to her like a kidney punch.

On top of everything, she was in Asia, thousands of miles out of her jurisdiction. Despite what they tell you on those stupid TV shows, other than a small, elite counterterrorism task force, the American FBI has no authority whatsoever outside of the country. She needed to report in somehow, get her superiors on the phone and let them sort this mess out, toss it to Interpol maybe. She needed someone to tell her what to do. But getting away long enough to make the call would be impossible and would definitely raise suspicions. She was on her own, with no idea how to proceed.

"I guess we're married now."

She looked up with a start. She hadn't heard him come in, hadn't even heard the shower shut off. He was drying his hair with a towel, another towel slung low around his hips. She watched a bead of water trickle down the white marble V in his abdomen and disappear behind the terry cloth. Jesus, she was acting like a schoolgirl.

"Why did you tell them that? That I'm your wife."

"It was the first thing I thought of," he said. "I couldn't let him shoot you."

"Why not? I'm just a random hooker Rocket sent to keep you company."

"Well," he said, "We both know that's not true."

Alarm bells went off as she searched his face. What did he know? He tossed the hair towel back into the bathroom and moved closer.

"At first," he said, "I thought Rocket had sent you along to kill me after I found his money."

"You thought I was an assassin? I think I'm flattered."

"But that's not it. I don't know who you really are, but you're no hooker. And I get the distinct feeling you don't want to tell me."

"You could beat it out of me."

"I doubt it," he said. They looked at each other for a few moments, then he continued, "Anyway, the shower's all yours."

On her way in, she paused in the doorway. "I could use someone to wash my back." He didn't hesitate.

Once they started, they couldn't stop. They had been together six weeks now, most of it alone in the cabin; it was a long time coming and when the dam broke, it burst. For Max, knowing she was not a prostitute and was making the choice to be with him was a green light, and he drove through it with gusto.

The first time, in the shower, was soapy and slippery and urgent. They did it twice more in the bed, each time just as passionate, but slowing down as they discovered one another's rhythms and responses. When they woke just before dawn and did it a fourth time, it was intimate and satisfying, the orgasms intense, as if they had known each other's bodies for a long time.

Max was pretty sure she thought it was happening despite the killing and danger around them, but he had been doing this kind of work for a long time and knew that the presence of death was a powerful aphrodisiac. Thinking he might die had driven him into more women's arms than love ever had.

Afterward, she went to shower again, then came back and climbed in bed, and nestled against his chest in the crook of his arm and he held her. Neither of them knew what this meant for them moving forward, and neither of them cared; right now, it was good. Their sex musk was strong in the small room. He wanted to run his fingers through her braids but figured that would be crossing a line, so he stroked her arm instead. He had forgotten the feeling over the last few years, but he had the idea that in that moment, he was happy.

That's when she said, "There's something I need to tell you."

CHAPTER TEN

Derek Moss lay awake in bed in his lavish suite at the Mandarin Oriental, watching Kelly sleep beside him, the deep rise and fall of her chest. His wife did everything with intensity, even dream, her eyes darting to and fro under her eyelids. It excited him. She dreamt in vivid detail and could always remember them the next day. She would tell Derek about them, and it filled a void for him, since he had never had a single dream.

"It's been that way since I was a kid," he told her once. "No dreams at all."

"What," she asked, "no flying or falling, no nightmares? No wet dreams even?"

"I missed out on that one."

"So what is sleep like for you?"

"I guess it's like anesthesia. I close my eyes and open them a few hours later, and it's like they were only closed for a moment."

"The sleep of the dead."

"When I was a kid bedtime scared the shit out of me, not knowing where my mind went while I was out."

"You ever see a doctor or a shrink about it?"

"No. I never told my parents. They bragged all the time to their friends about what a good sleeper I was."

He left out the fact that dropping off to sleep still scared him.

Watching her dream, Derek remembered the exact moment he knew he was in love with his wife, or as close to love as he was capable of, anyway. It was in Yemen, they had been married just over a year, and he was observing her interrogate a Taliban weapons smuggler. She barely had to touch the guy; the psychological pressure of being tortured, or even touched, by a woman was enough to break him, and she knew it. The man spilled his guts before she had removed as much as a fingernail.

That night, as they lay together after lovemaking, Derek told Kelly something he had never told anyone, that he had modeled himself after the man he considered to be the greatest criminal mastermind of the last century, Vladimir Putin.

"Oh, come on," she said, "seriously?"

"Dead serious. There are two things people generally don't know about him," he said. "The first is that when he was a teenager in post-war Leningrad, he was a street thug. The second is that he was kind of a nothing, unimpressive agent of the KGB. His moment of pure genius came when he realized he could combine his two worlds. The anything goes, strong-arm criminal tactics of the street wedded to the infrastructure and access to information of the KGB would make him the richest man in the world."

She had always thought he bore a strong physical resemblance to Putin, except the Russian president was better looking. "Okay, I'll bite. How'd he mix them?"

"For his first KGB assignment back in Russia after his posting in Germany, under the embargo the West had imposed at the time, he was put in charge of distributing trainloads of food that were brought in, legally, to feed Russia's hungry people. But instead of distributing the shipments, he hijacked and sold them, lining his pockets with millions of rubles. People starved, he got rich, and he never looked back."

"Yeah, that's the guy to model yourself after, for sure."

"I grew up basically the same way he did, I was a latchkey kid in Baltimore. I worked corners for dealers, rolled drunks, and robbed stores. I was a street thug, no question, just like he was, but I was also smart like him, too, and a secret reader. That was the key."

"How so?"

"I came across a biography of Putin someone had left in a bus station toilet, and my life changed. I quit the streets, applied myself, and got straight A's through high school."

"So, you were actually following Putin's KGB playbook when you applied to the CIA? You intended to use the agency for financial gain?"

"Better. I didn't apply; I got myself recruited. Went to the right university, Georgetown, got degrees in geopolitics and finance, joined the right frat. The agency approached me, just like I knew they would. I've been lining my pockets since day one."

"Smart. A little twisted, but smart."

He watched her closely to gauge her reaction. If she was a true believer, like Max, she would tell the brass what he had just told her. The truth was, he knew Max better than she thought he did. They went through The Farm together, and were on a similar trajectory, although Max was earnest, a patriot who actually thought that there were such things as good and evil. He was also smart enough to see what Derek was up to, and Max tried several times to expose Derek, until he eventually left the agency after the shit show in Laos. He also left Kelly behind, and Derek softened her landing.

He truly had not married Kelly as a way of getting at Max, but it was certainly a perk. She was beautiful, she was talented, and she would do whatever it took to get the job done. He married her out of admiration as much as anything, and for companionship, as well as pride of ownership, until that night in Yemen when he realized he might actually love her.

To his delight she did not turn him in, on the contrary, she embraced it. The next day they both resigned from the agency, moved back to Southeast Asia, and started to churn money.

Together they were solid gold. As private contractors they had performed assassinations, assisted coups, and smuggled everything from guns to an emir's wives and children. When Vinthu demanded they recruit Max to help move his gold, Derek came up with the plan to steal the bullion and kill Max in the process. He knew Kelly would be game, more than willing to exploit Max's unresolved feelings for her. His wife was practical that way.

"All you have to do is let Max hope," he had told her, "and we will walk away with a hundred and thirty-two million dollars."

"And if I have to sleep with him to get the job done?"

"I'll take that one for the team," he said.

She laughed. "That's big of you."

"What do you think? Can you do it?"

"Piece of cake," she replied.

Then Max showed up with a wife of his own, who was definitely more than she seemed. But Derek wasn't worried, they could handle it. It was just as easy to leave two dead bodies in the jungle as one. He fell away into dreamless sleep.

SEVEN YEARS AGO

THE RAID

The firefight raged all around them as Max dragged Kelly behind the pink and green stone lions guarding the General's front door. She had been hit, but it was through and through, she'd survive if she got medical attention relatively quickly. He took off his bulletproof vest and pulled his shirt over his head, wadded it up, and pressed it against the wound.

He still didn't know what was happening. They believed they had been sent on the raid through official channels, but that clearly wasn't the case, and the intel they had been given said nothing about American troops being stationed at the villa to support the Laotians. There were only a handful of them, Max guessed, in an advisory and training capacity, but they made self-defense almost impossible since there was no way the three of them could fire on Americans.

As he looked for an escape route through the chaos, he spotted Derek across the motor court, pinned down behind a Jeep. Derek looked at Max and his eyes asked the questions Max was struggling with: Who could have done this? Who had access to our authorization codes?

Max knew their time was up. Kelly would die if she didn't get to a medic, and they stood no chance against the soldiers pinning them down. He held up his gun to signal his intent to Derek. Derek nodded. Max took Kelly's weapons, then he and Derek threw their guns out onto the ground and raised their hands.

Kelly gasped, "Max, no!"

"I'm not letting the love of my life bleed out at the ass end of a pink lion."

He kissed her briefly, and then the soldiers were on them, pulling them in opposite directions.

“She needs medical attention!” he yelled in Lao. “Get her to a doctor!” A soldier hit him in the head with the butt of his rifle, and everything went black.

He was jostled awake by the movement of a truck. He quickly ascertained that he was sitting on a bench in the back of a Laotian army transport, his arms tied behind his back and his feet bound. His head throbbed and he was gagged with what felt like a bandana. Derek was tied up across from him, and had a bandana in his mouth, so he figured he was right. There were a dozen armed Laotian soldiers in the back of the truck with them. He couldn’t see Kelly. He tried to ask Derek with his eyes, have you seen her? Derek just shrugged.

Max nudged the soldier next to him, who pushed back. He nudged him again and made noises indicating he wanted to talk. The soldier looked at the others, who were indifferent. He lowered Max’s gag.

“The woman,” Max said in Lao, “where is she?”

“What woman?” the soldier asked.

“Please, just tell me if she’s alive or dead.”

“I know no woman!”

He went to replace Max’s gag, and Max struggled. “Please!”

The soldier hit him, threw him to the floor, and kicked him several times in the stomach and facc. He barked at him, “You stay quiet!” Max lay there, his head swimming with pain, his stomach spasming from the kicks. Once he had his breath he looked up at Derek, who was still sitting on the bench looking down at him, faintly amused.

Max rode the rest of the way on the floor, soldiers occasionally pushing at him with their boots. He had no way of knowing where they were going, but the trip took several hours. Finally he heard shouting outside, and the rumbling of gates opening. They drove a little farther and stopped. When they threw open the flap on the back of the truck, the sunlight was blinding.

Max was lifted and tossed out of the tailgate. He landed in dusty earth and barely had time to catch his breath before he was yanked to his feet and marched forward, just behind Derek. The stench of the place was overwhelming, hundreds of bodies that were almost never washed, layered in stifling humidity, combined with the sickly sweet smell of black dog grilling in the open air. As he looked around at the concrete block buildings, the desperate faces of the prisoners, and the cruel leer of the guards, he knew exactly where he was.

He'd been to Phonthong Prison before, but only as a visitor. Once known as the "Foreigners' Prison," it was originally built to house only non-Lao prisoners, but over the last few years, due to overcrowding, they had started adding Lao nationals. It wasn't like an American prison, where the inmates' every move is coordinated and regulated. Once you were within the walls of Phonthong, you were pretty much on your own, free to roam and form alliances. There were conventional cells, but they were left open most of the time.

It was also co-ed, male and female prisoners mixing freely, with all the issues you would expect with that setup. The women prisoners formed tight-knit groups for protection, never walked alone, and perfected a quick and lethal maneuver with a shiv they called a *chevonger*, a bastardization of the French word for gelding.

Max and Derek were separated. They took Max into a dark, concrete room and tied him to a chair, then removed his gag. They left him there, alone, which he knew was part of the interrogation itself. Derek would be sitting in an identical room. They expected Max to use the time to look around at the torture apparatus, so he did.

The first thing he noticed was that there was a drain in the floor, which meant they weren't fucking around. There was a bedspring attached to a car battery, and a bullwhip hanging on the wall. Fairly standard stuff. He assumed there was more gear behind him, but he couldn't twist enough to see the back half of the room.

He hadn't urinated in almost sixteen hours, and holding it in was getting painful. *Screw it*, he thought, *there's a drain in the floor*. He let it go.

He waited another half hour before the door opened and two prison guards entered, then stood aside and made way for his interrogator. He was a civilian, dressed all in black, the sleeves of his button-down shirt rolled up to his elbows. He sniffed the air and made a face.

"Filthy Americans," he said in perfect English.

"Hey," Max replied, "when you gotta go, you gotta go."

"Big Mr. CIA agent, sitting in his own piss."

Max smiled slightly and shook his head. The interrogator knew that the CIA called their operatives officers, not agents, and was trying to get Max to correct him. Instead he said, "You have the wrong guy. I'm a water purification expert. I was sent here by my company to sell your government reverse osmosis membrane systems."

"Yes, I see. Very well. I have questions. I hope you will answer them honestly."

"I'll try, but first I have a question of my own."

The interrogator lifted one eyebrow in curiosity.

"Yes?"

"Tell me," Max said, "what happened to the woman."

CHAPTER ELEVEN

Giuliana didn't want to die so young, but death seemed imminent as the tuk-tuk driver weaved through the Bangkok traffic. At barely 6:00 A.M. the streets were already crowded, the air heavy with humidity and exhaust mixed with the cloying smell of street vendors cooking heavily spiced meat on open carts. They had left the hotel less than five minutes before, and her life had already flashed before her eyes three times; this guy drove like the devil was chasing him. They barely missed a motorcycle that had a family of six aboard, mother and father, two kids hanging off the sides, grandma facing backward, and baby on the handlebars. Forget how dangerous it was, she couldn't figure out the geometry of how they got aboard like that in the first place.

Max was stoic beside her. He hadn't said anything since she told him she was an FBI agent except, "We need to get guns." She had told him everything, making sure to start with the fact that she wasn't there to investigate him. Her job was to get close to Rocket, a job she had clearly fucked up since she was now eight thousand miles away from him. She even told him she recognized Derek from the most-wanted list, but that it was meaningless because she had no jurisdiction to go after him. She told him that she wanted to stay at his side, but that she would get on a plane back to the States right now if he told her to.

To which he said, "We need to get guns."

So here they were, in the back of a tuk-tuk going forty miles an hour between a bus and a tanker truck, weaving to avoid the stray dogs that wandered casually around the streets of Bangkok as if there was no traffic at all. They turned down a narrow alley and came to a stop at a metal gate. Giuliana climbed out on shaky legs as Max paid the driver, who tore down the alley and out of view. Apparently, as long as he kept moving the devil couldn't catch him.

Max buzzed an intercom and looked into the camera mounted over the gate. He waited about thirty seconds and buzzed again, looking up at the lens with impatience. This time the gate unlatched remotely, and they went in.

They crossed a small cement courtyard and came to another metal door, which also unlatched electronically as they approached. She followed him in and down a long corridor with worn, purple shag carpeting. It appeared to be a home, inhabited by people who party too hard. There were bongs and beer bottles everywhere, and hard-core drug paraphernalia on the nightstands. They passed an open bedroom door, and she caught a glimpse of two naked Thai girls sleeping ass cheek to ass cheek, no covers on them. Giuliana didn't know what the age of consent was in Thailand, but she doubted they met it.

They stepped into the living room, which had a linoleum floor and windows that were blacked out and barred. It was built out as a full-on gun store. All manner of firearms hung on the walls, from small handguns to Uzis. There was even a counter with a glass case, like a real shop. The man behind the counter was so short that, at first, she thought he was a little boy, except that he was covered in tattoos and piercings. He and Max greeted each other in Thai, and she realized he was at least sixty. They exchanged a few more words, which Max translated.

"He said he was expecting us yesterday. I told him we were held up." Then he made introductions, also in English. "Jules, this is Iron Sam, so named for all his piercings."

"I assumed it was because you sold guns."

"Then I would be Polymer Sam, at least these days," the little man said in English. He seemed to decide that was enough chitchat and put on his business face. "What do you need?"

Max asked Giuliana, "Are you still on the 17?"

"No, I'm rated on the 19." She wanted to be surprised that he knew which weapons were FBI standard issue, and that they had recently been upgraded, but she wasn't.

Max nodded, and said to Iron Sam, "She'll take a Glock 19M. I want a .44 Magnum—preferably a Desert Eagle—and a compact nine mil. Also, a shoulder harness for the Eagle." Iron Sam nodded and started going through drawers. He kept glancing toward the back of the shop—the way they'd come in.

"Expecting someone?" Max asked.

"No, no," Sam said, "I just don't want to wake my girlfriends."

Max glanced at the security monitors, which showed the front of the house and the back way they came in. Both were quiet, empty. That made sense for the backyard, but there were no pedestrians on the street. Something was off.

Iron Sam had everything they asked for. He set their weapons on the counter, and they all went quiet as they looked them over, metallic clicks the only sounds as they checked the slides, the grips, the firing mechanisms. Giuliana smiled to herself as she stood beside Max, the two of them absorbed in the mechanics of the guns. *A couple needs a hobby to share*, she thought.

Max said, "Shells too."

Iron Sam knelt down, pulled boxes of ammunition from a drawer, and set them on the counter.

"Thanks," Max said.

Then he holstered his .44 Desert Eagle and punched Iron Sam in the face with a fist as big as Sam's head. The little tattooed man went down like someone cut his strings.

Max said to her, "Load up." Then he took out a wad of bills, counted some out and tossed them on top of Sam where he lay behind the counter.

"What are you doing?" she asked as she slid a full magazine into her Glock.

"Paying for the guns."

"Then why did you knock him out? I figured we were stealing them."

"I'm no thief. He set me up," Max said. "We walked into an ambush."

She shook her head. "That doesn't make sense. They'd get us on the way in, not on the way out, when we're armed."

"They meant to," he said, "Last night. Whoever it is must have a standing watch order out for me. Sam probably alerted them as soon as I called him. When I didn't show, they figured I wasn't coming, but when he saw me at the back gate, he called it in again. That was the pause, why I had to buzz twice. They'll be waiting for us."

"Who wants you dead?"

He shrugged. "If I get a chance I'll ask them."

They made their way back down the hall, past the sleeping girls. Max unlocked the metal door and opened it just a sliver.

The first bullet hit the doorframe an inch from Max's head.

CHAPTER TWELVE

Max fired two shots out the gap, the roar of the .44 deafening in the tight hallway. He pulled the door shut and locked it again as a volley of gunfire unleashed on the other side, bullets pinging off the steel.

"That'll hold for a while," he said, "but we're gonna need another way out."

The gunfire outside died down as they made their way back along the hall. The enemy, whoever they were, could afford to wait them out. Giuliana saw to her amazement that despite the noise, the two nude girls hadn't even stirred.

Back in the living room gun store, they loaded up on more weapons. Max preferred handguns and took a .357 Magnum. Jules chose an AK-47, opting for rapid fire, widely dispersed. As he loaded the Magnum, Max said, "He'll have an escape route somewhere, in case the law comes for him. We just have to find it."

Shoving a magazine into the AK, Jules went to the blacked-out window and pulled the heavy curtain back just an inch to look out. The window was peppered with gunfire that would have killed her instantly if the safety glass hadn't held.

"Front door is out."

Max ran his fingers along the edges of the cabinets, looking for a gap or a mechanism. He had to step over Sam's unconscious body. Jules said, "If you hadn't hit him so hard we could have asked him where his egress is."

Amused, Max said, "His egress, huh?"

"Rocket's not the only one with a vocabulary." She was looking down the corridor where the two girls were apparently still sleeping, an unformed idea nagging at her.

"I want to check something. Keep searching out here."

"Yes, dear."

As she walked back, Giuliana slung the AK over her shoulder and pulled the Glock from her waistband, gripping it in the ready position. Even as far back as training, she hated clearing rooms, especially if she was first through the door. Not many things scared her, but swinging around a doorjamb and getting shot in the face was at the top of the list.

She readied the Glock and swung through the door. The room was clear except for the two girls on the bed. She walked over and checked the first one for a pulse. She didn't have one, which wasn't surprising, because now that she was right on top of them Jules could see that they weren't girls at all—they were dolls. Ultrarealistic sex dolls posed side by side.

She looked at the half-filled glasses on the bedside table, the drug paraphernalia, the panties on the floor. Everything was covered in a fine sheen of dust. She called out.

"Max! Come in here a minute."

He came quickly. "Find something?"

"This room is staged," she said. "The escape route is in here somewhere."

As they searched for it, she continued, "I don't get it. If you don't want people checking out a room, why put naked girls in it? Seems like that would draw more eyeballs."

"It's a cultural thing," he answered. "Thai men will fuck prostitutes, and they'll watch strippers, because it's accepted in their culture. But they'd be too ashamed to ogle a woman who wasn't being paid. They'd avoid this room like the plague."

"Men suck everywhere."

"Can't argue with that."

Giuliana pushed on the headboard, and it clicked. Together they pulled, and the bed swung away from the wall, revealing a hole just big enough to crouch through.

"What do you know," Max said. "Egress."

He went through first and she followed, then they pulled the bed back into place to cover their escape.

It was pitch dark. Max felt around until he found a switch, which turned on a string of bare bulbs that ran down the length of a dirt tunnel. It reminded him of drug tunnels he had been through in Mexico, but built to one-third scale, like they would build it at Disneyland if Disney had Cartel World. They made their way along at a crouch, moving as quickly as possible.

"Bear in mind," he said, "they may know where this tunnel comes out."

He was right.

CHAPTER THIRTEEN

Thooey Kham hated his nickname. He had been chubby when he was a kid, there was no denying it, but he was a man now, and he was a member of the Ghosts, the biggest Laotian street gang in Thailand. More to the point, he was no longer a fattie, he was slim and muscular and, in his opinion, a bit of a badass. He deserved some respect. But his older brother had started calling him Thooey, the Lao version of Fatso, when he was three, and he couldn't shake it, especially since Som was higher up the ladder in the organization than he was. If he was going to get respect, he'd have to earn it.

Today was his chance. Sure, there was a cash bonus for the man who killed the farang, Max Starkey, but for Thooey the cash meant less than what it would do for his reputation if it was his bullet that brought Starkey down. Crouched behind a dumpster in the trash-strewn alley, he tightened his bandana around his face and double-checked that he had a round in the chamber of his Daewoo K5 pistol. The gun was a Thai military castoff, the serial number filed down. It was a ghost, like him.

He hated himself for thinking of his mother at this moment, but he always did, whenever something big was about to go down. She had begged him not to follow Som into the Ghosts.

She was afraid for him, which, in his mind, only meant she didn't see him as a man. His drunken father abandoned them when they were young, and Som had become a Ghost because it was the only way to earn enough money to feed the family and keep his two sisters out of the clutches of the Patpong pimps. One of them had become the girlfriend of a higher-up in the gang, which meant eventually she'd get turned out anyway.

Thooey had been jumped in at age fourteen, when he was just a kid. It broke his mother's heart, but she took the money he sent home every week. By then Som had made his rep, and the Ghosts helped Thooey along like they were all his big brother. They trained him on firearms and started him out on easy assignments, mostly collecting protection money from shopkeepers.

Today was his first big assignment. He had no idea why the bosses wanted the farang dead, but it didn't matter. Today he would prove his worth and get his respect at last.

The door on the shed rattled; he heard Tadpole yell "Pai Kan!" and it was on. He gripped his pistol in both hands, left hand on his right wrist, and finger on the trigger the way they had taught him, spun around the dumpster, and went for the kill.

Bullets ripped through his torso. He crumpled and rolled onto his back. He would never know if it was the farang who shot him, or the tall Black woman beside him. For all he knew, it could have been friendly fire or even a ricochet from a Ghost gun.

The sound of the firefight faded as he lay on his back watching a white cloud pass across the blue sky, pressing against his wounded stomach as he felt his life bleed out between his fingers. Sixteen years old, and it was all over. He thought of his mother, the pain this would cause her, and he wished he had stayed in school like she begged him to do. He thought of his brother, who nicknamed him Fatso, and who had encouraged him to go on this mission. He knew his brother would remember him, and honor him in death, but not in the way he hoped.

His last thought was, *Now I will be Thooey forever.*

CHAPTER FOURTEEN

The tunnel terminated at a wooden hatch in the ceiling. Max estimated they had gone one city block since they left Iron Sam's. There was no ladder, since crouched over as they were, Max could put his back against the hatch and push on it simply by standing upright. There was something heavy on top of it, but it rolled off.

He poked his head up slowly, emerging through the floor of a metal storage shed. It had been a gas-powered lawn mower that had rolled off the hatch. He climbed out and reached back down for Jules—Giuliana, he now knew—but she hopped up into the shed unassisted. She was nimble and strong, and maybe thirty seconds from dead.

"They're out there," he said, "I can feel them."

"I don't suppose you have a plan."

"Don't think there is one to be had. It seems like all we can do is go through that door and meet whatever's out there."

"Like the end of *Butch Cassidy and the Sundance Kid*." He just looked at her blankly. "It's a movie," she added.

"I told you, I haven't seen many movies. They make it out alive?"

She looked at him a beat before answering. "Yeah. Of course."

She readied her weapons, AK in her left hand, Glock in her right. She nodded. Max turned the door handle, heard a voice yell "Let's go!" in Laotian, and burst through the door, Jules on his heels.

A volley of gunfire came at them, and they shot back. Max's CIA training kicked in, what his training officer called SIPDE—scan, identify, predict, decide, and execute—all in a split second. He spotted a dumpster they could use for cover and headed for it, but a gunman with a bandana over his face popped up from behind it. Jules cut him down with a burst from her AK and they dove for cover as bullets rained around them. Max made it, but Jules was hit and fell to the ground. In the time it took Max to spray cover fire, grab her, and pull her behind the dumpster, she was hit twice more.

"Where are you hit?"

"Everywhere." From what Max could see she was shot in the shoulder, calf, and abdomen.

Shoulder and calf were survivable, but the abdomen would be a problem, maybe a big one depending on what the bullet hit once it got in there. Her breathing was already ragged.

"Wait here," he said. "I'll be back."

"*The Terminator.*" He looked at her blankly. "Never mind. There are three more distinct discharges. Not sure how many men, but three guns." He nodded. He had already clocked it, but the fact that she did, too, stirred something in him. He would not let this woman die.

He heard shouting, the same voice as before, and knew the man was telling his underlings to move around and flank them. He thought about rolling the dumpster and using it as a shield, but that would leave Jules exposed. There was only one way out of this, and he'd have to be fast, faster than he had ever been in his life before.

He put the AK in Jules's hand and told her to squeeze off a burst into the air every ten seconds or so. Then he ran at a crouch back to the shed and jumped feet first into the tunnel. He ran as hard as he could, bent over in the small shaft. He had thought about bringing her AK, but its extra weight would have cost him precious seconds he couldn't spare. He'd have to do this with his Desert Eagle. At the other end of the tunnel he shoved the bed out of the way and ran out the back door. Through the yard. Down the alley. He ran up the street in the direction the tunnel had led. Sweat poured from him in the humidity. He ran faster. His lungs burned.

He darted into the alley. He could see the shed, but no one was around it, so at least they hadn't seen him go back in, less than thirty seconds ago. He crept up to the corner.

Three gangbangers were closing in on the dumpster, coming at it from three sides, but hesitating every time she fired a burst. They all had their backs to Max. He gripped his Desert Eagle, stepped out, and fired three shots in rapid succession.

Three bodies dropped.

Max ran straight to the middle body, figuring him to be the leader, rifled the man's pockets, and came up with what he was after: the key to the BMW he had spotted on the street when he was running back. He looked at the dead man's face, and it stopped him for a beat. He had seen this face before, but he didn't have time to try to remember where. He ran back to the street.

He chirped the lock. Like most cars in Thailand, it was right-hand drive. He tore down the narrow alley like a bat out of hell and left the car running as he went to Jules behind the dumpster. She was alive, but she was pale, her breathing fast and shallow.

She looked at him and said, "You have to let me die."

CHAPTER FIFTEEN

Max couldn't put Jules in a fireman's carry because of her abdomen, so he took her under the arms and carried her backward to the car, her feet dragging. He got her into the passenger seat, fastened her belt, then ran around and jumped in. As they tore out of the alley, she said it again.

"Let me die or kill me."

"What the hell are you babbling about?"

"I'm an FBI agent, Max. I know everything. Where you're going, who with, and what you plan to do. If I survive . . ."

"You'll have to come after me."

"If that's what they order me to do. Very least . . ." She trailed off again. It was getting harder for her to speak. He finished the thought for her as he pulled out onto Thong Lo and headed north toward the hospital.

"Very least you'll have to tell your superiors what you know." She nodded.

Traffic was heavy on Thong Lo, but he knew the city well and there was no alternate route to the hospital from here. To the west of them were a bunch of streets that dead-ended in a few blocks. To the east was Sukhumvit Road, which would be more congested than Thong Lo. He leaned heavily on the car's horn, weaving, passing against traffic.

He looked at her, bleeding in the seat beside him, and realized this was the second woman who had gotten shot because of his mistake. Kelly had survived her injuries at the raid, obviously, but their relationship hadn't, and if she had died, he never would have forgiven himself. The same was true with Jules. Giuliana. If she died it would be his fault. He wanted her to come with him to Vinthu's palace, but the truth was he should have put her on a plane. She was on the verge of death because he selfishly wanted her at his side.

Right now, he needed to keep her conscious, keep her talking.

"So," he said, "I should dump you on the side of the road and let you bleed out."

"Unless you want me coming after you."

He honked at the bus blocking the lane ahead of him. "Maybe I want you coming after me," he said. "Maybe I'll miss you a little."

She didn't answer. He looked over and saw that her eyes were closed, her head lolled to the side. But her chest was still rising and falling with ragged breaths.

He whipped around the bus on the left, the Bimmer half on the sidewalk, plowing down shrubs, narrowly avoiding a cement trash can. He got back on the road, and the hospital was visible half a mile ahead. He covered it in less than twenty seconds, the Bimmer's engine screaming.

He skidded to a stop outside the emergency room and yelled for help as he ran around to the left side of the car. A doctor and several nurses came running, pushing a gurney. He lifted Jules out in his arms, carrying her under her shoulders and knees, and met the nurses halfway.

They took her from him, and as they laid her on the gurney, he told them in Thai, "Three gunshot wounds. The worst is in her abdomen, treat it first."

As they secured her to the gurney, he leaned down and kissed her gently on the lips. Her eyes fluttered open. He whispered to her, "Do what you've got to do."

Then she was gone, whisked away by the nurses. He watched until they took her inside, then he walked off, leaving the BMW where it sat. As he walked, he suddenly remembered where he had seen the dead gangbanger in the alley before and understood why they would still have people like Sam watching for him after all these years, with standing orders among their street soldiers to kill him as soon as he set foot in the region. He also knew they would come after him again the first chance they got. He would have to deal with it eventually.

But he'd have to figure it out later. Right now Kelly, Derek, and four thousand pounds of gold were waiting for him.

CHAPTER SIXTEEN

President Chavarat Vinthu was no fool. He knew he probably looked ridiculous, sitting alone on top of his pile of gold bars like Scrooge McDuck. But dammit, it made him feel better, and he needed to chase away his blues. Aside from his mistress, these cold stacks of gold bars were the warmest things in his life at the moment.

Everything was going to hell. The US had taken all his cash, seized his compound in Malaysia, his fleet of Rolls-Royces and his islands in the Bahamas. He had worked hard to siphon off those billions; it was completely unfair of them to take them. For God's sake, he had to have two different finance ministers assassinated. Did they think this shit was easy?

His beloved Suryaka, which had been so good to him, was on the verge of collapse. The rebels, under the command of that bat-shit crazy loon Chewy Chakri, had taken most of the north and dug themselves in on the slopes of the Sacred Mountains. His own army was amassing against him in the south, under the direction of that prick General Ruchuphan. He put the bastard in power and now he was staging a coup against him. No one has any honor anymore. And the list of countries that would take him in exile was very short; in all likelihood he was going to wind up in Libya. Fucking Libya! On top of all that, his acid reflux was back, and he was breathing it in his sleep, giving him a persistent sharp cough.

But none of that was on his mind now, he had bigger problems. His wife, Kaeo, had put her foot down about bringing Malai into exile with them. She was jealous of the younger girl, which made no sense at all. He loved his wife, worshipped her even. She had been by his side through it all, and he would never leave her. Malai was a plaything. He would never fall in love with this girl, but he genuinely cared for her, and she was eager to please in the bedroom.

It was possible for him to truly, deeply love his wife, and still have recreational sex with other women. He could never understand why Kaeo could not grasp this basic truth about men, and he was no ordinary man. He was the most powerful man in the country for God's sake. He owned all this gold. He was the harbinger of death for tens of thousands, and the source of life for hundreds of thousands more. If he was being honest with himself, he was half a god. He deserved whatever fleeting moments of pleasure Malai could give him.

Kaeo also refused to see the simple truth that if Malai was left behind, she would be considered an enemy of the people because of her relationship with him and would be tortured for information before being killed. Her life after him would be brutal and short. He couldn't leave her to that fate.

He needed to resolve this. The chopper carrying the former CIA officers who would move his gold for him was on the way, and after dropping them it would refuel and tomorrow morning it would fly him and his family to an undisclosed neutral location, which would sound impressive if he didn't know it was Tashkent, the armpit of Asia. It was the most depressing city he had ever visited, but it beat a tribunal and a beheading.

The answer came suddenly. Energized, he climbed down off his pile of gold and took his private elevator to the third floor. He knew that, ultimately, he had to side with his wife, but in a flash of inspiration he had figured out how to do both things, honor Kaeo and save Malai from death by torture. The elevator opened and he walked to Malai's suite, knocked perfunctorily on her door, and went in.

She was standing by the dressing table, naked but for a sheer robe that was hanging open. She was rubbing oil into her soft, brown skin. Her face lit up with genuine joy when she saw him, something he hadn't seen on Kaeo's face in years, and she put the oil down, ran to him and kissed him, long and deep, her sweet tongue massaging his. She broke the kiss and laid her head on his chest.

"I'm all packed," she said. "Just one suitcase, like you said." She looked up at him and brushed the hair away from his face. "You seem troubled."

"It's a big day, that's all. I'm tense."

She smiled again, took his hand and led him to the bed. His troubles melted away in her enthusiasm, the fragrance of her body, the tightness of her *jim*.

Afterward, as he lay in her arms, he heard the unmistakable sound of the chopper approaching in the distance. He kissed her, disentangled their limbs, climbed out of bed, and got dressed. As he buttoned his shirt he looked back at her, the dreamy smile on her face, basking in the afterglow of their lovemaking.

He took out his pistol and shot her between the eyes.

CHAPTER SEVENTEEN

The chopper flew low over the jungle, the skids nearly grazing the canopy, which grew thicker with every mile north, palms and bamboo groves giving way to sprawling banyans and thick tropical evergreens. Max had been in a lot of jungles and knew the endless ways they could kill you. He was not eager to get back to it.

He sat facing forward, Derek beside him. Kelly sat backward, facing her two lovers—past and present. She seemed perplexed to see them there, side by side, or maybe it was amusement on her face. Max felt pain when he looked at her, so he didn't. He watched the jungle and was surprised to find himself thinking about Jules. It had been just over five hours since he dropped her off; chances were she was still in surgery. It wouldn't be possible to check in with the hospital for a while, since he had told Derek and Kelly, who thought Jules was his wife, that her mother fell ill and she had to return to the States early that morning. That meant any call he made prior to the seventeen-hour flight time from Bangkok to Los Angeles would tip them off that he was lying. Meanwhile, he had to assume she pulled through. To think otherwise would cloud his mind and his judgment.

He had thought for all these years that he was still in love with Kelly, and in truth he barely knew Jules, but walking away from her at the hospital was one of the hardest things he had ever done. He had no choice, since gunshot wounds bring police, and police bring questions he couldn't answer. It was better to disappear into the jungle and let her work things out with her superiors and come after him if she needed to. He had no idea if she even wanted to see him again, but he already knew that if she didn't find him, he would find her.

Max saw two white spires and the Suryakan flag before he saw the rest of the palace. It wasn't the seat of government; it was a second home for President Vinthu and his family. It sat in the middle of nowhere, ninety-two miles north of the capital city and two hundred miles of hard jungle south of the Sacred Mountains. It wasn't supposed to be in the middle of nowhere, it was meant to be the centerpiece of a gleaming new city that was to be built quickly and all at once, the way Kazakhstan built Astana and China built Tianducheng. There were well-built roads leading nowhere in every direction, but once the palace was finished the project mysteriously ran out of funds. Rumor was the money bought Vinthu an archipelago in the Bahamas.

The rest of the sprawling structure came into view as they gained altitude to stage their landing. The last time Max saw the palace, it was gleaming and impressive. Now the parade grounds were cracked, weeds growing through the fractured concrete. One of the four barracks was gone, and Max could only guess why, not knowing that the soldiers had taken it apart for firewood. The palace walls were being taken over by vines, and one of the massive front gates was off its hinges. With no one to stop it, in six months the jungle would take over completely.

The chopper settled onto the helipad, which inexplicably had been built near enough to the swimming pool to make it impossible to keep water in it. It had never even been used once. As they settled, Max could see Vinthu's wife, Kaeo, waiting inside the glass doors for him, but no Vinthu. The three of them hopped out and went in.

Kaeo greeted each of them by taking both of their hands in hers and touching her nose to theirs. She had seen it done once on a vacation to Hawaii and had adopted it as her own. Their three children stood behind her. It took Max a beat to realize that the sixteen-year-old girl in the miniskirt and halter top, eyeing him from under her heavily made-up lashes, was their daughter, Cintha, whom Max last saw when she was nine and still calling him Uncle Maxie. Back then she wore black-rimmed glasses and spent all her time taking radios and household appliances apart and putting them back together; as a child she had a fascination with anything electronic and how they worked, and a naturally logical mind that impressed Max. Now she looked like she put more thought into makeup and clothes than anything else. The two boys were spaced about a year and a half each behind her, age-wise, making them fourteen and twelve.

Their mother, Kaeo, who was barely five feet tall, hadn't changed a bit, her hair still jet black, her front teeth slightly ahead of her lowers, her long dragon nails polished green, and she looked every bit as arrogant and avaricious as ever. Behind her smile, Max knew she would happily use his blood to water her flowers.

After exchanging pleasantries, Kaeo said that her husband was delayed getting rid of some trash, and that he would meet them in the basement. As the kids went off, the daughter, Cintha, brushed up against Max, which he thought was both intentional and alarming. Apparently, Kelly agreed, because she smirked at him as Kaeo led them downstairs.

Max had to admit, it was stunning to look at. Even in this poorly lit basement, the polished gold shone. It was the only thing he'd seen since he arrived at the palace that looked like it was cleaned every day. It was, if he was to be honest, mesmerizing. The gold bricks were in stacks thirty high, one hundred and thirty-two stacks in all, pressed together to form a cube. There were forty more stacked on top, making it an even four thousand.

Getting this stuff to the border would be extremely difficult; doing it without being intercepted by rebels or soldiers would be damn near impossible. Add the fact that Derek and Kelly almost certainly meant to kill him, and it was insane to even try. But he would. It was Max's job to figure out the route, to plot the way to his own murder.

CHAPTER EIGHTEEN

Kelly watched Max as he studied the large map on the wall. They were in President Vinthu's den, which was done up like an English study, with wood-paneled walls, a large mahogany colonial desk, the huge map of Suryaka, and shelves of war memorabilia, decommissioned weapons and the like. Kelly was certain that if he could, Vinthu would have the skulls of his political rivals mounted on pedestals.

Max was absorbed in the map, making notes on a pad. Derek and Vinthu were sitting in leather chairs in the corner smoking cigars, Vinthu drinking heavily, already half drunk, laughing and telling stories of exploits that Kelly had heard a hundred times before. She used the time to study Max. She had once known him better than anybody, but people change in seven years. Her initial plan to get him on board with the job had been to play on his residual feelings for her, even seduce him, if necessary, but she hadn't anticipated a wife. He kept checking his watch, and Kelly figured he was timing her flight back to the US. She expected at some point he'd call to make sure she landed okay.

She had clocked right away that they weren't wearing rings, but most people didn't in this line of work. Wedding rings told others too much about you and your possible weaknesses and could snag on things, which made them impractical. She was relieved that the gold itself was enough to get him to sign on, because Max wasn't the type to cheat, in fact he was loyal to a fault. He'd had plenty of women, but he wasn't a womanizer by nature. She knew for a fact that up until seven years ago he had never been with a prostitute, and she was confident that still stood. It's the one thing she was a hundred percent certain he would never do.

Part of the reason that she had fallen in love with him back in Prague was because of what he had overcome, and the lessons he had chosen to learn from his extremely rough childhood. It wasn't as bad as her own, but it was bad. She never did tell him her story, and he didn't tell her his until they had been together for over a year. He finally opened up about it one night nearly nine years ago as she sat between his legs and leaned back against his chest, beside a campfire at an archaeological dig in Abu Simbel, south of Cairo.

"I grew up in a trailer park in Texas. My dad was a long-haul trucker, and my mom was a waitress. She was extremely beautiful, and I don't mean just by rural Texas standards."

"The type of girl you never see in small towns," Kelly offered, "because they all moved to Hollywood or New York."

"Exactly, only Mom never got away. She had men hitting on her constantly. My dad was hardly ever there, and he didn't earn enough to make ends meet, and at some point, my mom started trading favors for things we needed."

"You mean, prostitution?"

"It wasn't that exactly, she just had a few boyfriends. Never mind that they happened to be our landlord, the grocery store manager, and her boss at the diner. She didn't think I knew what she was doing, but I did."

"How did you handle it?"

He let out a deep sigh. "I told my father."

"Shit. How old were you?"

"Eight. I wasn't trying to hurt her, I honestly thought I was protecting her, that my dad would step up and find more money so she could stop seeing those men."

"I take it, it didn't go that way."

"He beat her half to death, drove off in his rig, and we never heard from him again."

"Oh, Max. I'm so sorry."

His mother forgave Max immediately, told him it wasn't his fault and she knew he was trying to protect her. But he never forgave himself, mostly because of what happened next.

"The bastard left us deep in debt, and without his income we couldn't get by. Desperation took over, occasional boyfriends turned into regular tricks, and before long every man in town knew that forty bucks bought you an hour in Diane's trailer out at Dusty Acres. And I knew what it meant when she told me, Momma has a friend coming over so be a good boy and play outside awhile."

"That's rough, babe."

"I wasn't exaggerating about how beautiful she was. She was the prettiest woman in five counties, and the men lined up. She was like heroin to them. They spent their rent, their kids' 4-H supply money. Only a matter of time before the resentment and backlash hit."

"Was it bad?"

"Outside of her trailer, Mom became a pariah. The kids at school bullied me, son of the local whore, and no one was allowed to be my friend. When we went into town, the women glared at her and called her names, while their husbands pretended not to know her."

"Typical."

"As far as the good wives of Jasper were concerned," he explained, "the menfolk were not at fault, after all, they were only mortal men, weak of the flesh. Diane was, I guess, some kind of supernatural sex demon who had enchanted them, forcing them by the devil's own power to drive the two miles out to Dusty Acres Trailer Park and throw their grocery money at her. We lived that way for four years, then when I was twelve, we moved to Dallas."

"You get a new start there?" She tried not to sound too hopeful.

"Oh yeah. But not the one you're thinking. Through all those years in the trailer, Mom kept her looks and her figure, and it turned out she had been recruited by the madam of an upscale brothel. So we went up there and moved in."

"You lived in a whorehouse?"

"From twelve to eighteen."

"Jesus, Max. Not to be flip, but that sounds like every teenage boy's fantasy."

"Maybe if your mom's not one of them."

"Right. Sorry."

"Even up there in Dallas, Diane's looks made her a star, and she became Madam Brenda's top earner. The other working girls were nice to me, it was a clean, safe house, a strict no-drugs policy. The ladies kind of doted on me, made sure I did my homework, and helped me study the playbook when I went out for football."

"I bet they taught you other things too."

"They offered over the years, always the same way too. 'Let me make you a man.' But I turned them down."

"So who did make you a man?"

"A cheerleader named Mandy Carter, the old-fashioned way, groping around blindly in the back seat of a Buick."

Kelly watched the fire for a while, then asked, "Where's your mother now?"

"I haven't talked to her in a year or two but last I heard she had taken over for Madam Brenda and was running the place. If she hasn't been arrested, she's probably still there."

"Taking money off of men whose wives blame her girls instead of their husbands."

He laughed. "Yeah. But up in Dallas, the money's a lot better."

She asked him how none of this came up in his background checks, and he told her he had been completely open about all of it in his CIA application process, offering the novel, and ultimately successful, argument that no one could use the information to compromise him if everyone at Langley already knew it. She figured his stellar academic record, physical prowess, and movie star looks probably helped them accept that idea.

Watching him now, plotting out their route, she thought about how a childhood like his could fuck a boy up, not least in how he views and treats women. But rather than let it teach him that all women are whores, Max chose to learn that whores are human beings, and that people make the choices they need to make in order to survive. He didn't have a judgmental bone in his body. In the years they worked and slept together, Kelly had never seen him degrade or speak down to a woman, treat a woman harshly or unfairly, or raise a hand to one. Now he had a wife, and Kelly knew that he would honor Giuliana and stand by her.

"I'm ready." Max's voice pulled her out of her reverie.

Derek and President Vinthu got up and came over to the map. Kelly saw that Max had marked out three possible routes to discuss. He checked his watch again.

"Okay," he said, "let's figure out how to pull off this impossible task."

Yes, Kelly thought. *Let's.*

CHAPTER NINETEEN

In all the movies she'd seen, after anesthesia the actor's eyes flutter open like their lashes are little butterflies. Giuliana did not feel like she had delicate wings on her face. Her lids were pasted shut, thick with gunk. The light in the room hurt her pupils. And the first thing she saw come into focus was a Bangkok police detective whose sour expression made her think that if she did have a butterfly on her eyelid, he'd beat it to death with a hammer.

When Max dropped her off at the emergency room, she hadn't had time to think about what she was going to say at this moment, but she knew she had to lie. At least until she could get her superiors at the FBI into the loop. And since she was in deep cover, with no badge or identification under her real name, and since her bosses thought she was currently in Los Angeles, that could take a minute.

She managed to croak out, "Water."

She bought herself a few seconds to think as the cop held the cup for her so she could sip through the straw. The cool water was like an elixir, and she felt herself coming back to life, her brain starting to focus. The cop was impatient and pulled the cup away, set it back on the rolling table. He flashed his badge but didn't introduce himself.

"Who shot you?"

Giuliana shook her head slightly. "I didn't see them."

"Why did they shoot you?"

"No idea. I was walking down the street and gunfire broke out. It was terrifying. I think I was just caught in the crossfire of a gang war or something."

He looked skeptical. "What were you doing in that neighborhood?"

"Sightseeing. I'm a tourist."

"Sightseeing? In Sukhumvit?"

"I was lost." She remembered reading about a scam that the local cabbies pulled on tourists, and she incorporated it into her story. "I went to see the Grand Palace, but a tuk-tuk guy told me it was closed. He offered to take me to see a temple, but instead he dropped me off at a tailor's shop. I wasn't interested in buying any clothes, so I tried to walk back to my hotel. Not the smartest move, I guess."

The cop's sour expression didn't change, but she could see that he knew the scam, and believed that part, at least. He scrutinized her for a few moments, then asked, "Who drove you to the hospital?"

"No idea," she said. "The last thing I remember is being shot. Then I woke up here, in this bed."

"The doctor said the man whispered something to you on the gurney."

"If someone whispered something, I don't remember it." That part was true. She tried to recall if Max had said something to her, but everything after the alley was a blank.

She said, "May I ask you something now?"

"Go ahead."

"Can I see my doctor? It would be nice to know if I'm going to live or die."

She would live. The shoulder and leg wounds were superficial. The bullet in her abdomen had nicked her lower intestine, but they were able to remove the damaged portion and the bullet.

It would take her a while to get back to full strength, and she would have a gnarly scar, but there was no permanent damage. It was the best she could have hoped for under the circumstances.

She thought about Max, who was most likely deep in the jungle by now, and didn't know how to feel about him. They had spent all those weeks getting to know each other, without touching, then in the span of nine hours they had made love four times and been in a firefight together. After which, just like that, he was gone. It almost seemed like a dream now, or some fevered fantasy she had while she was delirious from being shot. Maybe it didn't really happen.

Except that the nurse told her he had called before she woke up to check on her well-being, and said he sounded extremely worried for her and very relieved that she had survived. "That one's a keeper," the nurse said. But could someone be a keeper after a nine-hour romance? Or was it a six-week romance with a nine-hour consummation? Up until a day and a half ago he thought she was a hooker. She was a cop; he was a criminal. It couldn't be real.

But when he lied and said, "She's my wife," it somehow didn't feel like a lie.

She wasn't going to figure it out lying in this bed, and right now she needed to get on with more practical things. She was relieved to find that one of the nurses had thought to plug her phone in, and it was fully charged. There was a text waiting for her from Fran Kellogg, the woman who recruited her for honey trapping and who had become something of a mentor. Her text said that she had just been fired and joked that she was chasing an opening in the security office at the National Zoo. She wrote, "From chasing the Ten Most-Wanted to guarding the tufted titmouse." Giuliana figured her text was a warning that her turn was coming, but her reply would have to wait. She asked an orderly to close the door to the room for privacy, and called her boss, FBI Assistant Director Jason Lin, in Virginia.

Then everything blew up.

CHAPTER TWENTY

Of the three possible routes from the palace to the border, Max chose the longest one. "Also," Derek pointed out, "the most treacherous and physically demanding. We take this route, we have to cross mountain passes and we have to ford two rivers."

"True," Max conceded, "but it also has the lowest chance of crossing paths with the rebels or the army, either of which would kill us and take the gold. There is one major problem with this route," he told the others. "We have to cross Phaya Nok Ravine. That bridge is old and not built to any kind of code. It was decommissioned; nobody is allowed to drive across it anymore. It's foot traffic only, on the pedestrian bridge a hundred yards east of it."

"How deep is the ravine?" Derek asked.

"Twelve hundred feet."

"You think the bridge will hold our trucks?"

"I made a couple of calls and have it on good authority that it's in working condition. But these M809s we're driving weigh ten tons already; there's no way it will support one of them carrying another four thousand pounds. Can't we get smaller trucks?"

"Only ones available to us. What is the bridge rated for?" Derek asked.

"It's not rated for anything; it was built by the locals fifty years ago. But I wouldn't try to carry more than half a ton across it in one of these behemoths."

"So we take five trucks," Kelly said, "four for the gold and one for supplies and weapons and extra men. Simple enough."

Derek looked to President Vinthu, who said, slurring his words, "Five trucks, ten. What do I care? Take the whole fucking fleet."

"Five will do," Max said. Then, to Derek, "You and I will drive two of them. Kelly, you're on tactical alert; we need your eyes on everything but the road. When do your men arrive?"

"They're already here," Derek answered, "out in the barracks. Fourteen of the best soldiers money can buy. Some excellent drivers among them."

"Good, we'll drive in shifts so we don't have to stop to sleep. If we move around the clock, we should make the port in Haiphong in eight days." He turned to President Vinthu. "But tell your ship's crew not to sound the alarm unless we don't show for two weeks. There are a lot of things that can slow us down out there." He yawned and said to Derek, "Tell your men to assemble at 0400 to inspect and load the trucks. We leave at first light."

They talked through a few more details, then split up to try and get some kip. Max took an empty, lavish suite close to President Vinthu's and showered, alternating scalding hot and freezing cold water four times, a routine he'd followed since his days in the field. On active duty he often went weeks between showers, so they were more than just a means to get clean, they were a way to revitalize. In the twenty-four hours since he landed in Bangkok, he had been ambushed by his old girlfriend and her husband, had a man shot in his hotel room, made love to Jules repeatedly, come under heavy fire, rushed Jules to the hospital, and flown over five hundred miles of jungle in a chopper. He needed sleep.

He dried himself off and fell into bed, naked. He worried he'd dream about the raid in Laos again, but he slipped into a sleep that was just this side of a coma. Over the years he had trained himself to sleep lightly. He would wake up at the smallest sound; a creaky floorboard, a lock being picked, but tonight, he was all the way out.

He didn't even feel her slip into the bed and didn't know she was there until she pressed her scantily clad body against his back and licked his ear. At first, in his exhausted slumber, he thought it was Jules, but as the cobwebs lifted, he realized it couldn't possibly be, she was in a hospital in Bangkok. This was Kelly. Her hands started to explore his body, but he grabbed her wrist before she could touch his cock. She was an octopus, for every hand he moved away, it seemed like three more made their way onto his skin. He could feel her breasts through her top, pressed into his back.

His body was responding, and he couldn't will it not to. He was rock hard. He had known Kelly would make a play for him, it had to be part of their plan, but he didn't expect her to just climb into his bed and try to fuck him. She was usually more sophisticated than this; as a chess player she was rated as a candidate master. This was rash and amateurish.

"What are you doing?" he protested. "We're both married."

She giggled and said, "Don't be silly, I'm not married."

Max bolted out of the bed like his ass was on fire, grabbing a robe to cover himself. Oh my God, how could he have been so stupid? As soon as she touched him, he had known it was bad, but he didn't know it was this fucking bad.

"What's wrong, Uncle Max?" Cintha asked, looking up at him from where she lay in her miniskirt, halter top, and ankle socks. Her pink sneakers were next to the bed.

He could be angry later. Right now he had to get her out of his room as quickly and quietly as possible. He figured this was some kind of rebellion against her father, and he understood her anger. Most of her life she was the privileged child of a president, and now, because of her dad's actions, she was going to live in some shithole country she'd never heard of, with no friends, no money, and no life. She was acting out, in the extreme, which wasn't unusual for girls her age.

But this girl's father had an army.

He whispered urgently, "What the hell are you doing? You need to get your shoes on and get out of here." *And I don't care in what order*, he thought.

She rolled over onto her stomach and looked up at him. Her clumsy attempts to be seductive only emphasized how young she was, and in a less urgent situation would have been laughable. But Max wasn't laughing.

"You don't have to worry," she said, "I'm not a virgin. I've done this before."

"Hooray for you. Just for the record, we haven't done anything, and we're not going to do anything. You have to get out of here—"

But it was too late. The door flew open and Vinthu stepped into the room. He flicked on the lights and took a moment as his eyes adjusted. Max saw that he had a pistol in his hand, and that he was now extremely drunk, swaying on his feet. Never a good combination, but it could slow his reflexes down enough for Max to survive this. He looked toward his Desert Eagle, in its rig over the back of the chair, but it was too far away.

"Mr. President, this isn't what it looks like."

He never got to offer his explanation. Vinthu took one look at his daughter sitting on Max's bed and fired a shot in Max's direction. His drunkenness affected his aim, and Max flung his robe at the president, covering him like a blanket. By the time he tossed it aside, Max was on him. Max grabbed Vinthu's wrist and tried to twist the gun from his hand.

"Calm down! Let me explain!"

Vinthu answered with a string of invectives in Suryakan. Max hadn't spoken the language in a while, but he got the idea. Enraged, Vinthu squeezed off a couple more shots, one of which grazed Max's inner thigh. He realized the older man was trying to shoot his dick off, and he couldn't blame him, really. The fight for the gun became a battle for survival. As they wrestled, Vinthu fired again.

The shot took off half of his head.

He dropped at Max's feet, and Cintha started to scream. Max picked up the gun as Kelly and Derek ran in, drawn by the gunshots.

They stopped cold and took it in. Vinthu dead on the floor, his daughter screaming in Max's bed. And Max standing stark naked, splattered in Vinthu's blood, bleeding from his inner thigh, gun in his hand.

Kelly was stunned. "Jesus H. Christ, Max."

He tried the line again.

"It's not what it looks like."

CHAPTER TWENTY-ONE

Giuliana's hospital room had been transformed into a circus. Her boss, Assistant Director Lin, was here, but so was his boss, Deputy Director June Martinson. There were several high-ranking Thai police officers, two men from the Thai government, and a jovial, mustachioed Austrian who turned out to be from Interpol. There was also a young, well-dressed woman from the State Department, whom Giuliana would bet her pension was CIA. Phone calls were flying furiously, underlings being reamed out in three languages. Conspicuously absent was the police detective who had first interviewed Giuliana, who had been unceremoniously shown the door when the big dogs showed up.

She had gone through her story six times and understood their confusion about how she had wound up in Bangkok since she wasn't totally clear on it herself. She had been investigating a criminal organization in Los Angeles and had accompanied one of the players to Thailand in her role as an undercover agent. That much made sense, but then it got harder to unravel.

"This Los Angeles criminal organization is behind the operation to steal President Vinthu's illegal cache of gold?"

"No, sir."

"Then this organization is attempting to gain a foothold in Southeast Asia?"

"No, ma'am."

"Then again, why are you here?"

She finally got her bosses and the Thai police to understand that she had only become aware of the gold after she arrived here, which is when they called in Interpol.

"So, *fräulein*, the man you traveled here with came to Thailand with the intention of stealing this gold?"

Deep breath. "No, sir." She explained again, "Max Starkey, the current subject of my investigation, was tricked into coming here by Derek Moss and Kelly Riggs, who are behind the whole thing. He only agreed to go see the gold; he hadn't signed on to any criminal enterprise the last I knew." She was careful to keep the concern out of her voice when she talked about Max. He was a target, nothing more.

"And the shoot-out in Sukhumvit is connected how?"

"I don't think it was."

"You expect us to believe it was random?"

"No, of course not. But it felt personal," she told them, "not political. Like Starkey was specifically targeted. Someone with an old grudge, maybe."

She had gone through every step of the gunfight with them several times and assumed that Iron Sam had been raided by now although it was just as likely that he had cleared that house out as soon as everything went down.

Her bosses were not happy that she had come to Thailand without authorization, but they could not deny that she had uncovered a massive criminal plot with international political ramifications, involving a president, mercenaries, former CIA officers, and two borders. And so they swallowed their annoyance. They'd be gritting their teeth right through her promotion.

She had already been told in no uncertain terms that her involvement in the case was over. She had argued hard for her place in the investigation, as the one who had uncovered the whole thing in the first place, but AD Lin pointed out, not unfairly, that at the moment she couldn't even walk. She only had one card left to play.

Lin knew that she was a honey trap, and although he found the whole thing unsavory and counter to his Christian values, he utilized agents like her to full advantage. Giuliana wasn't sure if Deputy Director Martinson knew, and if she didn't, telling her was a calculated risk. There was nothing old school about June Martinson, she was modern all the way, to the point of having her subordinates call her Sir. She had made her career fighting the systemic racism and overt sexism in the bureau, and had been surprisingly successful, which was why she was a deputy director at age thirty-four. The risk was that she might see Giuliana as part of the problem. Giuliana used sex to get information out of men . . . and once, a woman . . . and Martinson might lump her in with the distasteful elements she was trying to root out.

But she didn't want to be taken off this case, so she had to try.

"Sirs?" She gestured for Lin and Martinson to come over to her. They stood side by side on the left of her bed. She spoke directly to Lin first.

"Assistant Director, you know why I was with Starkey."

"Yes, Agent Abara, I do."

Giuliana looked to June Martinson. Her face revealed nothing. "She's been read in on the nature of your assignment," Lin said.

"All right," Giuliana said, "then you know I was ordered to get close to a criminal to gain information."

"Yes," Lin responded, "but not this criminal and not this information."

"The point is, Starkey trusts me. He actually thinks we're falling in love."

Lin sighed. Giuliana saw that Martinson wasn't moved by this, she'd have to go deeper. "The whole time I was with him in California, he wouldn't touch me. All we did was talk and play chess and get to know each other. Well, he got to know my cover anyway. It wasn't until I decided to come on this trip with him of my own free will that things finally got physical. Then he couldn't get enough." Giuliana noticed a slight tic of distaste on Martinson's face, but she pressed on. "Now he's like a puppy dog. When I got shot, I thought he was going to cry, for God's sake. I've got this poor bastard eating out of my hand. You need me out front on this." Martinson still hadn't shown what she was thinking. Lin sighed and looked to her.

"Deputy Director?"

Martinson took a few moments to consider, then asked Giuliana, "Is your cover intact?"

"Yes." It was a simple lie, but one she had to tell. If they found out she had told him she was FBI, it would call her judgment into question, and she'd never be allowed to work the case. To be honest, even she didn't understand why she had done it. All she knew was, she wanted, or even needed, for Max to know her true self.

She was put in charge of the case, and four minutes later she had access to the online files of Starkey, Moss, and Riggs, even the redacted files from the CIA. She started with Max's, and it didn't take her long to realize she didn't know him at all.

CHAPTER TWENTY-TWO

It wasn't hard for Max to convince Derek and Kelly of how things went down. They knew him well and would never believe in a million years that he was having it on with a sixteen-year-old girl. The events leading up to the self-inflicted death of the Honorable Chavarat Vinthu were clear. Much less clear was what would happen next. They were smack in the middle of an unstable country whose president had just blown his own head off, sitting on a fortune of gold and surrounded by hostile jungle, trigger-happy soldiers, and desperate rebels.

There was also the matter of the family. The gunshots and Cintha's screaming had brought Kaeo and both of her sons running, the older boy wielding a rifle. Now the four surviving family members were huddled together on the bed, Kelly covering them with the boy's rifle, which she had taken away from him like a toy from a child. Max could tell Kaeo believed his version of events by the disgusted way she looked at her daughter, but he also knew she would fight to the death to protect Cintha and her other children.

"All right," Derek said, "let's figure this out."

"What's to figure out?" Max asked. "We need to get in that chopper and get the fuck out of here before anyone outside of this room realizes he's dead."

"And just leave the gold?" Kelly asked.

"We're past the gold."

"I'm not past the fucking gold," she said. "There's zero chance I just walk away. Less than zero, Max."

Max indicated Kaeo and her kids. "And what about them? You want to just kill them too?" When she didn't answer right away, he realized she was actually thinking about it. "No, Jesus, Kel, we're not doing that. Derek, weigh in here."

Derek thought for a beat, then said, "We take them with us. Put them in the back of the supply truck. Let them out somewhere along the line."

"Sure," Kelly picked up the thread. "In the middle of the jungle. By the time they walk to civilization, or someone finds them out there, we'll be long gone."

Max shook his head. "If we leave them in the jungle, they could die."

"Shit, Max," Derek said, "everybody dies."

Max rubbed the bridge of his nose. He had forgotten how callous these two were about human life. Even Rocket and the other criminals he worked for now weren't this blasé about letting people die.

"May I make a suggestion?"

It was Kaeo, on the bed surrounded by her kids. Derek nodded. "Go ahead."

"The deal you had with my husband still stands," she continued. "My children and I will board the chopper as planned. We will tell the world that Chavarat shot himself, he could not take the humiliation of being forced to resign."

"Papa would never shoot himself!" Cintha objected.

Kaeo's dragon lady came out. She spat a string of words at her daughter in Suryakan that made the girl wilt with humiliation. She spoke too low for Max to catch it, but Kelly did, and she was grinning with perverse enjoyment.

Kaeo continued in English, "With the threat of his arrest no longer over our heads, we can live anywhere we like, Miami perhaps. I know the deal you made with him was for twenty percent of the value of the gold. I will give you thirty, and my word that no one will ever know what happened in this room."

She waited. Max looked at her with pity, Kelly with bemusement. Derek just looked annoyed. It took Kaeo a few moments, but she finally understood.

"You are going to take the gold," she said. "You have no intention of delivering it to my husband's ship." She sat with it for a few moments, then said, "Obviously this puts a different spin on things."

"Any further suggestions?" Kelly asked.

"No," Kaeo said bluntly. "At this point, my only goal is for my children to survive this."

"Enough," Derek said. "We put them on the truck."

CHAPTER TWENTY-THREE

They woke the mercenaries that Derek had hired earlier than planned. Max was impressed by them, a mix of ethnicities and sexes, all ex-military and in excellent shape. He knew these guys, in a few cases, literally. They were his brothers and sisters, warriors with skills that had no value in regular society, highly trained, with nowhere left to serve. Soldiers without a war, earning a living in this fetid jungle, with no moral purpose. Max had to give it to Derek, he knew how to find the best people who would follow any order, or kill anyone, for a buck.

They took the interruption of their sleep in stride and set about loading the gold onto the trucks, which was no easy task. The bars had to be stacked on the private elevator no more than two hundred at a time, so as not to exceed the lift's weight capacity. That meant loading and unloading twenty times. Then they had to be carried by hand to the staging area outside the kitchen and loaded onto the trucks, one thousand per truck. Next, they secured each load under a tarp, and winched it down tight, to keep the load from shifting. It was time-consuming and tedious, but they went about it so efficiently Max thought they could have been automated.

As the loads were being secured, he said hello to a mercenary he had worked with a few times before. Called Milo, he was a dichotomy, muscular, tall, and lethal, but also a straight-up nerd. He loved to explain things, in particular things that didn't need explaining.

"Good to see you, Milo." Max said. "It'll be nice working together again."

"Technically I'll be working for you, not with you. Derek Moss hired me but you're his partner, ergo, I'm your employee too."

Max grinned. "It really is great to see you."

The plan he, Derek, and Kelly came up with was simple enough. As they sat and talked it over, Max was amused and comforted to see that Kelly was geared up in her RATs. Some things are constant.

"Okay," Derek said, "the wife and kids are zip-tied in the back of the truck. Let's go over it again."

"One of the mercenaries will sneak onto the pad and take the chopper," Max said, "making a turn or two around the compound to make sure all the soldiers see them leave. Then he, or she, will fly ahead and scuttle the helo in the jungle, and meet us and the trucks en route."

"If any of the soldiers ask," Kelly added, "our story is President Vinthu didn't trust anyone, including his pilot, so he and his family were flown out early and in secret."

"And we are sure this buys us enough time?" Derek asked.

"It should do," Max answered. "Since his escape from the country was clandestine to begin with, it will be a few days before anyone even notices he's missing and sends up the alarm."

Derek nodded, satisfied, and closed his eyes to get an hour or two of sleep.

Before they left, Max needed to speak to Jules. He knew that the FBI and the State Department, and possibly the NSA, would be listening, but he had to be sure she was okay. Whether it was out of concern for her or to assuage his own guilt, he couldn't be certain. He borrowed an encrypted satellite phone from one of the mercs and dialed the hospital, then asked for her room. It rang several times, and he pictured the scramble in the room to turn on recorders and tracers, then someone pointing at her, okay, pick up.

"Hello?" Her voice made his confusion worse.

"Hi. How are you feeling?"

"I'm okay. My recovery will be slow, but complete. Rocket will have to wait awhile before he puts me back to work."

That was her way of telling him that the people in the room with her did not know that she had outed herself to him, that as far as they knew her cover as a prostitute in Rocket's employ was still intact.

"Screw Rocket," he said. "Or better yet, don't."

She laughed. "Tell me about the gold."

He sighed heavily. "There is no gold." He knew the alphabet soup people listening wouldn't believe him, but he had to try. "Vinthu was just worried about getting his family out safely, he wanted some extra help, and the gold story was how he got us out here. I think Derek found a million or so in cash in one of the safes, but the gold was total bullshit."

"Your instinct was right."

"Disappointing, but not unexpected."

"When will I see you?"

"I'll be back as soon as I can. I'll call when I get to the capital city tomorrow or the next day. I miss you, Jules."

"Really?" It came out a little too quickly, and a little too real, but no one on her end seemed to notice. Max heard a low voice in the background and assumed she had been fed a question. "Oh, by the way." She made it sound offhand. She was good at this.

"What's up?"

"I'm curious. You said President Vinthu *was* worried about getting his family out. What changed?"

"Oh, that. The old buzzard shot himself in the head before we even got here."

He ended the call, smiling as he imagined the frantic reaction to the bomb he just dropped in her room.

Max returned to the staging area behind the kitchen, and approached the mercenary in charge, a woman named Veronica Usher. She was tough as nails, tattooed, with short, spiky blond hair. She was also personable, with a great sense of humor, but you'd never know it when she was on the clock. Then she was all business.

"How's it going?" he asked her.

"All according to plan."

Knowing those four words were all he would get out of her, he went looking for Derek and Kelly and found them in the living room, engaged in an intense, whispered argument. She was saying, "You know I'm the best pilot in this compound."

"That's not the point."

"No, it's not. The point is that I'm also the only person here you can fully trust to do what I say I'm going to do and not set up some kind of play to take the gold off us."

Max asked, "What's the problem?"

"My better half wants to be the one to fly the chopper and scuttle it."

Max looked at Kelly and saw something, he wasn't sure what, but she really wanted this. Or needed it, even.

"Great," he said. "Excellent idea."

CHAPTER TWENTY-FOUR

Kelly felt at home behind the controls of the Eurocopter EC145 luxury helicopter. It was built by Mercedes-Benz, and the soundproofed rear cabin seated nine passengers in contoured leather seats, with a state-of-the-art entertainment system, but that was back there; up here in the cockpit it looked like any other helo. Kelly knew the base price on this bird was north of seven million. It was a shame to scuttle it in the jungle, but that's what had to be done.

As she warmed up the engine, she disconnected the transponder, went through her preflight checklist, and verified the fuel level. She eased the helo up from the pad and, as planned, made two slow rotations around the compound. The Suryakan soldiers down below jumped up and down, cheering and firing their guns in the air, not at the chopper, but in that weird macho way that men do instead of just yelling "yahoo." So far, the plan was working; they thought the president and his family were in the helo. She made a loop around the turrets, passed over Max and Derek and the trucks full of gold, and headed northwest over the jungle.

She was three layers down in her action plan. The first plan, the one she made with her husband, Derek, was simple enough; she would get Max to help them get the gold out, seducing him if necessary, and when they didn't need him anymore, they'd kill him and leave his body in the jungle for the insects and the tigers. That plan was going flawlessly. She didn't even have to seduce him, he came willingly.

What Derek didn't know was that she had a second plan, a plan of her own. This plan also involved Max, but in this case, she meant to enlist his aid in escaping from Derek, which inevitably meant killing her husband. This plan meant she would have to rekindle his love for her. Men only murder for women they love.

Derek had told her many times that if she ever tried to leave him, he would kill her, but Kelly did not consider herself an abuse victim. She knew abuse, and this wasn't it. She was six the first time her father came into her room at night, and he kept coming, while her mom was off flying strangers to Tokyo for three days at a time. He didn't stop until the night when she was fourteen and she wrapped a belt around his neck and almost choked him out, the result of martial arts classes he didn't know she was taking. Kelly was lethal by necessity, not choice.

Derek never physically abused her, and most of the time he was even nice to her. But she had come to realize, lately, that she had re-created her relationship with her father with her husband. His control over her and their life together was absolute, and she knew her happiness was of zero concern to him. In contrast, her happiness was all Max had cared about, and she threw him away like chewed-up gum, probably because she thought she didn't deserve his love and kindness.

She had also grown tired of the endless, pointless death, and the constant looking over her shoulder for law enforcement or old enemies, and that was before Derek had started aiding and abetting terrorists. The only bright side was, in one of the rare instances where systemic misogyny paid dividends, he had made the most-wanted list, but she had managed to stay off the law enforcement radar so far.

Her relationship with Derek was toxic, but she had walked right into it and had let him take over her life an inch at a time—accepting his decisions, following his lead—until she woke up one day a prisoner, with her jailer sleeping beside her. Once she raised the idea of having kids, and he had laughed and said, "Yeah, no." They never discussed it again. It was clear to her now that even if he did love her in his own twisted way, he had no moral compass, no compassion, and no conscience. Even if he didn't kill her, she would die if she stayed with him.

She looked at the moonlit jungle spread out beneath her and decided that she had followed Max's route far enough. She had reached the rendezvous point where they expected her to scuttle the helo and wait for them to catch up with her. Instead, she took her bearings and headed northeast, a route that would eventually get her to Laos, where she actually would scuttle the bird, and where she knew people that would help her. From there, she would be free.

She had been flying her new route for just over an hour when she caught a flash out of the corner of her eye, somewhere to the north. She turned toward it and saw the streak of an air-to-ground missile. She had only seconds to get clear, but the EC145 wasn't built for evasive maneuvers. She turned and dove, but the helo shook, the roar of tearing metal deafening her as the missile took off the back third of the chopper.

With her tail rotor gone she had no control, and all she could do was hang on as she spun out. The helo hit the canopy and flipped, still spinning as the rotor continued to turn. Something hit her in the head, and she was knocked out as the bird came to rest, upside down, thirty feet off the ground.

She might have been out an hour or a week, all she could tell for sure when she managed to squeeze her eyes open was that the sun had come up. She was hanging upside down in her harness, still strapped into the pilot seat. Her training kicked in, and before she tried to cut herself loose, she took a physical inventory, starting from her feet. The first problem she found was that her right ankle felt sprained. Worse, her left forearm was broken, but she couldn't tell if it was the ulna or the radius, or both. All she knew was that it hurt like a son of a bitch when she tried to move it. The good news was her spine, neck, and head seemed to be okay.

It was now or never; she had to move. Time, pain, and thirst would make it harder to get out, not easier, and although fire was unlikely the fuel tanks were still over half full. There were several large tree branches around her, the thickest of which ran past the cockpit. She would need to get to it, then climb across it to the trunk and shimmy down, with a broken arm and possibly a bad ankle. But first she had to get out of the harness.

She managed to twist just enough to get her right hand into her left hip pocket, where she kept her jackknife. She gripped the blade notch in her teeth and pulled it open and began to saw through the harness strap. When she was almost through, she used her right arm to raise her left and grabbed onto the metal seat frame with her left hand. It was excruciating, but her only other option was to cut herself loose and fall headfirst. She steeled herself and cut the last bit of strap.

She screamed as she swung down, hanging by her broken arm. As soon as she was upright, she let go and dropped to the inverted ceiling of the cockpit, absorbing as much of the landing as she could on her left, intact leg. The pain was unbearable. Her vision blurred, and she fell onto her back and lay there looking up at a family of macaques that were watching her from a nearby tree.

Once her vision cleared and she had her breath, she checked her ankle. It wasn't broken, in fact from what she could tell it was just twisted, not sprained. That was good news.

She started the crawl out onto the branch. Her broken arm felt like it was on fire as she dragged it, and her movements caused the helo to rock slightly. She had to move slowly and steadily, which was difficult knowing the helo could fall at any time.

She was half in, half out when the macaques hopped onto the fuselage, coming to explore. The helo lurched and resettled. She lost her grip and fell thirty feet to the jungle floor, hit the ground, and was knocked unconscious again.

When she came to this time, she was moving. She was on a gurney of some sort, surrounded by men and women with machine guns and machetes, chattering in Suryakan. Her head was pounding. She didn't know how many there were, but within her field of vision she counted eight. There was no use trying to fight or escape; she was too broken and battered. Instead, she tried to make out what her captors were saying. All she could get was a name.

Chewy Chakri. They were taking her to Chewy Chakri, the vicious, semi-insane leader of the insurgency.

She was in the hands of the rebels.

CHAPTER TWENTY-FIVE

Max drove the lead supply truck, with the president's wife and kids zip-tied in the back. Derek rode shotgun, or in this case, AK-47. He should have been sleeping, so he could drive the next shift, but he was too keyed up. The other trucks were behind them in a strict formation, exactly thirty feet between each of them. The sun was rising, and they were gliding through thick jungle on a brand-new road, meant to have been part of the new gleaming city but now just a four-lane highway to nowhere.

They were half an hour out when the pavement simply ended, becoming a rutted, uneven dirt road. With the end of the highway the jungle closed in around them like a living, cloying thing, wet branches and fronds brushing the sides and the top of the trucks so that after a hundred yards they looked like they had been in a rainstorm. The smell of wet jungle and rotten fruit was so strong Max could taste it, the humidity so thick that within two minutes his shirt was soaked through with sweat. The brush rippled with the movement of a million tiny creatures, just out of view. It was like being swallowed by a snake, the dirt road pulling them deeper down its gullet until they would disappear completely. It reduced their speed by two-thirds.

"How far are we from the rendezvous with my dear wife?" Derek asked.

It irritated Max that Derek kept referring to her as "my dear wife" and "my better half," especially since he didn't believe Derek had real feelings for anyone other than himself, including Kelly.

"Twenty miles or so. But it'll be slow going from here." He took a beat. "Listen, Derek. Something happened in Bangkok."

"Hey, my friend, what happens in Patpong stays in Patpong."

"I'm serious," Max said. "When I went to Iron Sam's to buy guns yesterday morning, I was ambushed by Ghosts."

"No way at all to identify them?"

"Not that kind of ghost, the Laotian street gang, the Ghosts."

"Ahh. So that is the real reason you sent Julie home."

"Giuliana. I didn't want her getting in the line of fire."

"Why did they come after you?"

"At first, I thought maybe you sent them. Or at least told someone with a grudge that I was in town."

Derek nodded. "Since you are telling me this, I guess you rethought that."

"If you wanted me dead, you'd kill me yourself."

"There is that."

"Plus I think you're sincere about needing me to guide you through the jungle. I can't see a scenario where you had anything to gain by killing me in Bangkok, so I thought I ought to read you in. Just in case they try again."

"So, why did they attack you?" Derek asked.

"No idea." It was a lie, he knew exactly why they had come for him. "But one of them was in Phonthong Prison at the same time we were. I remember him, a gangbanger they called Tadpole."

"You knew him?"

"We shared a papaya once."

Derek thought about that for a moment, then shook his head. "Coincidence. There were a lot of lowlifes in that shithole."

"A gangster we were in a Laotian prison with, ambushing me seven years later when I've been in Bangkok for less than twelve hours? Even you don't believe in that much coincidence."

They drove in silence for a few moments. Then Derek offered, "Well, whatever it was, they are not going to find us out here."

"Probably not."

Derek's radio squawked, and Veronica Usher's voice said, "Auric One, this is Auric Five. We have company, approaching at speed from the rear."

Derek and Max exchanged a glance as Derek keyed his radio. "Can you identify?"

"Looks like a regular army patrol."

"Okay," Derek said, "that's fine. I have a letter of passage from President Vinthu that should satisfy them. Under no circumstance do we go hot unless they fire first."

"Copy that."

Max slowed and pulled over, which on this narrow jungle road meant stopping with the right tires up on the berm and the rest of the truck still on the road. The other four trucks pulled into tight formation behind him and cut their engines. Max and Derek hopped down, leaving the AK in the cab, tucking handguns into the back of their waistbands.

As they walked toward the rear of the caravan, Max said, "If they find the wife and kids, we're dead."

"Then let's make sure they do not."

The army patrol pulled up behind the last truck just as Max and Derek arrived. There were two Jeeps, with four soldiers in each. They were well armed, but there were eight of them and fourteen mercenaries, plus Max and Derek. Max figured they could take them if they had to, but not without incurring losses.

Derek approached with a smile and outstretched hand, but their leader, who wore the seven-pointed star of a captain, started barking at them in Suryakan.

"Who are you? What are you doing out here?"

Derek answered him calmly, also in fluent Suryakan. "Transporting freight."

"On behalf of who?"

"Your Honorable President, Chavarat Vinthu. I have a letter . . ."

He reached into his jacket pocket, and seven machine guns came up at once. Derek flashed his most reassuring grin and held up his left hand, then slowly pulled the envelope out with his right, between two fingers. The captain snatched it, took out the letter, and read it. Then he looked at Derek for a moment.

"Show me your cargo."

"Captain, that is the seal of your president. The letter is legitimate."

"Show me your cargo."

He took a step toward the back of the truck, but Derek moved between him and the vehicle. He stepped to the side, but Derek moved with him. The captain glared at him for a moment, then signaled to one of his men to open the truck. As the man stepped forward, Veronica and several of the mercenaries stepped around the truck with their weapons raised.

There was a lot of shouting on both sides, until the captain quieted his men. He asked Derek, "Would you die here today?"

"I am loyal to President Vinthu," he answered. "I assume you are too."

The captain balked. He shouted an order, and his men got back into the Jeeps. He and Derek were still face-to-face. Derek nodded to Veronica, and the mercs lowered their weapons and stepped back. Derek took two steps back himself, then turned to walk back to the lead truck.

Max caught the motion out of the corner of his eye as the captain raised his pistol and aimed at the back of Derek's head. Max had a split second to pull his gun, raise it, and fire. His bullet went through the captain's neck, and he grasped at it as he fell in the mud.

Gunfire erupted all around them. Max squeezed off a couple of shots at the soldiers on the Jeeps, then knelt by the wheel well and joined the volley of gunfire. It wasn't a fair fight. The mercenaries had the trucks and the jungle to give them cover, but the soldiers were exposed in the open Jeeps like ducks in a shooting gallery. It lasted a minute and a half, and when it was over two of their mercenaries and all eight soldiers were dead.

"Listen up," Veronica said. "We don't have time to bury our dead, so grab their tags and pile them on the Jeeps with the others." She nodded at the dead soldiers. "Gather their weapons and ammo, and any gas cans that weren't punctured by bullets, then drive them deep enough into the jungle that they can't be seen from the road and drain the tanks."

The mercenaries got to work, scavenging and stacking the dead bodies with the same cold, unemotional precision with which they had loaded up the gold. Max and Derek sat in the cab of the lead truck while they drove the Jeeps into the thicket.

"You saved my life," Derek said.

"Reflex. Don't take it personally." Derek laughed. The mercenaries returned from scuttling the Jeeps, and the caravan started their engines up again. As he pulled out onto the road, Max said, "Well, so far, I'd say this is going great."

SEVEN YEARS AGO

FIVE WEEKS AFTER THE RAID

In his unlocked cell, Max lay face down on the straw mattress while the old woman, whose name was unknown to him since everyone in Phonthong Prison just called her Old Woman, tended to the deep lacerations on his back from the bullwhip. She slathered his wounds in some kind of poultice she had made from available ingredients in the prison. It smelled like an outhouse, and he figured he was better off not knowing what was in it, so he never asked, but it made his back feel better, so he let her plaster it on, smell be damned.

He'd have tomorrow and the next day to recover. That was the pattern for five weeks now, one day in the torture room, two days to recover. It was crueler than simply keeping it going day after day, as his wounds would begin to heal, then the whip would open them up again. He hadn't told the interrogator anything, sticking to his story about being in the country to sell them water purifiers.

The Old Woman spoke Lao in a quiet yet somehow also harsh voice. "Much more of this and you will die. You should tell them what they want to know."

"I can't."

"Would it really be so bad?"

"You don't understand," Max said. "I can't, because I don't know. It's impossible to cave when you don't know the answer."

The Old Woman grunted and continued to apply the poultice. Max knew they wanted him to name the CIA as ordering the raid on General Vong's villa, but that was the one organization he knew for a fact hadn't sent them, because whoever hijacked their codes had. As for Kelly, he still had no idea if she was dead or alive, and that was worse than the whip.

He and Derek were kept in separate parts of the prison, so they couldn't synch their stories up, but he had seen him from a distance a couple of times. He seemed to be holding up well, better than Max, anyway, and looked to have a small harem of female prisoners around him. Max wondered if they were as comforting to him as the eighty-year-old woman slopping shit onto his back was to Max.

A shadow fell over him. He looked up to see a Laotian man squatting down beside him.

He had seen this guy around the compound but had never spoken to him. He was a mid-level member of the gang that ran the cellblock, the Ghosts. Max had heard the other prisoners call him Tadpole.

"Sabaidee, farang," he said, "I have message for you. From outside. Sorry for my English."

"It's better than my Lao," Max said. "I appreciate the effort. Hang on a sec."

He nodded to the Old Woman, who laid his shirt over his shoulders, covering the poultice. He got to his hands and knees, then somehow managed to turn and sit, facing Tadpole, who was smiling.

"They fuck you up pretty good, huh."

"Yeah. Pretty good."

"You don't break, huh."

"They have the wrong idea. I just sell water filters."

Tadpole laughed. "Good, good. Water filter." He shook his head and laughed again.

"You said you had a message from outside for me?"

"They come to break you out," Tadpole said.

"Who's coming?"

"No idea. I take you to the spot, they take you out. Arrangements made with Ghosts outside prison, I just follow orders."

"When?" Max asked.

"One week from tonight, midnight."

"Is the other farang coming too? The one that arrived with me?"

"Yes, both. Other Ghost bring him, I bring only you. One week."

"One week. Thank you."

"How much you pay me to take you to breakout spot?"

"Look around. I have nothing," Max said. "I suppose you could have my one pair of dirty underwear."

Anger flashed across Tadpole's face, then he understood and relaxed. "You make joke."

"Not a very good one."

"I tell you what," Tadpole said. "I help you, you owe me favor. Do something for me one day."

Max caught the Old Woman give him a sharp look of warning in his peripheral vision, but he needed to get out before they killed him, and he needed to find Kelly. He had nothing else to bargain with. "Deal," he said.

It was the longest week of Max's life. They continued to torture and whip him every third day, but knowing that meant just two more sessions, he found it easier than ever to resist. The prospect of breaking out of this hellhole buoyed his spirits and strengthened his resolve. Still, the torture was excruciating, and the whip was shredding his back so badly that he wasn't sure it would ever recover. His straw mattress was soaked with blood, and even the Old Woman's mud wasn't helping anymore. He didn't think it could get worse.

Then, on day four, Tadpole called in his favor.

CHAPTER TWENTY-SIX

The ride in the back of the truck was rough. They had heard the gun battle when they stopped, but Cintha guessed the bad guys must have won because they were moving again. Her wrists and ankles were zip-tied, her hands behind her back. She was still wearing her short skirt and halter top, and the older of the two guards in the back with them kept staring at her underwear, but at least she was cool. It was hot as balls in the back of the truck and Cintha was the only one, her mother included, who wasn't sweating like a pig.

She was seriously angry. Not at her mother, not at Max, not even at the men holding them hostage. She was mad at herself. She had been an arrogant, stupid little girl, right up until the moment her mother told her it was her fault that her father was dead because she was such a slut. When her mother said that all the fight left her, and she realized what a dumb little kid she really was. She felt small, petty, and stupid.

Her mother was only half right, though. It was her fault that her father was dead, but on the other thing she was dead wrong. Cintha was still a virgin. Her mom thought she was loose because of how she dressed, which, for real, wasn't very feminist of her. Plus, when did her mom think she was doing all this hooking up? She had barely ever been alone with a boy, every time she went to a party or a club her bodyguards stuck to her like glue. Maybe her mom thought she was doing one of them, but that was too gross to think about, they were like, thirty. And her dad would have had them shot if he even suspected they had touched her. Besides, her mom was a total hypocrite. Her dad had a girlfriend barely three years older than Cintha, that lived in the house with them and traveled with the family, and she never got all morality police about her.

She didn't even know why she went in there and crawled into Max's bed. She'd had a crush on him when she was a kid, and he was still super handsome, but also now he was kind of old and nasty. Actually losing it to him would have been totally disgusting.

That was a lie though, she did know. She did it to get at her mom, to show her, okay, you think I'm a whore, I might as well be one. That part of the plan, at least, had worked. Now the only way to fix what she did was to get her mother and her brothers out of this situation. That would be her redemption. She didn't have any idea how she would do it, but it was fully up to her to save the day.

She tried to work her hands free from the zip cuffs behind her back, but every time she shifted even slightly, the skeevy guard leered at her. She ignored him. They went over a big bump, and she found herself sitting back against the sharp corner of a wooden crate. She stared at her pink Nike Dunk Lows and slowly rubbed the zip tie up and down against the edge.

It took two hours, and she kept having to reposition herself because of the bouncing of the truck, but at last the plastic broke. She almost yelped with joy but caught herself in time. She saw the guard turn to look at her in her peripheral vision, but she kept staring at her shoes. Over the last two hours she had memorized every square millimeter of those shoes, every stitch, every contour. The left one had a scuff on the midsole, so once they landed somewhere she would need to get a new pair.

Her hands were free, but she had no idea what to do next. Since they were tied up, the guards weren't holding guns on them. They both had knives strapped to their legs, but the old perv had set his rifle down and leaned it on the bench where he was sitting, and the younger guy only had a handgun, and it was in his holster. Cintha had been shooting with her dad most of her life and was good with guns, so she could go for the rifle, but she knew they were trained mercenaries or whatever and would beat her to it. Maybe she could try to seduce the old geezer who kept looking up her skirt, but last night proved she wasn't very good at that either.

The geezer said, "I gotta piss."

"So piss," the younger one answered. They were speaking English.

"Where? You got a bottle or something?"

"Just hang it out the back."

The geezer considered it, shrugged, then got up and headed toward the back, without his rifle. Unfortunately he remembered, came back and grabbed it, and slung it over his shoulder. He went to the back and opened the canvas, unzipped and started peeing off the back of the truck.

Cintha saw the driver of the next truck back give him the finger. The geezer tried to raise his arc to hit the other truck, but it was too big a gap. They were all laughing.

The younger guard was watching, grinning, his head turned toward the back and away from Cintha. The knife on his leg was only a few feet from her. She had to go for it. She took a deep breath and got ready to jump into action.

Just as she started to move, her mother lunged forward, her hands also free. Her mom pulled the knife from the leg sheath and plunged it into the man's throat before he knew what was happening. He tried to call out, but she had stabbed him right through the larynx. His blood was spurting out in pumps, and her mother's hands were covered in it. It was epic.

The man at the back was shaking off and zipping up. Her mom tried to pull the dying man's pistol (it looked like a .45) but her hands were so slick with blood that she couldn't get a grip. Cintha pushed her out of the way and yanked the pistol free from the holster (it was a .45!) just as the pervy guard closed the canvas flaps and turned around.

He found Cintha aiming at him, sitting with her elbows on her knees, her feet still bound together, and both hands on the gun the way her father taught her. He looked surprised, then amused. He looked her in the eyes.

"Okay, sweetie," he said, "put the gun down before you hurt yourself."

Instead of complying, she held eye contact with him while she reached up with her thumb and flicked the safety off. His expression hardened.

Her mother dried her hands on the dead guy's shirt, then pulled the knife out of his throat and cut her own feet loose, then Cintha's. Then she quickly freed both of her brothers. The truck was jostling, but Cintha held the gun steady. Her mother walked back to the guard.

"Give me the rifle."

He started to comply, then the truck bounced through a pothole and her mother lost her footing. The man shoved her aside and Cintha fired the .45 just as they hit another pothole. Her shot went through the canvas and out the back. The geezer lifted his rifle. Her mother stabbed him in the leg and Cintha fired again. This time the bullet hit him in the chest, and he looked surprised as he fell out the back with the knife still in his leg.

He hit the road and rolled to a stop. He sat up and thought, *Hallelujah, my vest saved my life*, just as the second truck slammed into him and the front bumper caved in his head.

In the cab of the lead truck, Max, who was still behind the wheel, and Derek heard the shots. Over the engines and the other sounds of trucks careening over the rutted road, they weren't sure at first.

"Were those gunshots?" Derek asked.

Max looked in his rearview mirror. "Truck two is stopping." He eased his truck into first and rolled to a stop. He killed the engine and took the keys as they both hopped out and headed back.

The second truck had stopped about a hundred feet behind them, and they were halfway to it before Max saw the mangled body of the guard under the front axle.

"What the hell happened here?"

"Max, look."

He looked up at the cab and saw a spiderweb of glass around a bullet hole in the windshield, the driver sitting behind it with a neat hole in his forehead.

"Where'd that shot come from?" Max asked.

Veronica Usher came around from behind the truck, rifle in her hands. She asked, "What's the situation?"

"Sniper in the trees, maybe?" Derek answered.

"Why would they shoot the second truck?" Max asked.

He looked ahead at his own truck. Something caught his eye. He jogged over, Derek and Veronica on his heels. There was a bullet hole in the rear canvas; someone had shot through the canvas from inside, and the bullet had gone through the windshield of the second truck and killed the driver.

On a signal from Max, Derek and Veronica raised their weapons and covered him. Derek nodded, ready, and Max flung the canvas aside. There was another dead guard on the bench, drenched in blood, but otherwise the truck was empty.

President Vinthu's wife and kids were gone.

Derek spun around and looked at the jungle, started going one way, then the other.

"Forget it," Max said, "we'll never find them in all that, and we were going to let them go eventually anyway."

"Actually," Derek said, "I planned to kill them."

"I know you did. But this works too. It'll take them a month to find their way back, if they even manage to do it."

Derek nodded, but muttered under his breath, "Loose ends." He took a moment. "We're down a driver. Looks like I'm up," Derek said.

"Take the lead, I'll drive truck two."

"It's your route, you take point. I might get us lost."

Max nodded. He exchanged a fleeting glance with Veronica as Derek walked to the second truck, pulled the dead driver out so he fell to the ground, and climbed in behind the wheel. Veronica pulled the dog tags from the dead men, rolled them out of the road, and headed back to the rear of the caravan.

Max walked back to the lead truck, got in, and started the engine. As he pulled out, he thought, *Yep, this trip gets better with every mile.*

CHAPTER TWENTY-SEVEN

The field hospital Kelly was laid up in was poorly equipped, but sterile and well run. The doctor who set her broken arm, who introduced himself as Dr. Phan, was clearly a fully trained physician and not a field medic. The nurses were fastidious and efficient. She felt like she was in good hands, medically anyway.

During the day they kept the wall flaps rolled up for ventilation, and Kelly could see a good portion of the rebel camp from her bed. The jungle was thick here, too, and Kelly could tell they had gained some elevation by the dwarf palms and ginger plants which only grew in abundance higher-up. They had cleared some of the foliage away to build the camp, but hadn't killed the oldest growth trees, so camp life flowed around them. The largest was a banyan tree at what she figured was the center of camp, its spreading trunks covering half an acre. Meals were served under its canopy. From her bed she could hear the chittering of insects, the chattering of distant monkeys, and the grating, screechy call of a koel bird.

The camp itself was not what Kelly had expected. Sure, there were all the things she thought would be there. Tents for sleeping, camouflage nets hanging over their heads, some Jeeps that had seen better days, and a couple of dozen horses, mostly Thai ponies which were smaller than other breeds, but nimble and strong and better suited to the jungle than larger breeds. There were even a couple of elephants. The camp housed six or seven dozen fighting-aged men and women with a hodgepodge arsenal of weapons, from machetes to machine guns, and from the amount of food preparation going on in the open-air kitchen, she figured there must be at least that many more fighters outside the perimeter of the camp.

All of that she expected, but there were also families. When she was still groggy from her injuries and whatever painkillers Dr. Phan was feeding her through her IV, she thought she was imagining the sound of kids playing, a delirium dream of the children Derek had unilaterally decided she would never have. But as the cobwebs cleared, she realized there actually were kids running around. Between the fighters, the support staff, and the families, Kelly estimated there were five hundred people in the camp, at minimum. It was a small town.

"Dr. Phan," she asked as he was checking her ankle, "where did all these women and children come from?"

"Some belong to our soldiers and staff," he explained. "My wife and children are here, just up the hill there. Some are the families of men killed in the dictator Vinthu's purges. Others are from villages we passed along the way who just decided to join us."

"Why would they choose to follow Chakri?"

He glanced at her before continuing. "Chakri the madman, you mean?"

She didn't answer. She had heard the stories about the rebel leader and his habit of settling arguments by chopping his opponent up with his machete, as well as his use of rape as a weapon of war, which fortunately no rebel had tried to use on her yet (fortunately for them, she meant). He was known for his hair-trigger temper, which could be set off by something as simple as too much salt on the pork, and which erupted into operatic displays of arterial blood spray and death.

"If wanting this country to belong to the people who live in it is insanity," Dr. Phan said, "then I guess I am crazy too."

He went to inject more pain meds into her IV line. She held up her hand.

"No, please."

"You will be in a lot of pain."

"Pain and I are old friends."

"As you wish. Let the nurse know if you change your mind."

Kelly had several reasons for turning down the pain meds, chief among them that she could see their supplies were meager, and she didn't want to use meds that a child or a wounded fighter might need down the road. She also wanted to keep a clear head, knowing that as soon as they thought she was up to it, she would be interrogated. And lastly, she needed to learn the camp, not just the layout but also the rhythms, the comings and goings, because as soon as she could move well enough, she would need to mount her escape.

That first night, she regretted her decision. She had been prepared for the pain of her broken arm and sprained ankle but hadn't counted on the battering she took both in the crash, and in the fall from the canopy to the jungle floor. She could barely move her stiff neck, but she managed to look under her hospital gown, and found that her body was essentially one big, ugly purple bruise. She laid back and concentrated on her breath, willing her mind to ignore the pain in her body. She managed to catch a few minutes of sleep here and there before a throb or a twinge would wake her up again.

He came to her early the next morning. She awoke to a commotion outside the tent, an excited murmur, people pressing together on the main path through the camp as if a rock star were walking down the street. The crowd parted in front of the hospital and Chewy Chakri emerged, smiling. Women and children were touching his hands, kissing his fingers like he was the pope. *Is that all this is*, she thought, *a cult of personality?*

She sized him up as best she could in the ten yards he had to cross to reach her bed. She had heard he was physically small, but he looked to be about five-foot-six, fairly average for a man in this part of the world. He was wearing fatigues but didn't appear to have a weapon on him. He had long black hair, tied back in a ponytail, and a razor-thin mustache like a 1930s movie star, or John Waters. Still, he was handsome, even if he was overdoing it a little bit.

A nurse dragged a chair over for him. He said, "Thank you," smiled at her, and sat down beside Kelly's bed. The nurse walked off, blushing.

"The doctor tells me you have refused pain medication."

"I like to keep a clear head," she said.

"What was it T. E. Lawrence said? The trick is not minding that it hurts."

"I'm not sure if that's a real quote, or just something from the movie."

"Either way." He looked over the cast on her arm, then met her eyes and smiled, the way a spider might when a fly hit its web. "Kelly Riggs. We've met before, you know."

"I don't think so. I would remember meeting the infamous Chewy Chakri."

"It was a long time ago, and I wasn't Chewy Chakri the famous madman then. I was simply Charles Chakri the supply clerk. I was there the day that you and, now what was his name, Max Starkey, that's right, helped then presidential candidate Vinthu stage a raid on the Hap Phong fuel depot. I was one of the three survivors."

She remembered the day well. It was supposed to be a simple seizure of government oil, but under Vinthu's command it turned into a bloodbath, the first of many. Chakri was there? If so, she was in a lot more trouble than she thought.

He waved a hand dismissively. "As I said, a long time ago. So, you were piloting Vinthu's helicopter. My men scoured the landing area, but we could not find him."

"He wasn't aboard. I stole the helo and was making a run for it. He's still back at the northern palace, safe and sound with his family."

"What were you running from?"

"That's my business."

"Why should I believe you?"

"Honestly, I don't give two shits if you do or don't. You said yourself, you searched the crash zone and he's not there. No one is there, and if I couldn't walk away from that crash, that soft old prick sure as hell couldn't. You wasted a ground-to-air missile on me, and from the looks of things around here I doubt you have much armament to spare."

Irritation flashed in his eyes, and she knew she had hit a nerve. He looked at her for a long time. She returned his intense gaze, then looked away first, and hated herself for giving him that small victory.

"You have the run of the camp," he said. "When you are up to it, feel free to explore. Talk to people. Ask questions. But do not try to leave or you will be shot."

He walked out. She lay there for a long time watching the movements of the camp and thinking about the Hap Phong fuel depot raid. It was a shit show, a straight-up massacre. If he really was there, one of the few survivors as he claimed, then she was fucked and needed to escape sooner than later. Everyone knew his lust for vengeance was insatiable, and her death would be slow and painful. She would take him up on his offer to explore the camp. She would prod its defenses and learn its perimeter. But she would not let her guard down for an instant.

Stay vigilant, she told herself, as she finally drifted off to sleep.

CHAPTER TWENTY-EIGHT

Giuliana leaned on her hospital-issued cane and looked down at the corpse of President Chavarat Vinthu while an older bureau photographer who looked exactly like Luigi from *Mario Kart* took photos. Vinthu's gun was still in his hand. He hadn't been dead long, the room still smelled of nitroglycerin and graphite from the gunpowder, mixed with the rusty odor of blood.

A younger agent cataloging evidence said, "There's gunshot residue on this sleeve, and the shot was point blank, from under the chin. It certainly looks like suicide."

"It does," she agreed. "But there's also a void in the blood pattern, here, see that?"

"Meaning?"

"Meaning someone was standing very close to him when he shot himself." That held no significance in and of itself; there were dozens of people it could have been standing there. But Giuliana felt a cold foreboding just the same.

"Right." The younger agent turned to the photographer. "Make sure you get shots of that void there." Luigi met Giuliana's eyes for a fleeting second, can you believe this kid telling me my job? Giuliana smiled.

A Suryakan policeman stuck his head in the door. "We found another one."

"Another what?"

"Corpse. Another dead person."

Giuliana limped out of the room and followed him down the hall, thinking, please God, don't let it be Max.

So far at least, the local cops were being extremely cooperative. They were a rural station, five officers total, and had no desire to take the lead on the death of a president on the eve of being deposed. In fact, they were grateful that the Americans were taking charge and had agreed to keep Vinthu's death quiet for now to avoid national panic. The CIA suitcase stuffed with hundred-dollar bills also helped ensure their discretion.

To their credit, her bosses had tried to obtain official permission to enter the country and investigate, but with Vinthu dead and the country under martial law, there really wasn't anyone to ask.

"Constitutionally, with the president dead, it's supposed to be the prime minister, followed by the vice president," Lin had told her.

"Okay, so where are they?"

"Good question. Two weeks ago, in a last-ditch attempt to consolidate his power, Vinthu appointed his wife, Kaeo, as prime minister, and one of his kids, I believe it was the daughter, as vice president. They're missing, and I doubt if either one of them even knows he did it."

"The chopper is gone too," Giuliana pointed out. "The family is probably in Tashkent by now, anyway."

Two of the five FBI agents assigned to her for the investigation were waiting when she walked into another ornate bedroom, following the local cop. There was a beautiful young woman lying nude in the bed, a neat round bullet hole in the middle of her forehead. The smell was worse in here, due to the woman's bowels letting loose at the moment of death.

"Who is she?" Giuliana asked.

The male agent, Wojciehowicz, said, "No idea. There's no identification in the room, and she's not one of the first family. Mistress, maybe?"

"Murder suicide?"

The female agent, Carver, jumped in. "She's in full rigor. She died at least eight hours before Vinthu."

"That doesn't rule out murder suicide, it could be that it just took him some time to get up the courage to off himself. All right, we're done here."

She turned to go. Carver asked, "What about her?"

"Let the local cops deal with it," Giuliana answered. "It's a civilian death, and I doubt it has anything to do with our mandate, which is finding the stolen gold and arresting the thieves."

"Should we at least get Luigi in here to take photos?"

Giuliana smiled slightly; so, she wasn't the only one who saw it. "Sure."

Carver nodded and the two younger agents followed Giuliana out. She noticed each of them hesitate at the door and glance back at the dead girl, wrestling with their innate empathy and their desire not to leave her alone. They were just a couple of years out of Quantico, but they were smart and dedicated, and Giuliana knew that the sentimentality would be ground out of them soon enough. For now they still had it, and she was a little bit jealous.

She was moving fairly well but wasn't quite ready for stairs, so she rode the elevator down to the ground floor and made her way to the ballroom, where several high-tech consoles were set up. Two men from the NSA, and the woman from the State Department that had been in her hospital room, were monitoring satellite images that were coming in, in real time. Giuliana had been told all their names, but she hadn't prioritized the information, and it was long gone.

"Anything?" she asked the room in general. An NSA man answered.

"We have one satellite in fixed position over the jungle and two that pass once every ninety minutes and every four hours, respectively. So far, we haven't found anything."

"It's a large country," the State Department woman said. Karen something, Giuliana suddenly remembered. "Small on a map, but in reality, it's a lot of ground to cover, about fifty thousand square miles. And most of the roads are completely under the jungle canopy. Spotting five trucks in all of that is like a needle in a haystack."

"Seven trucks," Giuliana said.

“The gate guard told us five trucks left early this morning.”

“According to the motor pool manifest, there are seven trucks missing, not five. Of course we don’t know how many of them they’re responsible for. They could have taken one and the rest went AWOL some other way. Or they took seven. Or none, maybe they went by horse-drawn cart. Maybe the guard is right and they took five, maybe he’s wrong. Or he could be lying. All we can do is keep looking.”

“We’ll do our best.”

They returned to their monitors as Giuliana walked down the hall and back into President Vinthu’s study. She was convinced this was the last room Max had been in before he left, maybe even the room he called her from. The smell of cigar smoke was still in the air, and some unwashed glasses sat on the desk and table. She couldn’t smell Max in the room, but she felt him and knew he had been there.

She spotted the corner of a piece of paper under the desk. Her agents had searched the room, but not forensically, and they didn’t move furniture. As she bent forward her abdomen felt like it was going to rip open, but she gritted her teeth and reached down, pulled the paper out and stood back up, taking deep breaths until the pain subsided.

She unfolded and smoothed out the rumpled paper. It was a map, with their route to the border marked in red ink.

“Gotcha.”

She took the map and walked back to the ballroom as quickly as she could manage. “Focus all of your satellites on the northern half of the country,” she told them. “Anything above our location.”

An NSA agent asked, “Why?”

“I found this map in the study. It has their route clearly marked out.”

The others examined the map. Confused, State Department Karen said, “But Agent Abara, the route on this map goes south.”

“Exactly. I know Max Starkey, and he isn’t stupid enough to leave a map of their route behind, unless he wanted us to find it.”

“You think it’s a decoy?”

Giuliana nodded. “They went north.”

CHAPTER TWENTY-NINE

This absolutely fucking sucked. Cintha had been following her mother and her brothers through the jungle for hours now, and she def wasn't dressed for it in her skirt and halter top. Her legs, arms, and tummy were shredded from sharp branches and prickly bushes. Not to mention she was getting itchy bug bites all over her limbs. She couldn't believe she had been worried about a scuff mark on her Dunk Lows, which were now completely fucked. They were caked in mud so you couldn't even tell they were pink anymore, they were torn, and one sole was flopping half off.

She had carried the .45 for the first two hours, but she didn't have anywhere to put it. She had to hold it in her hand, and after a while, her arm went numb from swinging the weight of it. Her mother had taken it and given it to her brother, who tucked it in his waistband and strutted through the jungle like he was in a Tarantino movie. She was just getting feeling back in her arm.

Sunset was less than two hours away and the jungle was turning spooky. Once or twice she heard something in the bushes, like someone was following them, someone big, but she chalked it up to her imagination. There was nobody but her and her mother and her two idiot brothers for miles in any direction.

"Mom," she said, "I need to rest."

"We keep moving," Kaeo answered tersely.

"I'm getting eaten up by bugs, I want to put some mud on my arms and legs to keep them off. And look at Beavis and Butt-Head." Her nicknames for her brothers. "They're barely able to walk. We need a break."

"Keep moving, end of discussion."

Cintha sighed and kept trudging. There it was again, the sound in the brush. For a moment she was afraid it might be a tiger, but no, a tiger wouldn't stalk them. She had learned in ninth grade that tigers don't like human flesh, that only forty or fifty people get attacked by tigers every year in all of Asia, including India, and that was usually because the person had done something boneheaded and got themselves mauled. Tigers that had eaten human flesh before might do it again, but they didn't get a lust for it like in movies, and the wildlife people always killed a tiger that attacked a person, just in case. So whatever she heard, it wasn't a tiger.

They walked past a mud hole and Cintha couldn't take it anymore. She was a little behind the others anyway, so she would do what she needed to do and then catch up. She sat on a rock at the edge of the pond and started spreading mud on her legs. It felt amazing, so soothing. She saw a twenty-foot-long Burmese rock python, as thick as her torso, curled around a tree branch on the other side of the pond, but she didn't react. She knew enough about the jungle animals to know that it would ignore her too.

She finished caking both legs in mud, then started on her arms. As she patted it on, she thought back to shooting that skeevy guy on the truck and smiled. She thought, *How do you like my underwear now, asshole*, then thought, *Wait, that didn't make much sense*. She looked up and the snake was gone. Everything was in shadow. How long had she been sitting here anyway?

She heard a gunshot in the distance. Then another one. She was trying to figure out what it meant when she heard her mother scream. It was faint and far away, but it was the sound of sheer terror. Cintha yelled "Mom?" at the top of her lungs, then thought, *Maybe I should shut the hell up*. She took off running after her family.

This time she didn't notice the branches tearing her arms up, or how tired she was. She just ran. She pulled up every ounce of energy and every bit of determination and bolted through the jungle like a gazelle. Okay, a hella clumsy gazelle, but still. She ran until she reached the edge of a large clearing that led to a thick bamboo forest, then she skidded to a stop.

They were dead. All three of them, and they had died violently and painfully, her brothers mangled almost beyond recognition. Cintha nearly passed out as the blood rushed to her head. The world spun and her knees buckled, but she somehow managed to stay on her feet. She forced herself to focus and saw her mother on her back in the middle of the glade.

The tiger was still feasting on her.

It was a full-grown male, and a big one. In that moment Cintha wasn't sure how she remembered what she knew about tigers, but she knew this one was larger than average. It was at least ten feet long and must have weighed five hundred pounds. She was sure of this, but then again, she had been sure about the whole tigers-won't-eat-people thing too.

Cintha didn't move. She fought the urge to sob, or scream. She was a statue, barely even breathing. She only moved her eyes, which were stinging with tears that she didn't dare wipe away, scanning the clearing until she saw the gun. It was on the ground near the pile of twisted meat that used to be Beavis and Butt-Head. There was no way she could reach it, the tiger would be on her before she covered a quarter the distance. She remained still.

She couldn't stand here forever. Eventually the tiger would spot her or pick up her scent. She couldn't hesitate like she did in the truck, because her mother couldn't step in and save her this time. She took one step backward, then stopped.

The tiger raised its head and looked directly at her.

CHAPTER THIRTY

The rendezvous point was the intersection of two muddy roads, the one they had followed since the palace, and another, smaller road heading into the remotest part of the jungle. There was a peat swamp nearby, with enough space between the seventy-foot trees for Kelly to scuttle the helo, but there was no sign of it, or of her. Under Veronica's direction, the nine remaining mercenaries formed three search parties and went out to look for her. Derek refused to leave the gold, and Max didn't want to leave him alone for reasons of his own. So the two of them sat on a fallen tree on the side of the road and waited. Max noticed a huntsman spider the size of his head sitting on the trunk of a nearby acacia tree.

The roar of the engines had muted the sounds of the jungle, but now they were loud and oppressive. Aside from the bird calls and insects, he could hear movement in every direction, big things, little things, slithering things, every leaf vibrating with abundant life. He watched a nine-inch centipede, as thick as his thumb, crawl over his boot and estimated there were a dozen things that could kill him within a thirty-yard radius. There was nothing to be done about it, so as the centipede slinked off into the foliage, Max took out two protein bars and offered one to Derek. "Hungry?"

Derek shook his head. He was staring at the ground, his brow furrowed. Max ate his quickly and started on the other one.

"She's gone, Max."

"Don't catastrophize. I'm sure she's alive, she probably just drifted off course."

"I do not mean she is dead, I mean she's gone. My soulmate has left me."

Genuinely surprised, Max asked, "You think she took the helo and just bolted?"

"That is what I am saying. I had a feeling. A premonition when she was taking off."

"Bullshit. I've seen the way she looks at you."

Derek looked up at him. Max didn't see hope in his eyes, he didn't see anything. Derek's eyes were empty, like a shark's eyes.

"You really think so?"

"Sure," Max said. "And we both know how materialistic she is. She wouldn't leave the gold. When I suggested it, she nearly bit my head off. We'll find her on the way, guaranteed."

"Good. Thank you," Derek said. Max nodded but Derek wasn't finished. "Because if she left me, I would have to kill her. I would have to find her, and I would have to kill her."

Before Max could formulate an answer to that, Veronica's three-person search party emerged from the direction of the swamp.

"We looked everywhere, did a grid search," Veronica said. "She's not here."

Max asked, "What about the helo's transponder?"

"It's not working," Veronica answered. "Either she turned it off, or . . ." She stopped herself.

Derek looked at her and finished her thought. "Or it was destroyed in a crash."

Veronica nodded. They all stood there for a few moments as the other two search parties returned, shaking their heads, no luck.

"What do you want to do?" Max asked Derek.

He took a deep breath, blew it out, then stood up. "Get the trucks ready to move. We keep going, we don't have time to delay."

Veronica nodded and gestured to her mercenaries, and they headed for the trucks.

"Listen," Max said when he and Derek were alone, "we have to alter the route."

"We cannot."

"We have to. What if she was caught? What if someone has her, right now, and is torturing her as we speak?"

"She would never break, you know that."

"You willing to risk your life on that?"

Derek took a beat. "Of course," he said. "You are right, of course you are. I'm sorry, I wasn't thinking clearly, because of my missing bride."

"Understandable."

"You have an alternate route worked out?"

"I have several routes worked out, just in case."

Derek nodded and clapped him on the shoulder. "I'm watching you, Max."

It took about half an hour on the muddy road to get the trucks backed up and reoriented, time Max spent studying the new route on his maps. They headed north into the deepest part of the jungle, on a road even narrower than the one they had been on. Max was concerned about Kelly, but the fact was that she made his life easier by disappearing. He would have found a reason to change the route one way or the other, but by not showing up, she did it for him.

SEVEN YEARS AGO

DAY OF THE ESCAPE

Max was in more physical pain than he had thought possible. The whipping he took the day before went to new heights of intensity and brutality. They added barbs to the ends of the lashes, and today his back had the consistency of raw hamburger. It was so bad that, at first, he thought the interrogator must know about the impending breakout, but it never came up. Now he was lying face down, trying to rest so he'd have energy for the escape. He didn't even raise his head when the Old Woman came in with her poultice.

"Not today," he said softly, in Lao. He would be grateful for the soothing effects, but he didn't want to smell like shit when he got out of here.

"I didn't bring it," she said. He looked up and saw that she was empty-handed. "I came to say goodbye, and to wish you luck."

"Thank you," he said. "But I'm not out yet."

"What Tadpole asked of you. Will you do it?"

He wanted to tell her the truth, to say no, not a chance in hell. But in Phonthong you never knew who was listening, or who the Old Woman might report his answer to. So instead, he said, "Yes. Of course I will. I gave my word."

She nodded, a little sadly, and for a moment he wished he had been honest with her. The moment passed.

Two days ago he was sitting in the main quad eating half a papaya, one of less than a dozen that had been smuggled in, hidden in the laundry. He wanted to savor it, but instead he ate quickly and kept his eyes open. There were men in here that would kill you for half a piece of fresh fruit.

Tadpole came and sat beside him. For a while, neither of them spoke. They could hear a baby's cries echoing in the cells. Max saw the gang member eying his papaya, so he forced himself to stop before he finished and gave the remainder to him. Tadpole ate it quickly, scraping the inside of the skin with his teeth. When he was done, he tossed the skin in the dirt, and someone immediately picked it up.

"Three more days, go home."

"Yes."

"Time for favor." He looked at Max, who nodded.

"I'm listening."

"After you are out, you kill General Vong."

Max almost laughed out loud. "What?" He looked at Tadpole for a few moments, thinking he had to be joking, and the real favor was coming, but Tadpole was dead serious. Max asked, "You want me to assassinate a Lao army general?"

"I want nothing. I deliver message. Price for help breakout is life of Vong."

"No way. You must be joking. I'm not going to do that."

"Okay. You stay here, maybe die next week, maybe live here five, ten, twenty years. Life outside go on, woman find new man, family forget you. You stay, no problem."

He clapped his hands together and spread them, done, and started to walk away. "Wait." Max watched him walk back and arch an eyebrow as he sat.

He asked, "Why do you want Vong killed?"

"How do you Americans say, beyond my salary level. It is yes, or no."

Max thought about Kelly on the outside. He knew she would be loyal for a reasonable length of time, but Tadpole was right, of course, eventually she would move on to another man. Max couldn't fault her for that, she would have every right, and he wanted her to be happy. But just the thought of never seeing her again felt like a knife in his heart. He nodded.

"I have to hear you say it."

"I'll do it. Get me out of here, and I'll kill Vong."

"Word is contract. Don't fulfill contract, Ghosts kill you."

"I understand."

He did understand, but he had no intention of murdering someone, especially someone high up in another nation's army. So he made up his mind sitting on that bench. After his debrief he would resign from the agency, and because of the torture he was currently enduring, the agency would happily sign off on it, probably even give him an early pension. He would propose to Kelly, marry her, and they would leave Southeast Asia together and never return. He was pretty sure a Vientiane street gang wouldn't track him overseas. As long as they never came back to this part of the world, he'd be fine.

Tadpole came for him ten minutes before midnight, his finger over his mouth, signaling quiet. Max followed him out and they moved along the wall. The night air was oppressively humid, and Max's shirt was sticking to the bloody gashes on his back, causing the skin to feel like it was ripping open all over again with each step.

Tadpole stopped him at the corner to the quad, and they peered around. There was a guard on the wall, pacing, watching the open area. Tadpole stepped out first, the guard saw him and turned so his back was facing them. Tadpole signaled Max, let's go. They crossed the center of the quad, the guard keeping his back to them all the way. Just part of the service, Max supposed.

They went into the rear cell block and Tadpole led him along past the open doors. Each cell Max passed was like a diorama of horror and vice. Men kneeling around homemade dice; male and female prisoners zonked out, needles still dangling from their arms; a desperate woman trying to breastfeed a scrawny baby that would rather scream itself to death than latch on; several men waiting in line for their turn on top of one woman, clutching the scraps of food and clothing they would use to pay her. The human misery in Phonthong was bottomless. Max tried to keep his mind on what lay ahead.

Two more guards turned their backs as Tadpole led him through the kitchen. The Ghosts wielded a lot of power inside the prison walls. When they reached the back door, Tadpole tried it and found it unlocked.

"Good day when everyone do job."

They slipped out and ran across a small patch of grass to a heavy iron door in the outer prison wall, thirty feet from a tower where two guards kept watch, one of them sweeping the outside perimeter with a searchlight. Derek and his Ghost guide arrived at precisely the same time, as if it were choreographed. Max and Derek nodded to each other but didn't speak. Derek looked to be in much better shape than Max, but he had probably been tortured just as badly, and it didn't show. Different interrogators had different methods, all horrific.

They heard a high-pitched whirring on the other side of the door, which Max guessed was the sound of a handheld drill. The noise stopped when the searchlight came back their way, then started up again after it passed.

"Careful listening," Tadpole said. "Other side of wall, thirty meters open ground to trees. Wait for light to pass, run like hell." *I guess they don't own all the guards*, Max thought. "Once in trees," Tadpole continued, "go five hundred meters straight, find road. Car waiting."

"Who's in the car?" Derek asked.

Tadpole held up his hand, *I have no idea*. He watched the guards on the tower, timing their movements. When they were both facing away, he knocked once on the door and whoever was on the other side opened it.

"Go through," Tadpole said, "but stay close to wall, wait for light."

"Aren't you coming?"

Tadpole shrugged. "I do my time. Go."

Derek went through first and Max followed. There was a woman waiting for them, hair pulled up under a cap, dressed all in black. Max had never seen her before, but she was a standard-issue mercenary.

The three of them pressed back against the wall, watching the searchlight sweep the ground. When it moved away, they ran.

Thirty meters is a big distance when you think you might get shot in the back, but, even injured, they covered it in under six seconds and were safely in the trees before the light came back. Running through the jungle was impossible, every tree branch or scratch from a bush hitting spots that had been beaten or whipped, so they walked.

Derek asked the woman with the drill, "Who are you?"

"I'm your driver," was her only response.

Max asked Derek in a whisper, "What did you have to promise them to get out?"

"You first," Derek said.

"I'm supposed to kill someone."

"Me too. Who is your target?"

"You first."

The woman said, "Talk about this later. Right now let's just get the fuck out of here."

It took less than three minutes to get through the jungle but felt like an hour. Max was fighting to stay conscious through the pain and the blood loss.

They came out on a narrow blacktop. There was a Range Rover waiting for them, a few years old and caked in mud. They ran to it. Derek jumped into the front passenger seat, the woman got behind the wheel, and Max pulled open the back door and crawled in.

He saw her high-end RATs first, and he had never been so happy to see a pair of boots. Kelly was in the back seat waiting for him and she looked beautiful, but more importantly, she looked whole, like she hadn't been tortured. He climbed in and they held each other.

Their rescuer looked back. "Hang on. I'm Veronica, by the way. Veronica Usher."

Max fell forward, his head in Kelly's lap. She kissed his forehead, and she said his name, and all was right with the world.

CHAPTER THIRTY-ONE

Kelly walked the rebel camp just before sunset. She had slept a good portion of the day, and her ankle was wrapped tightly and had been shot full of cortisone, so she could move fairly well without a crutch, but she had found a heavy wooden cane in the med tent and was using it to keep weight off the ankle. She probably could have walked without it, but in a pinch, it would serve as a fairly decent weapon.

The open-air kitchen was in full dinner prep mode, and it was a massive undertaking, even if they did do it every day. There were six whole pigs roasting on spits, and massive pots of rice being stirred with big wooden ladles. She passed downwind of the kitchen and realized she hadn't eaten in over twenty-four hours, and her stomach and her head both ached from hunger. She approached a table where a young male baker was slicing fresh loaves of bread.

"May I please?" she asked in Suryakan.

The baker looked annoyed, but when he looked up and saw her, he smiled, tore off the end of a loaf, and handed it to her. She thanked him and ate it as she walked away, feeling his eyes on her ass.

It was a massive camp, like walking through a village, except that there was nothing in this village that couldn't be packed up and moved inside of fifteen minutes. Some of the children watched her with curiosity, but the adults largely ignored her, as if they had foreign women limping through their midst every day. The camp was alive with activity. With few exceptions, the women did laundry, mended clothing, and tended to the children, while the men chopped wood, maintained the tents, and cleaned their guns. The division of labor was decidedly old school, along clear gender lines. She did pass a tent where men and women worked side by side filling shells with gunpowder, so the business of death was gender neutral, at least.

She noticed a tent with the side flaps down, which was odd in the oppressive heat and out of synch with the rest of the camp. She walked over to it and circled it, looking for the door, which was on the back side. She stopped to listen when she heard voices from inside, a heated discussion in Suryakan. One of the voices was Chakri's.

"I can't move my army south until we get more ammunition. Half of our rifles are empty, and we wasted our last missile on Vinthu's helicopter."

"There is no more money," one of the other voices said.

"General," another added, "we are going to run out of food in less than a week."

"I understand that," Chakri answered. "We must try the Americans again."

"They were very clear, they will not finance us," the first voice said. "Vinthu is their man, they put him in power. They are not going to pay for an attack on him."

"It is not about Vinthu!" Chakri shouted angrily. "He is going to be killed or flee the country, either way he's not our problem much longer. But if we are not strong enough to stop him, General Ruchuphan will step into power. He has the army behind him. Then nothing will have changed, we will have traded one dictator for another, just as bad."

"Maybe worse," the other voice said.

A new voice added, "I am old enough to remember the purges when the monarchy fell. I was forced to dig graves in the killing fields. We will see the same again. General Ruchuphan will burn this country to the ground in his lust for power."

"That's why we must be strong enough to face the army," Chakri said. "Find a way. I don't care if we have to go to Tokyo and rob a bank. Find me money."

Kelly realized he was coming out, and she scrambled back. When he emerged, brow knitted in thought, she did her best to look surprised and said, "Oh, hello."

He stopped and looked at her a beat, then back at the tent, then at her again.

"Is this your quarters?" she asked.

"No." He looked at her for another moment, then his countenance softened. "How are your injuries? You seem to be moving well."

"The trick is not minding that it hurts."

He smiled. "It's time that you and I had a more substantial conversation," he said.

Here it comes, Kelly thought. She was ready. She had been interrogated many times and was not afraid of it. She would feed him bits of information, just enough to keep him from killing her. She would hold back the fact that Vinthu was already dead until she really needed it. It was her trump card.

"I've saved you a spot in my circle for dinner," he said. "I hope you'll join me."

"Yes, of course." She was surprised but didn't show it. "I'd be honored."

He looked at her a moment longer, as if trying to decide something, then nodded and walked off. She watched the adoring faces of his people turn toward him as he passed, and thought to herself, *What is this guy's tactic? To kill me with kindness?*

At dinner, they sat on blankets on the ground, in a semicircle around a fire, Kelly on Chakri's right in a spot he had saved for her. The rest of the people in his circle were essentially the voices she had heard in the tent, the camp's leadership and their families. Before dinner some of the camp's children performed a traditional song and dance, which delighted Chakri, and signed Kelly's cast with colored markers, which amused her. She was ready to eat her own foot by the time dinner finally came and had to force herself not to wolf it down. It was basic fare, shredded pork over rice with a side of pan-fried eggplant, but like all food in the region, it was five-alarm. When Kelly had first started eating Suryakan food, every meal had made her sweat profusely and break out in hiccups, but now she was used to it, and she enjoyed the simple food.

After the dishes were cleared, someone came and poured them rice wine. *I see you have enough money to buy booze*, Kelly thought.

"So, our more in-depth talk," Chakri said to her as small conversations started up around the fire. "Ask me anything you want."

"Me, ask you?"

"I'm an open book." She hadn't prepared for this, but she would play along.

"Okay," she said. "Why do you want to rule the country?"

"I don't."

"So all of this is just for fun? You murder, rape, and pillage for the hell of it?"

He smiled. "You read too much propaganda."

"Sure. I bet you don't even own a machete."

"Of course I do. This jungle is full of coconuts that need splitting. And we are trying to overthrow a corrupt government, a certain amount of killing comes with the task."

"You want to overthrow the government, but you don't want power."

"Once we have liberated the people, there will be a free and fair election."

"Which you'll win, naturally."

He shook his head. "I won't run. I am a leader right now because an army needs a general, and a movement needs inspiration. But I'll step aside when the job is done."

She tried to read his face, to see if he was even a little bit sincere. He seemed to mean it, but she had met enough psychopaths to know that they faked sincerity very well. To his followers, Charles Manson appeared to have a clear handle on things.

"So the stories about you, the butchery and the cruelty. All made up by your enemies?"

"I have done my share of killing in this war, of course I have. But you were there, that day at the fuel depot." He poked at the fire with a stick, sending up sparks. "You saw the face of barbarity. Vinthu could have taken the fuel without violence, there was no need to slaughter the workers. He enjoyed it. And after America helped him into power, he murdered thousands of his own citizens. So tell me, Ms. Riggs, who has inflicted more carnage on my country?" He looked her in the eye. "Me, or you?"

Kelly felt warm, from the shame or the wine, she couldn't tell. She wanted to defend herself, to laugh at him and tell him he was wrong. But she couldn't, because he was right. She could have pointed out that she was just following orders, which was true, but the fact was Vinthu had been a murderous tyrant, and she had helped put him in power.

She sipped her wine and stared at the fire until he asked, "Any more questions?"

She thought about it but could only come up with one. "Am I your prisoner?"

"Unfortunately," he said, "you know my location, you know my numbers, and by now I'm sure you have a pretty good idea of the strengths and weaknesses of my little force here. You will be treated as a guest, not a prisoner, but yes, I am afraid I must keep you from leaving."

"Then just one more question," she said. "May I have another glass of wine?"

CHAPTER THIRTY-TWO

When Cintha woke up she was still safely in the tree, which was good, because if she had fallen out she would be dead, either from the fall itself or the tiger. He was asleep, too, curled up in a ball at the base of the trunk. Waiting for his breakfast to drop into his jaws.

After he looked her in the eye in the grove by the bamboo forest, the tiger had lowered his head again and gone back to feasting. To Cintha it didn't look like, *I have no interest in you,* but more like, *Meh, I can catch you whenever I get around to it,* which was definitely true. She started moving backward, away from the clearing, slowly, one small step at a time. He looked up at her once and she froze, but he went back to his meal. His meal being her mother. Her eyes welled up with tears for like the tenth time, and she wanted to vomit, but she forced herself to swallow it. She didn't want to make any sudden noises.

As she reached the trees, the tiger moved around the carcass (her mom!) to get a better angle at whatever part of her he was digging into, facing away from her, and Cintha turned and ran, as hard and as fast as she could. Her eyes were bleary with tears, and the physical exertion broke her resolve. She began to sob uncontrollably, but she kept running. She imagined what she must look like, tears and snot flying out in a trail behind her, running in her miniskirt, her limbs caked black with mud. It only made her cry harder.

Then she heard him coming, crashing through the underbrush behind her. She looked back but couldn't see him yet. She looked forward again, a beat too late. She tripped over a banyan root and went sprawling, sliding on her exposed belly, scratching it up even worse. As she got back up, she frantically looked for a climbing tree. Tigers can climb trees, too, of course, and one this big could probably jump thirty feet, but he'd kill her for sure if she stayed on the ground. She picked one that was not too thick, so he wouldn't be able to get a good grip, and not too scrawny, so his weight wouldn't knock it over. The tiger came charging out of the jungle just as she jumped and caught the first branch. He was maybe a hundred yards behind her and closing fast.

Cintha hadn't climbed a tree since she was twelve, but she used to be really good at it, and you'd be amazed how quick stuff like that comes back to you when a tiger is trying to bite you on the ass. She swung around and got up two more branches before she felt the tree shake as he jumped on and started climbing after her. She kept going, scampering up the tree as fast as she could.

There were a lot of branches in this tree, which made climbing easier, and, she realized, also gave her an advantage. The tiger would have to navigate the thicket of branches, which would slow him down. At least she hoped so.

She hadn't looked back since she started climbing, so as she cleared the next two branches, she looked down. It was terrifying. The tiger was only ten feet below her, and despite having to continuously change its course to avoid the many branches, he was closing the gap. He had blood on his fur, and bits of flesh between his teeth. Bits of her mother. This time she couldn't help it, and she vomited.

She kept climbing even as she was retching. She was running out of tree, and he was still coming. With nowhere else to go, she started climbing out on a limb. There was a Menara tree, which only has branches at the very top, next to this one. Maybe she could get to it, but if she could, the tiger probably could too.

The branch she was on was about twelve inches in diameter. She scooted out along it, scraping up her bare inner thighs. She was halfway to the Menara tree when she felt the branch sag. She looked back over her shoulder and saw him coming, stepping carefully out onto the branch, his hungry eyes fixed on her.

If she fell from up here, she would die, but she had no choice. She scrambled to her feet and ran along the narrowing branch, hearing him snarl behind her. She heard a loud crack and jumped, grabbing a branch of the Menara tree as her perch broke off under the tiger's weight. She hung there in the air, watching him fall, scraping the other branches on the way down. He hit the ground and lay there for a few moments, then got up and shook it off. He looked up at her, baring his teeth. The fall didn't kill him, but it definitely pissed him off.

She pulled herself up into the branches of the Menara and watched him. He made a couple of attempts to climb the trunk, but it was too thin for him, and he finally decided it was easier to wait, since she had to come down eventually. The sun was down now, and once she was sure he wasn't coming up, at least for the time being, she had wedged herself into a crook between two branches and tried to get some sleep. She was certain she would never fall asleep, but she was exhausted and nodded off within minutes.

Now the sun was up, and she had to figure out what to do next. Her stomach was cramping with hunger; her lips parched with thirst. Come on, she told herself. You're not going to sit here and starve to death, that would be lame. You need a plan.

She had a pretty good view of the surrounding area from the tree; she could even see the open glade where her . . . The open glade that led to the bamboo forest. She scanned a full circle around her. There was nothing but jungle for miles in every direction. She had never been good with all that north south stuff, so she had no idea which direction led home.

Home. Not anymore. Her entire family was dead; she was the only one left. She looked back at the glade. Even if she could get to it, she could never reach the gun. It was practically in the middle of the clearing; the tiger would be on her like a chew toy. Her eyes drifted to the bamboo forest. She could tell even from here that it was a very old-growth forest.

The bamboo! That was the answer! The bamboo stalks were a foot in diameter, they would be strong AF, there was no way even a five-hundred-pound tiger could break bamboo that thick. And they were very close together, she wasn't even sure that she could squeeze through them, but she was certain he couldn't. If she could get to the bamboo, she would be protected from him. But it was easily half a mile away.

She heard a snuffle and some movement and looked down. The tiger was awake now, on its hind legs, its front paws on the tree, looking up at her like a house cat waiting for you to open a can of tuna. She had half hoped it would forget about her by the morning, but it was laser focused. It even licked its chops.

She couldn't go back down to the ground. She looked from the tiger, back to the bamboo forest. There was only one way she was ever going to get there.

She would have to go across the canopy.

CHAPTER THIRTY-THREE

Max and Derek stood at the front of the caravan, getting drenched in the warm rain, looking at a river that shouldn't be there.

"What do you mean, shouldn't be there?" Derek asked.

"There's no river on any of the maps," Max answered. "Nowhere in this area."

"Let me see the maps."

"You think I'm lying?"

"Jesus, relax, I didn't say that. I just want to see the maps."

They walked around and stood at the back of the lead truck, where Max spread the maps out on the bed under the canvas cover to keep the rain off. As Derek looked them over, Max glanced at the bench that was still soaked with the blood of the mercenary the Vinthu family had killed in their escape. He idly thought, *I hope they found a place to stay out of the rain.*

"So," Derek asked, apparently convinced Max was telling the truth, "what is it doing there?"

"Could be a hundred reasons. A landslide somewhere in the hills that diverted an existing river. A sudden breakthrough in erosion somewhere in the mountains. It doesn't really matter. There's no way around, so we have to cross it, and we have to do it as soon as possible."

"Why?" Derek asked.

"All of this rain is going to swell it; it's going to get wider and deeper. Not to mention the risk of flash flood. We either get across now, or we wait for the rain to pass and the river to settle, which could take days."

"Okay," Derek said. "Let's get moving." He headed back to his truck.

Max explained to Veronica how they were going to handle it, and while she got the drivers organized, he walked down to the edge of the river to assess the situation. The banks were gentle slopes on both sides. It was about fifty feet wide, twice the length of one of their trucks, but he couldn't tell how deep it was, and there was only one way to find out. He tore a large elephant ear off a Thai Giant plant and tossed it as far as he could out into the water. It floated downriver at a leisurely pace, indicating that the current wasn't too fast, at least not yet.

He tied a rope to a tree, set his Desert Eagle on the seat of the truck and walked out into the river. He waded all the way across, unspooling the rope as he went. At its deepest point it came to the middle of his chest, about four and a half feet deep. He stood on the far shore and looked back at the trucks. The big M809s could easily handle the crossing, as long as these conditions held. He tied the other end of the rope to a tree on this side, then waded back across using the rope as a guideline. He went to the second truck, where Derek was already sitting behind the wheel.

"Slow and steady," Max said. "Follow my lead."

Derek nodded. Max looked back at Veronica in the third truck, and she gave him the all systems go. He went back to the lead truck and climbed up, retrieved his Desert Eagle, and got back behind the wheel. He turned the engine over and shifted into low gear, then slowly started easing the truck forward into the river. He felt a little resistance as the water started pushing against the front tires, but the massive truck didn't budge. He was halfway across, the water up to the level of the cab door, when Derek drove the second truck in behind him. The rain was heavier now, the wipers barely clearing the windshield.

Max's eight rear wheels spun slightly in the mud, but not enough to cause problems, and he drove up onto the far bank. He shifted into a higher gear and pulled far enough ahead on the narrow road that the other trucks would have space to stop behind him, then shut the engine down, hopped out, and ran back to the shore. On the way, Derek passed him in the second truck, and Veronica in the third. When he reached the river, the fourth truck was halfway across and struggling. The fifth truck hadn't started in yet.

The river had already swelled. The tree Max had tied the guide rope to was now in six inches of water. The current was stronger, but still navigable. He waded out along the line and climbed up on the running board on the driver's side of the cab.

"Try going to the left a little bit. I think you're getting stuck in the wheel ruts of the other trucks."

The driver nodded and eased the truck to the left. It raised up about half a foot and found traction. Max hopped off and continued across the river to the last truck as the fourth one drove out onto dry land, or as dry as it could be in the now torrential downpour.

The driver leaned out the driver's side window. The trucks had no glass in the side windows, so he was wet enough already.

"I'll drive," Max said. "The two of you go across and get the rear winch ready on truck four in case you have to pull me out of there."

The two mercenaries hopped out and headed across the river, following the guide rope. Max went around back and climbed up into the truck bed, where he double-checked the tarp holding the bullion down. He tightened the winches all the way around, all but vacuum sealing the block of gold bars under the tarp.

He hopped down and went back to the cab, put it in gear, and started easing forward, into the river, which was moving faster now, and rising quickly. The water pounded against the side of the cab, but the tanklike truck held its ground. It was built for this. He was halfway across before he lost traction. He tried changing his course slightly, but he couldn't find an area of the riverbed that hadn't been dug out by the forty 14 x 20 tires that had gone through ahead of him. He stopped spinning his wheels before he dug himself any deeper.

He climbed out the window onto the hood of the truck and signaled for the tow line. The mercs on the far bank activated the drum and started unspooling the chain. Max saw Derek standing to the side, watching as Veronica waded in with the hook, the chain dragging behind her. Max hopped off the truck to meet her, the water nearly to his shoulders now.

He moved along the guide rope until he reached Veronica. She said, "If the tarp comes off of those bars, we're fucked."

"I tightened it down. It'll hold."

She gave him a look that said, *It better,* as he took the hook from her and worked his way back to the front of the truck. Veronica quickly returned to the far bank.

The tow ring on the front of the truck was two feet under water. Max groped around until he found it, then took a breath and went under. He clipped the hook to the ring, popped back up, and made his way around to climb back in the cab.

Once behind the wheel, he put the truck in first gear and signaled Veronica, who started the drum, pulling the tow line taut. The truck began to inch forward.

They call it a flash flood for a reason. Max heard a roar and barely caught movement out of the corner of his eye before a four-foot wall of water slammed broadside into the truck. He dropped into the wheel well and wrapped himself around the steering column as the cab instantly filled with rushing water, trying with all its might to tear him free.

He hadn't had time to shift out of first, and the truck stalled right away. He felt the movement as the truck was pushed a few feet downriver. That meant that the water was strong enough that it had dragged the truck on shore, on the other end of the tow chain, a few feet too. He imagined, or at least hoped, that they were doing everything they could to pull him out, but he knew that they would cut him loose before they let a second truck get pulled in.

To help them save him, he needed to get the truck into neutral, but he couldn't let go of the steering column or he'd wind up dead three miles downriver, and Giuliana would never know what happened to him. He used his rear end to feel around behind him until he located the clutch, then sat back, his ass pushing the pedal into the floor. He let go with one hand just long enough to knock the gear shift into neutral. The arm that was still wrapped around the column was almost torn off during those two seconds, and he was in intense pain as he grabbed hold again. This time he wrapped his legs around the column, too, as best he could in the tight space.

His lungs were burning. There was the slim chance of an air pocket at the top of the cab, but if he let go to find out, he'd be swept away. With the water rushing through the cab, he couldn't even tell if the truck was moving forward. For all he knew he was still in the middle of the river, with no chance of rescue.

He looked up at the underside of the box-like dashboard and thought, *This is a billion-to-one shot, but it's better than dying without trying.* He tightened his legs around the column, reached down and pulled out his tactical knife, and wedged it into the seam of the box. After a couple of tries he popped it off and stuck his face up into the hole. There was enough air trapped in there to give him one good breath before it, too, filled with river water. The powerful current ripped the knife out of his hand. He was still fucked, but at least his lungs were full.

The current had lost none of its power, but the water level was dropping. Another minute or two and he would be able to breathe, if he could hold his breath that long. He clung to the steering column as his lungs burned. He began to see spots. He wasn't going to make it.

The passenger side door opened, and the water rushed out of the cab. He was on the bank; they had pulled him free. Veronica jumped in as he sucked in huge breaths, grabbed him under his arms around his chest, pulled him out, and laid him on the ground.

"The bars," he said.

As much as he wanted to lie there for the next few days and just breathe, he scrambled to his feet, ran around back, and climbed into the bed of the truck, following on Veronica's heels.

One bar was poking out under the corner of the tarp, but otherwise it had held. He pushed the bar back under and tucked the tarp down around it as Derek came around the back of the truck.

"The gold okay?"

"Yeah," Max answered. "I'm okay, too, if you have any interest."

Derek grinned. "You're a maniac, Starkey. A stone-cold fucking maniac."

Max climbed down out of the truck and walked to the edge of the river, which was now twenty feet wider and two feet deeper than it had been when he first waded across it. As he watched it rush past, he realized with surprise that when he was about to die, it was Giuliana he thought about never seeing again. Kelly hadn't entered his mind.

At least it had stopped raining.

CHAPTER THIRTY-FOUR

The corpses were stacked haphazardly on the two Jeeps, and for a moment Giuliana thought of a scene in an old Monty Python movie, "Bring out your dead." She wasn't laughing this time, but she privately smiled when she realized Max would most likely have no idea what Monty Python was, and wouldn't laugh at it anyway, because he never laughed. When she was nine, she had a pet python that she kept in a terrarium and fed live mice. She named him Monty, and she was the only one in her whole school who understood why. Philistines.

The bodies had been spotted by one of their satellites during its hourly pass over the region. The satellite image was crystal clear, so clear that she could read the license plates on the Jeeps. But she couldn't see the faces because of how they were piled, so they had driven out here in a Jeep of their own to see them in person. She was still relying on the cane and couldn't walk into the jungle to look at them, so she had them carried out one by one and laid out in a row on the dirt road.

There were two dead mercenaries and ten dead Suryakan soldiers, including a captain.

The deaths of the soldiers would elevate this thing to a new level, but luckily there were no local cops out here with them to report it. It was Giuliana, the two agents working under her, Wojciehowicz and Carver, State Department Karen, Luigi the photographer, whose real name, believe it or not, turned out to be Mario, and an NSA agent whose name was Blane. She didn't know if that was his first name or last, but he had such a frat boy look about him that she assumed it was his first. It took the five of them nearly half an hour to lug the ten bodies out onto the road, but it had to be done. Investigation-wise, she needed to know if Max, Derek, or Kelly was among the dead. Personally, she only cared about Max. She could have had them take pictures of their faces on the Jeep and saved all that physical labor, but she needed to see for herself if he was one of the bodies. Thankfully, he was not.

Which meant that he was probably involved in killing them, directly or indirectly. She couldn't dwell on that, she had to think like an investigator, at least for now.

Wojciehowicz said, "They've been stripped of weapons and ammo, and the Jeeps' tanks are empty, they took the gasoline. There are no IDs or dog tags on the mercenaries."

"What do they need gas for?" Carver asked. "The trucks they're using run on diesel."

"There are other uses for gas," Giuliana answered. "They can run generators with it, certain kinds of power tools."

"It's a resource," State Department Karen said. "Maybe they just took it because it was there. My father used to say all the time, it's better to have it and not need it, than to need it and not have it."

Carver and Wojciehowicz nodded and looked at her like she had just said something incredibly profound. She hadn't, but to be fair, it was a good adage to remember. Giuliana's own father had taught her two similar adages to live by. The first was "Pack out your trash," which was literally a hiking thing, but which was really his way of saying always be responsible for yourself and any mess you might cause. To this day she couldn't leave a popcorn box in a theater without feeling guilty. The second was "Never turn your back on the ocean," which made no sense to her at all growing up in Chicago where the nearest ocean was eight hundred miles away, but which became crystal clear in an instant when she was sixteen and bodysurfing in Hawaii. She had been nearly drowned by a six-foot wave that hit her from behind while she was waving to her friends on the beach. Her whole life she had been trying to figure out the metaphor of what her father told her, when what he meant was, literally, don't turn your back on the ocean or it will fucking kill you.

"What do we do with them?" Wojciehowicz asked.

"Luigi," she said, "get photos of all of their faces."

"It's Mario."

"Right, my bad. Wojo, fingerprint the mercs. We should be able to identify them through their military records."

"I don't think we have a fingerprint kit out here."

"So improvise. Break open a Bic and use the ink, print them on your tighty-whities if you have to."

"Right."

Carver asked, "And after we print and photograph them?"

Seeing how hard they had labored bringing them out, Giuliana didn't want to break the news. Luckily, State Department Karen did it for her.

"We have to put them back and leave them here."

A collective moan went up as Carver asked, "What? Why?"

Giuliana took this one. "We can't let the Suryakan army find out about this. It will turn into a massive manhunt."

"Isn't that a good thing?" Blane the NSA frat boy asked. "Find the thieves faster."

"They may be thieves, or they may not."

"How do you figure?"

Karen jumped in. "The ownership of the gold is, at best, murky. Does it belong to President Vinthu? He bought it with stolen money, and, not incidentally, he's dead. Maybe his family has a claim, maybe they don't. Can the gold be traced back to any particular theft of actual funds? Extremely doubtful. So you tell me, are they thieves or are they not?"

"Either way," Giuliana continued, "they are American citizens who served their country." They all nodded. That they understood.

"To clarify," State Department Karen added, "they're American citizens who served their country and know a whole lot of nasty shit about what we've done in the region, so it's imperative we find them before anyone else does."

So, they put the bodies back. Giuliana waited in the Jeep and thought about Max, and about the things she had learned from his file, and how some of those things made her fall for him even harder. The stuff about his mother, Diane, for instance, and how he was raised in a brothel. Those five weeks at the cabin, when she was "bought and paid for" and he wouldn't touch her, she figured he just wasn't attracted to her, or, in her worst moments, that he knew she was an undercover agent. When she learned that he would never sleep with a prostitute because of what he saw his mother go through, it made her see him in a whole new light.

From what she read, Max Starkey had been a straight arrow, a company man all the way, and a true patriot. He and Riggs had dutifully reported their relationship to HR at Langley, a relationship that lasted for nearly five years before he quit the CIA. He had been tortured for weeks and not given up any information. He was Captain America, bleeding red, white, and blue, right up until he resigned from the agency and fell in with Rocket and his network of criminals.

So, she wondered. What the hell had changed?

SEVEN YEARS AGO

NINE WEEKS AFTER THE RAID

Max's debrief lasted two weeks. It was intense, but not unpleasant, certainly better than the questioning he had gone through in prison. He had a great team of doctors treating his physical wounds, an attractive and crazy strong physical therapist, and a middle-aged Wizard, CIA code for a psychiatrist that treats field officers, whom he had to see once a day whether he wanted to or not. The Wizards' identities were closely guarded secrets, because their heads contained a wealth of personal information about officers all over the world. They were required to have extremely good memories, since they were not allowed to take notes. Hell, the Starbucks in the lobby at Langley wasn't even allowed to ask you your name when you ordered a latte, let alone write it on a cup. Psychiatrists' notes were out of the question.

He was held in isolation at a CIA safe house just outside Chiang Mai, which was clean and comfortable. The house, not Chiang Mai. The doctors, PT, and Wizard came to him. The chef he never saw provided healthy, satisfying meals. The only bad part was that he and Kelly were separated again. They had the ride from Phonthong Prison to the border in the Range Rover together, but that was it.

On the car ride, she told him that, because she was wounded, she had been pulled out of General Vong's by the American soldiers stationed there, the ones who had been shooting at them ten minutes earlier, and was treated by American medics. There was a quick on-site negotiation, which spared her but sent Max and Derek to be questioned about the raid by the Laotians. Her debrief had been done weeks ago, while he was in prison, so he had no idea what she was doing on the outside while he, and Derek in another safe house somewhere, were undergoing theirs. They had not had a chance to be intimate since they reunited, and he had surprisingly vivid sex dreams about her every time he fell asleep.

He missed her in a deep, aching way, but he concentrated on his recovery and on giving as much information to his debriefer as he could. He was an older male officer named Carmichael whom Max had run across a few times over the years. Their sessions were held in a soundproof room in the house specifically for this purpose, and they were recorded. He was friendly, but he was thorough, and if Max had had anything he wanted to hold back, which he did not, Carmichael would have dug it out eventually.

"So," Carmichael said on the first day, "explain the codes to me like I'm a civilian."

Max nodded. "Every field officer has an activation code, a series of numbers and letters unique to him or her, that changes at random intervals every month or so. No one knows these codes except the officer him or herself, and their handlers at Langley."

"Not even your field partners?"

"No."

"So, for example, you don't know Kelly Riggs's personal activation code, even though the two of you are in an intimate relationship?"

"That is correct. And she doesn't know mine."

Carmichael nodded and made a note, which was an affectation since the session was being recorded. He looked back up and nodded, and Max continued.

"When we receive an assignment, in this case it was to evacuate an asset from General Vong's villa . . ."

Carmichael raised a hand. "Let's keep it nonspecific for the time being."

"Of course. When we receive an assignment, it will be accompanied by our code. Or often, by part of our code. The codes are quite long, over twenty places, so a code with every other digit omitted is still proof of legitimacy."

"How do you get your assignments?"

"It varies. Sometimes you'll see a chalk mark on a mailbox, which tells you to check a certain drop spot. I once had an assignment handed to me by a waiter on the back of my dinner check, and another by a little kid on the street in Mexico who was selling lottery tickets. Those types of notices are B-A-R." It stood for Burn After Reading. "But to be honest, nine times out of ten someone at Langley just calls you on a secure line and says, 'Here's your assignment and here's your code.'"

"What about in this case?"

"Officer Riggs and I were awoken early in the morning by texts on our secure phones."

"Separately?"

"Well, we were together in bed, but yes, we were pinged separately. As I said, we have never seen each other's codes, and according to regulations, never will."

"Derek Moss was also pinged?"

"Yes," Max nodded. "The three of us were sent on the raid together."

"The raid that turned out to be unsanctioned and unauthorized."

"Correct."

"How do you remember your codes? Do you write them down somewhere?"

"God, no. That would be a major breach of protocol. We memorize them."

"You memorize a twenty-digit code that changes every few weeks?"

"Yes."

Carmichael nodded, impressed. "How do you think your codes were stolen?"

Max took a beat. "I've thought about this a lot. In my opinion, it had to be someone at Langley. We don't share our codes with anyone, and we don't write them down. Langley is the only place where all the codes are stored. However it was done, it had to be done in Virginia."

"Any idea why it was done? What the purpose was?"

"Perhaps an attempt to assassinate General Vong. Although killing him was not part of the assignment I received."

"So why would you think that?"

"The prison gang that the agency employed to get me to the extraction point wanted something from me in exchange. I had to contract to kill General Vong once I was free."

"You're kidding."

"I have no intention of doing it, of course, but at the time I agreed to gain my freedom." Carmichael nodded, go on. "I assume if they want him dead now, they wanted him dead six weeks ago."

"Makes sense. But why wouldn't killing him be explicitly outlined in the assignment?"

"That I can't answer. Maybe one of the other two officers got that part of the assignment. I'm just guessing here, but again, to be clear, I have zero intention of carrying it out."

Over the next two weeks they went over that day again and again, getting into minute detail. By the end of it, Carmichael knew that Max was brushing his teeth while Kelly peed. He knew which shoe Max put on first that morning, and most importantly, he had a timeline of the raid itself, broken down into thirty-second intervals. Nothing was left out.

Then it was over. On the day he was set to leave, Max asked to see Carmichael one last time. They stood in the foyer and shook hands.

"Promise me," Max said, "that when you find out who did this, you'll tell me."

It was an unfair request and he knew it. Whatever the truth turned out to be, it would be highly classified. Carmichael offered, "I promise to tell you what I can."

Max nodded, picked up his small suitcase with his few belongings in it, and walked out the front door, where he broke into a grin as wide as the sky.

Kelly was waiting for him at the gate.

CHAPTER THIRTY-FIVE

It had literally taken Cintha all day to navigate the treetop canopy to the spot where the jungle met the bamboo forest. Sometimes it was easy moving tree to tree, but sometimes they were too far apart, and she couldn't reach, or had to jump, or, more often than that, find another way around that added time and distance to her journey. Some of the branches were thin and she had to crawl or scoot along them. To make things worse, there were aggressive, territorial monkeys that simply wouldn't let her go certain ways, and spiders, snakes, and other creepy crawlies that made her choose not to go others. Turn around, go back, find another way.

As a result, it took her nine hours to travel half a mile. She had always been good at math and could have figured out what that was in miles per hour, but she was starving and her brain hadn't thought about anything for the last three hours except cheeseburgers and Skittles.

The tiger had paced her all the way, always directly underneath her on the ground, waiting for her to misstep. A couple of times he leapt up the first ten feet or so and started climbing the tree she was in, but by the time he made any progress she would be in the next one, so eventually he gave up and just shadowed her on the ground. Watching her. Waiting. Frazzling her nerves. Once or twice he disappeared for a while, she assumed to find water or maybe to eat more of her family, but he always came back.

In some ways she was grateful that the journey across the canopy was so difficult, since it forced her to focus on what was right in front of her, rather than dwelling on the fact that her entire family was dead. When the thoughts did intrude, she mostly thought about her dad, maybe because she actually saw his head get blown off. She had found her mom and brothers dead, but she hadn't actually seen them die.

She would miss her dad, of course she would, but also, she was kind of conflicted. He was a good dad when he was around, which wasn't all that much, to be honest. Still, she had a hard time reconciling the dad that played stupid board games with her, and Marco Polo in the pool, with the monster she heard people whispering about. She had been pretty sheltered, in her private school, with her bodyguards and drivers and maids and nannies. Everyone was super careful around her, and nobody ever said anything bad about him in front of her, including her friends and even the bitchy girls at school. But she had the internet, and she overheard things. They said he was a tyrant, they said he was a criminal, they even used the word genocide. She had to look it up and couldn't grasp the idea that it was something her dad could do.

The sun was starting to go down, and if she stayed in the top of this banyan tree much longer, she would fall for sure, either from exhaustion or starvation. She thought about that thing they learned about in Mr. Sale's class, a pyrrhic victory; at least there wasn't that much meat on her bones for the tiger to gnaw on.

She had gone as far around the clearing as the jungle canopy would take her. She wouldn't have to cross the whole clearing to get to the bamboo, which she never would have survived, but there was still about twenty feet of open ground she would have to cover. The tiger was lying down about fifty yards away, near the bodies of her brothers—there were those annoying stinging tears welling up again—swatting flies with his tail and keeping an eye on her. The only edge she had was that he had been awake all day, too, tracking her, and so he had to be tired. She just had to stay awake longer than he did.

They sat there watching each other for what felt like three hours but was probably twenty minutes. At long last he put his head down on his front paws and let his eyes close. She waited a little longer to make sure he was asleep, then started climbing down.

She wanted to jump out of the tree, but she forced herself to move slowly and very, very quietly. Halfway down she figured she was at the point of no return; if he heard her now, she wouldn't be able to climb back up fast enough to escape. Finally her toes touched the earth, and she eased herself down and stood on solid ground. She was shielded from the tiger's view by the tree's thick trunk.

The twenty feet she had to cover to reach the bamboo looked a lot farther from down here than it had from up in the tree. But she had no choice, there was no other way, and she couldn't stay here. Her life depended on running twenty feet before he ran fifty yards. She took a couple of deep breaths, steeled herself, and bolted.

Almost immediately, she heard him growl and charge, but she didn't look back. She could hear his paws pounding on the earth, and she swore she could feel his breath on the back of her neck. Her legs pumped.

She almost made it clean.

As she ran into the tight space between the massive bamboo stalks, the tiger swiped at her with his claw and one of his razor-sharp talons ripped down the back of her right leg. It was the most painful thing she had ever felt, and although she didn't know at the time, ever would feel. She screamed and fell, but she kept moving forward, crawling on her hands and knees deeper into the bamboo.

The noise behind her was deafening, like a thunderstorm happening right on top of her.

The tiger was roaring in anger, his frenzied attempts to get at her clacking the huge bamboo stalks together like thunder sticks. She thought her ears were going to burst.

When she was about twenty feet into the bamboo, she simply couldn't crawl anymore. Her leg was on fire, and she had no energy left. She rolled onto her back and looked back. She could barely see him through the close-together bamboo stalks but could tell the tiger was in a state of pure, white fury, trying to squeeze in, reaching for her, roaring, manic. But he couldn't get to her. The bamboo was too tight, and too strong. Her plan had worked. She was safe, at least for now.

She passed out.

CHAPTER THIRTY-SIX

At Chewy Chakri's invitation, Kelly spent the next day meeting with some of the soldiers and families that traveled with his army, and hearing their stories of life under President Vinthu. They were predictably awful. Friends and neighbors disappearing without a trace, relatives murdered, homes and farms that had been in families for generations seized under the guise of eminent domain, only to be gifted to Vinthu's closest friends and advisors. By the end of the long day, she needed a drink. Or several.

On her way back to her tent, one of the laundresses caught her eye and signaled for Kelly to follow her. The woman led her through the rabbit warren of clothing vats and hanging drip dry, to a small tent among dozens of others. Her name was Sarai, and although she was only a few years older than Kelly, she looked worn down to the nub. She lived in the tiny tent with her four children, who ranged in age from three to seven. It appeared to Kelly that the middle two were twins. Kelly sat on a large rock outside the tent, and they talked in Suryakan while Sarai built a cooking fire.

"You are gathering stories?"

"Well, in a way."

"You're writing a book?"

"No. Chakri just thought I'd benefit from hearing them."

Sarai looked her over. Then she switched to flawless English.

"I was a professor at Nusantara University. Do you know it?"

"I do. What did you teach?"

"Literature and Suryakan history. My husband was a writer; he had a column in our biggest national newspaper. His stories were often reprinted in English, in the *Bangkok Post.* He was critical of Vinthu and investigated allegations of corruption against him. I suppose we were what you classify as intellectuals."

"Sure," Kelly said.

The fire going now, Sarai opened a can of green curry and placed it over the flames with a tong. She set a pan of water beside it to boil.

"At first my husband's editors were tolerant, but as the regime cracked down on the press, they stopped publishing his columns. He tried other papers, but no one would touch his writing. The entire media in our country was paralyzed with fear. But he was determined to get the information he had out."

"Why was he so determined?"

"His parents had been killed in the purges after the monarchy fell. He knew what unbridled power could lead to, and that censorship was just the beginning."

Kelly nodded. The water was boiling, and Sarai removed it from the fire. She grabbed the can of curry with the tong and used a wooden spoon to scoop the curry into the pan. As she mixed it all together, Kelly realized she was using the water to stretch the curry.

"Why don't you eat with the others?"

"Food supplies are dangerously low. The fighting men need it more than we do."

As she continued her story, she parceled the watered-down curry into four tin bowls. Four, not five. None for herself, Kelly noted.

"At the same time, I began receiving instructions from the government on how to amend my curricula. They were attempting to change our history. It was made clear that I would be fired if I did not comply. We lived in university housing, our oldest was in private school, we owned two cars, and our refrigerator was always full. Our life was good."

"So what did you do?"

"I complied."

She said it without emotion, but Kelly could sense the shame behind it. Sarai whistled, and her oldest child, a girl, came out of the tent. She told her in English to distribute the plates to her siblings.

"And be careful. They're hot."

"Yes, mama."

When the girl was gone, Kelly said, "I'm impressed. Are all your children bilingual?"

"They also speak French, and we are beginning to work on Mandarin. Where was I? Yes. My husband was unable to publish, so he and a few other dissident writers formed their own underground paper. There were six of them all together. They bought a very old printing press, and Dusit was able to cobble together a clandestine distribution network. They did everything, those six, from writing the stories, to layout, to driving around tossing bundles of papers onto street corners. They operated on contributions, but he was also draining our bank accounts. The newspaper was called *Khuaamching*."

"Truth," Kelly said, realizing. "Your husband was Dusit Makok."

"Then you know what happened."

"Yes." Kelly nodded. "I'm so sorry."

"They were laying out the front page, preparing for a press run. A government paramilitary unit kicked the doors in. They didn't bother arresting them, they simply shot them where they stood. I'm told all six of them were brutally murdered within fifteen seconds. I didn't have time to grieve, I knew they would come for me and my children, so we took whatever we could carry on our backs and fled the city. Eventually we wound up here, with the rebels."

"But why Chewy Chakri?"

"He's what we have. Dusit's parents were killed in a purge. He was murdered by his own government. That's two generations of my family scarred by political violence." She glanced toward the tent, where her children were eating their watered-down meal. "I cannot let it be three."

“Aren’t you worried Chakri will turn out to be the same? He might kill just as many journalists and professors as the last guy.”

“Until he does, he is all the hope we have.”

Kelly took a long time to walk back to her tent. The conversation with Dusit Makok’s widow had cut her like a knife and had opened a wound she didn’t know was there. She accepted certain things about herself, for instance, that she was selfish. She always had been, the way she treated Max at the end was proof enough of that. She was okay with being selfish. She was also callous, and she was okay with that too. For her, the political machinations she pulled off as a CIA officer were a game, nothing more. Put this guy in office and take that guy out. Make sure this general is arrested, and if it’s with a prostitute, all the better. She never thought about the human costs because they weren’t within the parameters of the game she was playing. The rules on the inside of the box cover didn’t say anything about dead journalists.

Her own life had been remarkably consequence free. She had been shot once, and shot at more times than she could count, but she had never been seriously injured or lost anyone important to her to violence. She had never been in jail or officially sanctioned. Even the time she spent in the “prison” of her relationship with Derek resulted in twenty million dollars in a Cayman Islands bank. She walked through the violence and turmoil like she was still the prom queen at Waimea High School, where she had carelessly left a string of broken-hearted boyfriends and betrayed girlfriends. The truth was, she treated people like shit, even back then.

Once she and Derek left the agency and went freelance, the jobs were just a payday, nothing more. Human cost? What human cost? They were just moving things around, money, guns, whatever. And sometimes gathering information. Like in the Truth case.

It wasn’t her fault. She didn’t even take the job. Derek, in his usual way of handling things, took it without consulting her. He walked into their suite one day and announced, “I took a job for el presidente.

A hundred grand. All we have to do is figure out where some people are printing a newspaper."

That's it. An address. She couldn't have known what was going to happen.

But of course you knew, Kelly told herself. *You just chose not to think about it.*

CHAPTER THIRTY-SEVEN

The trucks inched their way up a steep, narrow grade at ten miles per hour. Derek had to concentrate, or he'd stall out again. He had already stalled out twice, once after almost rear-ending Max in his truck. He was a good driver, he was just distracted, and this snail's pace was excruciating. Max was adamant that this was the way to go, saying the grade wasn't the worst of what they were going to face before they got to the bridge at Phaya Nok Ravine.

Derek was tired, but not overly so, as he had managed a few hours' sleep in the cab while someone else drove. They needed to keep moving around the clock, since they had lost nearly half a day flushing the systems of the truck that got caught in the flash flood. He had wanted to take the tarps off to check the gold, but Veronica, the woman in charge of the mercs he hired, said it would take another forty-five minutes to properly batten everything down again, so he only checked one, the one that had been caught in the river. The tarps had held, and they hadn't lost a single gold brick.

He did almost lose Max there, which would have been a disaster. Max was the only one who knew how to get from wherever the hell they were to the ravine. If Derek lost Max, he might drive around this jungle for the next five years. Derek never liked the jungle and hadn't spent much time in it. He was fine with tigers and snakes and angry monkeys, but mud and bugs, no thank you. Derek was a city guy, give him urban warfare and backroom deals, and leave the dirt to people with cheaper shoes.

During his time as an active case officer, Max had been all over this jungle, out in the bush for months at a time. He knew the route. After Phaya Nok, Derek would be fine, he could find the border from there. But until they got there, he needed Max, and Max knew it. As soon as they were across Derek would put a bullet through the smug son of a bitch's condescending smile.

Kelly, who was Max's girlfriend at the time and was now Derek's wife—his missing wife—had spent maybe half of that time in the jungle with Max. Which meant that she didn't know the area as well as he did, but she knew it too well to lose her way, especially in a helicopter.

Which was why Derek was distracted and stalled out for the third time. As he cranked the engine over, the merc sleeping at the other end of the cab opened one eye and looked at him, as if to say, really?

"Look at me sideways again," Derek said. "See how that goes for you." The guy shrugged and went back to sleep.

No, Derek thought, as he eased the truck back into motion, there is no way she drifted off course. She knew the area well enough, and she was a goddam good pilot. Plus she was only meant to fly sixty miles, following a road the whole way. How do you get lost in sixty air miles? Meaning there were two possibilities. She crashed, or she ran.

He was going with ran. The fact was, she had been uppity the last couple of months, challenging him on which jobs he took for them, and offering her opinion when he didn't fucking ask for it. She was becoming difficult to control. He had come close to smacking her a couple of times, but Kelly was no ordinary woman. If he hit her, he stood a good chance of sustaining real physical damage himself. He could take her, definitely; in fact he was positive he could kill her with his bare hands, but he wouldn't come out of it whole. That thought made him smile. His wife was a badass.

So what was she up to? He desperately wanted to reach their bank, to check on their accounts, but he had tried several times and there was no cell service in this godforsaken part of the world. It all came down to the money. If it was gone, she ran out on him. If it was still there, she was most likely dead in a crash. For her sake, he hoped it was the latter.

Or . . . for fuck's sake, he just thought of this . . . were she and Max up to something together? Max had an arrogance about him that made Derek grit his teeth. Maybe he was feeling his oats because he was plowing Derek's field. He had changed the course, maybe Kelly was lying in wait to ambush him somewhere on this new route, with mercenaries of her own.

He needed to put all of this out of his mind right now and just drive. There was only one thing for it, anyway. If she had ripped him off, he had to kill her, too, whether they were working together or not. The gold was all he needed. So, as soon as they crossed the ravine, he'd execute Max Starkey. He'd do it quickly, even though he'd rather do it slowly.

Then he'd hunt down his dear wife and put a bullet in her head. Wherever she was, recovering from a helo crash in a hospital or spending his money on the French Riviera, he'd find her. If it took him five years, ten years, thirty. He'd find her and he'd put her down.

The grade evened out a little and the driving got easier. They were able to speed up to twenty-five, which seemed like Le Mans after six grueling hours of ten miles per, and Derek had another inspiration. Once they were both in the ground, he'd look up Starkey's widow, that tall slice of ebony. Tell her how sorry he was for her loss. They could help each other through their shared grief.

That thought made him smile too.

CHAPTER THIRTY-EIGHT

General Ruchuphan and his army arrived while Giuliana was still in the jungle. After they replaced the bodies, they had followed the rough dirt road for another twenty miles, to a small junction where Max and the others had apparently turned the trucks and headed up a narrow tract. Giuliana was in a lot of pain when they stopped, the sutures in her abdomen having been strained by every bump in the road. She forced herself to get out and look around, taking the cane in case she needed it on the uneven surface, but trying not to rely on it.

The road was muddy from the recent rains and completely torn up from the heavy trucks. She couldn't tell how many there were, but it was more than one or two. She turned to Carver and Wojciehowicz, whom she had started to call Frick and Frack, at least in her mind.

"Why do you think they took so many trucks?"

"What do you mean?" Carver (Frick) asked.

"The M809s can carry five tons. Say the gate guard was telling the truth, and they took five trucks, that's a capacity of twenty-five tons. They're only moving four thousand pounds, that's less than half of what one truck can carry. Why so many vehicles?"

"There's a lot of mud," Carver said. "Maybe they're worried about getting stuck. Spread the load out among more trucks?"

"These trucks can roll through anything."

Wojciehowicz (Frack) offered, "Maybe they're moving other expensive things from the palace, you know, knickknacks, furniture?"

"If you were stealing a hundred million worth of gold," State Department Karen asked, "would you take the lamps?"

Giuliana said, "There has to be a logistical reason. If we find it, we find them."

"Meantime, do we follow these tracks into the hills?" Carver asked.

Giuliana thought about it. They could move faster than the trucks, and would catch up with them eventually, but she had no idea where they were headed or what the terrain was like on the smaller road. Anyway, the key was in the number of trucks. Maybe it was smarter to go back and figure out why they took so many.

She never got the chance to decide. Her secure sat phone rang, one of the NSA agents they had left behind to monitor the satellite feeds was calling, whispering urgently.

"You need to get back here. The army just arrived."

"Damn. How many?"

"It looks like all of them."

The drive back took nearly four hours with Frack behind the wheel, even though they were going faster than they had coming out. The Jeep wasn't built for comfort, and every jarring bump threatened to split open Giuliana's abdomen. When they hit the smooth blacktop that had been laid for the city that never was, she wanted to get out and kiss the asphalt.

The NSA guy wasn't exaggerating. They hit the outer perimeter of the Suryakan army half a mile from the palace. There were Tigr armored vehicles and a few tanks, all Russian made, but most of the vehicles were manufactured in the good old USA, and all of them had the green-and-red star insignia of the Suryakan army. They had to show their IDs at three different checkpoints just to get through the gate. As they rolled up to the palace steps, Frick nudged Giuliana and nodded. She followed her gaze and saw the Jeeps with the bodies piled on them, the ones they had left in the jungle; they had found them and towed them back here. They weren't through the door yet, and this was already a clusterfuck.

Giuliana climbed down off the Jeep and waved off the cane, not wanting to appear any weaker than she absolutely had to. By the time she got up the palace steps she regretted it but gritted her teeth and stayed the course. They showed their credentials one more time at the door, and a soldier led them down the long corridor, both sides lined with paintings of Vinthu in various heroic poses. Her favorite was the one where he was rescuing an armload of babies from a burning orphanage, his foot on the head of a wild-eyed rebel soldier. She would see that movie.

The soldier stopped them at the door to the president's study, and asked in broken English, "Who is leader?"

Giuliana half raised a hand. "That would be me." The soldier took a beat, glanced at Frack, then back at her, as if he was waiting for someone to say, "Just kidding."

He finally nodded. "Others wait here."

Giuliana went in. General Ruchuphan was sitting behind the presidential desk, shuffling papers, the large map still pulled down behind him. He was in combat fatigues, the chevron on his shoulder the only sign of rank. He was smoking a cigar and wearing a sidearm. Through all the checkpoints to get in here no one had frisked Giuliana for a weapon, so he was clearly confident in his ability to outdraw whoever came into the room.

He gestured at a chair without looking up at her, and she sat down across the desk from him. She had seen him in photos, of course, but in person he was different. For one thing, she realized that they must have shot every picture of him from a low angle, since he was maybe five foot two. In all the photos she had seen he looked imposing, but in person he was Kevin Hart short. His black hair, which was clearly dyed to hide the gray, was slicked back with what she assumed was a gallon of Crisco. The only things that carried over from the photos were his eyes, which were intense and focused, and a strange shade of amber with a fleck of green in the center. His eyes made her wonder if he blinked sideways.

He set the papers aside, sat back, and puffed his cigar, looking her over. Then he nodded and said, in English, "FBI Special Agent Giuliana Abara."

He didn't say anything else, so after a few moments passed Giuliana said, "General Alphonse Ruchuphan."

He smiled. "President Ruchuphan. In light of the tragic suicide of Mr. Vinthu, I have declared martial law and seized temporary control of the government."

"Temporary?"

He ignored the question. "We found the bodies of the former president and his concubine, but there is no sign of the family. Do you know where they are?"

"No. We were just out looking for them."

"If you are harboring them somewhere, it will not bode well for relations between your country and my new government."

"Temporary government." She saw his snake eyes twitch. "We don't have them. I honestly have no idea where they are."

"And the gold?"

She didn't miss a beat. "What gold?"

"Vinthu had a basement full of gold bars."

"If he did, they were gone when we got here. You're welcome to search my pockets."

He regarded her for a few moments. He clearly wasn't used to sparring with a female, and she idly wondered if he had ever met a Black woman in his life. "Why exactly are you here?"

"The truth is we came to help him get out of the country, but when we got here, he was dead and his family was gone. So we started looking for them."

"You divert satellites to look for a woman and her children?"

"We're the United States of America; we don't do anything half-assed."

"And the bodies on the Jeeps?"

"I'm sorry, you lost me again."

"Eight dead Suryakan soldiers and two dead Americans."

"They have nothing to do with us. My word, Mr. President, that is not our mess."

"Unless I choose to make it your mess."

"I sincerely hope you won't."

"My soldiers were murdered. Someone has to pay." He puffed his stogie. She was certain he knew exactly who was behind the killings, and who took the gold, and he would track them down and kill them. She had to get to Max before he did.

"A helo will fly you and your people back to the capital city, and we'll put you on a plane to Bangkok. I don't care where you go from there, but do not come back to my country." Then he added, "You're leaking."

He meant that blood was seeping through her shirt, but she had stopped listening. She was looking over his shoulder, at the giant map of the country, and she had her answer. She knew why Max needed so many trucks.

CHAPTER THIRTY-NINE

The first thing Cintha did when she woke up in the morning was locate the enemy. For a glorious moment she thought he had left, but her hopes were dashed as she saw him pass, like a shadow through the bamboo. He was pacing in the clearing just outside the grove, patiently walking back and forth, waiting for her to stray too close to the edge.

The next thing she did was tend to the wound on the back of her leg. The talon had cut a slash about eight inches long, from just under her butt to almost the back of her knee. It was deep, but he didn't seem to have hit anything vital. The tendons in her hamstring must have been intact, because she could move her leg okay even though it hurt like an MFer, and if he had hit an artery she never would have woken up, so she figured she was lucky.

There was no water that she could find to wash the wound out with, and if there had been it would have been full of bacteria and unusable, so she took off her miniskirt, which wasn't covering all that much anyway, and used the cleanest part of the inside of it to wipe the dirt out of her leg wound. It hurt like a bitch, and she screamed, which brought a restless growl from her unseen stalker in the clearing. She pulled a bamboo shoot out of the ground and bit down on it as she finished cleaning the wound, so she wouldn't scream again. No use working him up.

When the wound was as clean as it was going to get, she wrapped the skirt around it and tied it off, securing it with hair ties that she found in the skirt's hidden pocket. This left her in her halter top, her Nike Dunk Lows and ankle socks, and her underwear, which at least was cotton and sturdy, not silk or a thong or something. Her mother never let her buy that kind of stuff, and she had been embarrassed in the locker room at school about how childish her underthings were, but at this moment, she was grateful. At the thought of her mother she started crying again, and she sat there for about fifteen minutes, sobbing. Hunger finally stopped her.

She was starving, and she knew she was weak from losing blood, but she had been bitten by mosquitos in her sleep and had a few itchy bumps on her arms and legs, so job one was to get her limbs covered in mud again. Foraging for food would have to wait. She limped around for about half an hour looking for mud, the combination of her leg wound and her one floppy shoe slowing her down, but there wasn't any mud in the bamboo that she could find, so she made some. She peed on a soft patch of dirt and mushed it up. As she spread it on her arms and legs, she thought, *Three days ago I was the most popular girl in school, the most famous teenager in my whole country, and now I'm slathering myself with pee mud.* Oh well, it was better than catching dengue fever or Zika from a mosquito.

Next it was time to fill her stomach. She found a broken piece of bamboo about four feet long, and used the jagged, pointy end of it to dig in the dirt at the roots of one of the biggest stalks. She uncovered a large nest of bamboo worms, which are a hundred percent edible and a million percent gross. She watched them slither over each other for a minute or two, then decided to put off eating as long as possible. She was, like, literally starving, but she wasn't literally starving.

Instead, she went to find the part of the bamboo forest that was closest to the gun in the clearing. She took the four-foot-long sharpened bamboo pole with her. It helped to use it like a walking stick, putting some of her weight on it to keep it off her wounded leg.

From some places she could see the bodies of her brothers through the bamboo, if not the actual gun itself, but she knew it was on the ground right next to them. She worked herself around to what seemed like the closest point and estimated it was about forty feet from the edge of the bamboo to where her brothers lay. From this far back in the stalks, though, she couldn't see if the gun was there, and she wanted visual confirmation. She stood still for at least ten minutes, listening for him. She didn't hear anything. No padded footfalls. No snuffling. Usually if he was near, she could at least hear him breathing, but now there was just silence.

She took a couple of steps forward through the stalks and stopped again, ears cocked. She stood there another five minutes, no sound at all except the occasional grumbling of her hungry tummy. When she felt secure that he wasn't close, she moved to just a few feet from the edge of the bamboo.

The gun was in plain sight, on the ground forty feet away. She knew she would have to get it sooner or later, because this tiger wasn't going to let her walk out of here any other way. She was certain he would wait until she either came out or died in here.

The world exploded as the tiger leapt at her through the bamboo, roaring. She instinctively thrust her broken piece of bamboo forward, like a spear, and it stuck him in the face, a few inches below his eye. She was startled and he was enraged. She pulled the spear back and as he swiped at her she thrust it out again, hitting him directly in the paw this time. It sunk in deep and he yelped and pulled back, taking the spear with him, wrenching it from her hands.

Cintha backed away deeper into the bamboo as he shook his paw, finally jarring it loose.

He came back for her, but she was out of his reach now. He was in an absolute frenzy, but there was no way he could get to her. She squeezed deeper into the grove, feeling almost giddy. She had hurt him. *She* had hurt *him.* She knew the reality was that he could kill her with almost no effort, a flick of his paw or a snap of his jaw, but right now, at this moment, she felt like the baddest bitch in the world. She-Ra. Samus Aran. She had lost her spear, but she would find another one.

She found a short sharp stick and dug up another nest of bamboo worms, held her breath and shoved a handful in her mouth. It was gross, but she was ravenously hungry, and she knew from her conversations with the palace chef, Binty, that they were loaded with protein, fiber, and even B-12. She was going to need her strength if she was going to beat the tiger. She ate two more handfuls.

An hour later it started to pour. She was happy to let the piss dirt wash off her, since after the rain there would be plenty of mud to replace it with. She tilted her head back and opened her mouth, and drank as much of the cool, clear water as she could catch.

CHAPTER FORTY

Max had planned to sleep while Derek drove his truck for a couple of hours, but he wasn't able to. He rested, eyes closed, and thought about the man behind the wheel. Derek's wife had disappeared in a helo and could be dying in the jungle, and he hadn't expressed a single word of concern. He hadn't seemed at all conflicted about whether to stick with the gold or go look for her, and when he did talk about her, it was only with anger. "She's going to regret it." "She thinks she can make a fool out of me?" Even, "I'll show that ungrateful bitch."

From everything he knew about Derek, none of this was out of character. Derek thought only about Derek, even at the expense of his wife. He was selfish and greedy, and Max knew that for months before he left the agency Derek was using his job to enrich himself. On that front, he and Kelly were perfect for each other.

Kelly had always been self-centered, even when she was truly in love with Max. He had seen past it and known it for what it was, a form of self-protection. He knew about her childhood sexual abuse at the hands of her father, even though she never told him. When they were first dating, her best friend, Marcy, having had way too much eggnog, pulled him into a corner at a Christmas party and warned him that he better be good to her, because here's why, and proceeded to spill the beans. Mercifully the friend was so drunk she didn't remember that she did it or at least was so embarrassed that she pretended not to.

Max never told Kelly that he knew. He figured it was her trauma, not his, and if she wanted him to know she would tell him. He gave her plenty of opportunity. He chose a night when they were isolated in the Egyptian desert, just them and their campfire and not another soul for twenty clicks in any direction, to tell her about growing up in the trailer and the brothel, thinking she might return the gesture. She was genuinely moved by his story, but didn't offer hers, and he didn't push.

Instead, he took on a role that he saw as a protector, but which was, in hindsight, more like an enabler. So what if she was a little selfish and cut off emotionally? She had earned the right to wear some armor. And the ways in which her selfishness manifested were small and unimportant and didn't cause any real problems in their relationship.

Until that night in Chiang Mai. Then it brought their world down.

"Hey, Starkey, are you awake?"

Max sat up and let his eyes adjust to the late afternoon sun. There was a six-hundred-foot, nearly vertical hillside rising about five miles ahead. He had to squint to see the switchback road carved into the thick foliage, but it was there.

"Is that where we're headed?" Derek asked.

"Yeah, that's it."

"Remind me why we came this way again?"

"It's safer."

"Right. Forgot for a minute there."

"We'll stop at the base, rest the men and the trucks. Check the fluids, top off the tanks. Each truck is going to burn a full load of fuel climbing that hill. We'll start up again at sunset."

Derek glanced at him. "You want to go up that thing at night?"

"It's the most exposed we'll be, there on the cliff face, so we ought to go under cover of darkness. There's enough moon to light our way." He took a moment. "I won't lie to you, Derek. Aside from the bridge itself, this is the most treacherous part of the journey."

"You have my permission to lie to me next time."

"Noted." They drove in silence for a while, then Max asked, "Who were you supposed to kill?"

"You'll have to be more specific."

"When we contracted with the Ghosts to get out of Phonthong. You never did tell me who your target was."

"You first."

Max hesitated, then thought, *What the hell difference does it make now?*

"They wanted me to assassinate General Vong." He waited. "Go on, then. Who was yours?"

"You."

"What?"

"After you killed Vong, I was supposed to kill you. I guess you could say I was batting clean-up." He laughed at the look on Max's face. "Relax, Starkey, I was never going to do it, Jesus. For one thing, my contract didn't kick in until after you fulfilled yours, and I knew you would never kill Vong. Besides, I don't kill friends."

"I wouldn't exactly call us friends," Max said. "Not even back then."

"I still wouldn't have done it. Can you imagine?"

They had reached the bottom of the sheer rise. Derek rolled to a stop and killed the engine. He looked up at the narrow switchback and whistled.

"It's not as bad as it looks," Max offered.

"The last time you said that you had a president's brains all over you."

"Okay, it is as bad as it looks. But if we go slowly and carefully, we'll be fine."

They spent an hour servicing the trucks, checking brake lines and radiators, and topping off fuel. Veronica personally checked each load, making sure the tarps were winched down as tight as she could get them. Max was looking up at the switchbacks when Milo came and stood beside him.

"How far are we?"

"This rise will take us into the foothills of the Phukhao Saksid Mountains."

Milo said, "*Phukhao* means mountain in Lao. You just said the Sacred Mountain Mountains. That's like saying panini sandwich, or queso cheese."

"Thank you, Milo."

"Or support bra."

They ate a quick meal, then the mercenaries sat down with their backs against the giant tires and tree trunks and went to sleep. They were trained to fall asleep instantly and got some quality rest before Max woke them an hour later. They were on their feet and in position within sixty seconds.

Derek went back and got in the cab of the second truck, as Max pulled the last truck around. He would drive it up first, the others behind him. The supply truck was going last this time, the four trucks with the loads going first, the theory being that it was better to lose some diesel fuel and MREs than thirty-three million dollars. Veronica had volunteered to drive the supply truck, bringing up the rear, and pulled it to the side as Max and the others passed her.

Max eased onto the narrow switchback. He had been up and down this road a few times in the past, but never in anything bigger than a Toyota Hilux Revo. He pulled the mirrors in so that he could get closer to the side, yet he still had less than two feet between him and the edge of the drop-off.

Slow and steady, he thought, as he eased the truck forward. Then he thought, *I must be fucking insane.*

CHAPTER FORTY-ONE

The first leg of the switchback was a little over half a mile and took about ten minutes to drive up. The switchbacks were all different lengths, varying from short ones like this, to over two miles. The total distance of the road up the hill was nine miles, all to climb six hundred feet. It would take them all night.

The roads were treacherous, no doubt. Max knew that on some of the switchbacks, no matter how closely they hugged the side, part of their outside rear tires would hang over the edge. But even with the constant threat of plunging hundreds of feet to your death, the straightaways weren't the most dangerous part. The challenge was the turns.

As he reached the first turn, Max slowed to a stop, locked his brakes, and walked out onto the dirt turning pad to look it over. It was big enough that a car or even a pickup truck could have made the turn in one go, but their big trucks would need to do several point turns, and their margin of error was extremely narrow. If your rear tires went off the pad, the rest of your vehicle would follow, taking you and your load with it.

This was one of the bigger pads and built entirely on solid mountain. There were turns up above where the pad was so tight that the army had extended them by building heavily fortified wooden platforms and anchoring them to the mountainside with massive concrete pylons. They were built for military vehicles, even tanks, but that was five regimes and sixty years of no maintenance ago. They would have to turn their trucks around on those platforms and pray that they held. Max knew they were strong, people still used them all the time, but he doubted if anything as heavy as an M809 had challenged one of them in decades.

Derek and a couple of the mercenaries came forward to join him on the turning pad. "What's the plan?" Derek asked.

"Guide me through my turn. Once I'm back on the road, I'll come back and guide you and the others through yours."

Derek nodded. Max climbed back into his truck and started it up. Before putting it in gear he radioed Veronica Usher in the supply truck, at the rear of the caravan.

"Hold your position. We'll bring the trucks forward one at a time."

"Roger that. Holding."

He eased the truck onto the pad. Derek waved him forward, then signaled him to start turning. Max turned until the nose of the truck was touching the hillside. Then he popped his rearview mirror back into place and looked back at Derek, who signaled him to back up. Max put the truck in reverse and started inching backward while turning, as slowly as he could.

"Good, keep coming," Derek said, also using hand signals. "Come. Come. Stop!"

Max stopped and saw in the mirror that his rear tires were right at the edge. Another half inch and he would have gone over. It occurred to him that Derek could kill him right here, simply by not saying the word stop. But he would take 25 percent of the gold with him, so he figured he was safe for now.

He eased the truck forward again, turning until the front corner of the cab met the hillside. Then they did the whole thing over again. It took two more times back and forth before he was able to drive ahead onto the next level of the switchback. Maneuvering his one truck around the corner had taken about five minutes, which meant twenty-five minutes at each turn, if everything went smoothly at all of them. With twelve more turns ahead of them, that was nearly six hours just for the corners, not counting the drive time between each one. It was looking unlikely they would reach the top before dawn.

Once they had all the trucks past the turn, Max called Derek and Veronica together. "From here on out," he told them, "once a truck makes the turn it should head straight for the next one and not wait for the ones behind it. Otherwise we'll never be done by morning." He could see that Derek was skeptical about letting the trucks out of his sight, so he added, "There's one road up the side of the mountain, it's not like there's anywhere for someone to run off to. But if you like, you can drive point and wait for the rest of us at the top."

Derek looked up at the dark, twisty road ahead of them. "No," he said. "No, I trust you. You stay on point." He headed back to his truck. When she was sure he wasn't looking, Veronica rolled her eyes. Max smiled and got back behind the wheel.

They reached the first turn that had a wooden platform extension at around 3:00 A.M., at an elevation of four hundred feet. Max got out and walked out onto the suspended deck. It felt sturdy enough under his 215 pounds, which of course meant nothing. Three-foot-wide teak planks were laid on massive trunks, also teak, considered the strongest wood in Southeast Asia. They were held in place by concrete pylons that were sunk into concrete bases anchored to the mountain. Engineering-wise, it was as strong as a wooden platform could possibly be. He was about to find out if it was enough.

He told the mercenary riding shotgun with him to get out and wait while he tested it. The man was reluctant but followed orders. He stood on the side of the road and watched as Max eased the nose of the truck out onto the platform. There was no give, no pliancy. With a short prayer to a God he wasn't sure he believed in except in moments like this, Max drove the rest of the truck out onto the wooden platform, turning as he went.

Under the full weight of the M809, there was no creaking or groaning, nor the slightest sign of movement. It felt solid. The merc guided him through a three-point turn, and he was back on the road.

The rest of the trucks followed. There was no problem with the first platform, or with the two after that. The last one was where everything went to shit.

The final turn was only fifty feet below the summit. When they reached it, just before dawn, Max felt like he was near death. The drive was one of the most physically demanding things he had ever done and was just as taxing mentally. His nerves were frayed, he was exhausted, and he was drenched in dirty sweat that kept running into his eyes. He figured the other drivers must have been in similar shape, if not worse. The final switchback was only two hundred yards long, short but steep. They were so close.

He could tell right away there was a problem with the platform. As he eased the nose of the truck onto it, he felt a slight dip, as if the platform was sloping slightly. It was too subtle for the eye to see, but he felt it. A cold wave of fear shot through him, but he pushed it away. Unless they wanted to back the five trucks all the way back down the mountain, there was no choice but to go forward.

As he turned the rest of the truck out onto the platform, he heard a low, plaintive creak, as if the wood was saying, *I'm too old for this shit.* He looked down at the nearly straight drop, five hundred and fifty feet to the jungle below. He was grateful they had spread the load out over the four trucks, pretty sure that another three thousand pounds would have been too much for the platform to bear. He fought down his impulse to go quickly and made his four-point turn as slowly and steadily as he had the previous three, guided by the mercenary. The platform held.

As soon as he was back on the road, he drove the two hundred yards to the summit, parked the truck, and jogged back down to help guide the others through the turn. He had everyone but the drivers get out and walk around to the final switchback, making the trucks as light as possible. Truck two, driven by Derek, and truck three made it through without incident. Like he had, the crews of those two trucks parked at the summit and walked back down to see the last two through.

Truck four was halfway through its turn when there was a loud groan, and the outer edge of the platform dropped two feet, increasing the slope. Rocks and earth jumbled loose from somewhere underneath the platform and tumbled down the mountainside into the abyss.

Everyone on solid ground cried out or gasped, but to his credit the driver didn't panic. He sat still and waited for things to settle.

When they had, he continued his turn. The platform groaned in protest through every inch of it, but it didn't move again. Before long he pulled up onto the road, and everyone applauded with relief. He drove to the summit to park his truck, and perhaps, Max thought, to change his underwear.

There was one truck to go, the supply truck, with Veronica at the wheel. Max went to her and stood on the running board.

"Do you want me to drive it?"

She shook her head. "I'm fine. Really, I'm fine, I can handle it."

"Have your men unload the supplies and carry them around. It will lighten the load, and the trucks are nearly empty. If we lose the fuel, we're dead in the water." She nodded, understanding that what he meant was, if you plunge to your death, we can't let the fuel go with you.

While the crew unloaded the barrels and rolled them around the bend, Max grabbed a tactical flashlight and found a place where he could hang onto a tree and climb down enough to look under the platform. He spotted the problem right away, a large crack in one of the concrete footings holding the braces in place. The brace itself was intact, but the one next to it had a wide, lengthwise crack in it, presumably from the added stress of the first brace's load. Max was certain that if the supply truck survived the turn, it would be the last thing that ever did.

By the time the supplies were offloaded and moved up the hill, morning had broken, giving Veronica the added burden of the sunrise shining directly in her eyes. She put on dark black sunglasses, and Max gave her a nod and walked out onto the sloping platform to guide her. The truck was only halfway onto the wooden surface when he heard something give and the platform dropped another six to eight inches. He nearly lost his footing, which most likely would have resulted in his rolling over the edge. He met Veronica's eyes, and she nodded this time.

He raised his hand and guided her out, told her when to start her turn. By the time the truck was fully on the platform, it was snapping and groaning like a wooden ship in heavy seas. They both tried to ignore the sounds and concentrate on maneuvering the truck. The rest of the crew, including Derek, watched from the road, as quiet as stone. After what seemed an eternity, the truck was fully turned around.

Just as she got the front wheels onto the road, the platform dropped again, and the truck lost traction and started sliding backward. Max fell to his knees and slid down a few feet before he was able to stop himself. He looked toward the road and realized that he was looking up, the platform now sitting at almost a thirty-degree angle. He ran up the slope and shouted to Veronica in the cab.

"Leave it!"

"I can pull it out!" she said. "Get to ground!"

Max climbed up onto the road and watched as she fought to gain traction, the back wheels spinning on the wood. The wheels finally caught, and the truck lurched forward a couple of feet, the front tires finally on solid ground. She gave Max a thumbs-up.

There was a crack like a sonic boom, and the platform dropped again, the front tires of the truck lifting completely off the road.

Max shouted, "Get out!"

This time she didn't hesitate. She jumped out of the truck and ran up the slope, leaping into the air just as the platform dropped out from underneath her and the truck went over backward. Max caught her hand and managed to hold on as she slammed into the side of the mountain. He felt someone, who turned out to be Derek, grab his ankles and pin him down so she wouldn't pull him over with her weight. He helped her climb up and the three of them watched the truck careen end over end down the side of the mountain.

"Are you okay?" Max asked her.

She looked at him, white as a sheet, and said, "I lost my sunglasses."

The three of them walked up the last switchback together, slowly and silently. When they were almost to the summit, Derek asked, "To be clear, you said that this was the second most dangerous part of the trip?"

"Wait," Max answered, "until you see the bridge."

SEVEN YEARS AGO

THREE MONTHS AFTER THE RAID

Max and Kelly had barely left her bed in the last week. She had rented a beautifully crafted Lanna-style house on the banks of the Ping River, just outside of Chiang Mai.

Constructed entirely of golden teakwood, it was mostly balconies and open walls that let the mountain breeze cool the house. After she picked him up, they had talked on the drive out about the raid and the aftermath. She hadn't learned anything more and told him that aside from recovering from her gunshot wound, she had spent most of the time he was in prison working to convince the agency that they were set up and pushing them to arrange his escape.

The conversation ended when they arrived at her rental, and it hadn't come up again.

They went to bed right away, taking each other with the intense neediness of two people who had cheated death. It was a little bit comical as they tried to find positions that didn't aggravate either of their many wounds. But once they got into the groove, their love-making was more intense than it had ever been before, and it was constant. It was almost as if they were afraid that if they stopped, death would catch them. For the first week they broke only for meals, showers, and Max's daily doctor visits.

They slowed down after a few days, more out of exhaustion than lack of ardor. As Kelly put it, with her usual poetic flair, they had plain fucked themselves out. Still, Max couldn't stop, and between bouts of intercourse he used his tongue on her. He became obsessed with that too. He loved the taste of her, the smell of her, exploring her particular nooks and crannies and folds. He was driven crazy by the way her thighs clamped around his head when she came. He would have kept going forever, if she hadn't grabbed him by his ears and pulled him up, reminding him that he needed to breathe.

On day seven they lay together on a chaise lounge on the balcony overlooking the river, both naked, under a mosquito net, playing a quiet game of chess. On the far bank a farmer was grazing half a dozen water buffalo. They were working animals, used to pull plows and carts, and they were eating voraciously. Kelly was lying in the crook of his arm, casually running her fingers over the old bullet holes in his shoulder, moving her men with the other hand. He had never felt so serene in his life. He had never felt so much in love, either, and he said so.

"I love you."

"I know."

It wasn't the answer he had expected, or wanted to hear, but he could see that she was half asleep, and anyway, she must have felt him tense up because she mumbled, "I love you, too, dumbass." He laughed.

He wanted to propose right then. He had been with her twenty-four hours a day since his debrief, so he hadn't had time to make any arrangements, or even buy a ring, but he knew he wanted to marry this woman, so why wait?

He was confident she would say yes to the marriage, but he was less certain about the rest of it. He had mapped it all out in his mind, their resignation from the agency, returning to the States, buying a house. In his imagination he even saw the white picket fence and the yellow Labrador, which was just that, a fantasy, since they would more than likely wind up working for a security firm in a major city. He had also thought through the alternative if she didn't want to give up her career. She could stay in the CIA but leave the field. She was more than qualified, and had the experience, to be a chief of station or even to run officers from Langley. He could find a job wherever they sent her. Berlin, London, Istanbul. His resignation and their marriage could be the catalyst for her promotion, if she truly didn't want to leave the company.

He wanted to ask her properly, in a nice restaurant, with a diamond ring, but as he watched two teenage boys lazily punt down the river on a raft loaded with dragon fruit and guavas, he thought, *Will there ever be a more perfect moment than this?*

"Hey, Kel."

"Hmm?"

"I want to ask you some . . ."

His phone rang inside the house. It was jarring in the peaceful afternoon.

"That's you, babe."

"Ignore it."

They waited for it to stop ringing, and he started over.

"I've been thinking a lot the last few days, and I think we . . ."

It rang again. She sighed and rolled off him. "You'd better see who it is."

He reluctantly moved the chessboard aside and went inside. He didn't recognize the number, but he answered.

"Starkey."

It was Carmichael, the man who had conducted his debrief. "Listen, Max. I got something for you. I'm on a bar phone; they'd hang me if they knew I was telling you this."

"Okay."

"We still haven't found out who at Langley compromised your codes. They were sold, but we don't know who did it."

"I knew that already."

He briefly lost concentration as Kelly sashayed through the room naked and smiled at him on her way to the bathroom.

"Hang on. We still don't know who sold them, but we figured out who bought them. We don't know why yet, but we know who sent you on that fake raid."

He gave Max a name. He didn't write it down because he didn't have to. He had never met the man, but he had heard the name before, he was a prominent French businessman based in Marseilles and Hanoi.

"Are you going to bring him in?"

"Our hands are tied. He's a French national and a well-known figure. We can't just rendition him."

"Any way I can help?"

"Absolutely not. You're on rest and rehab. Off the clock."

"Right."

"We have absolutely no control over you at the moment."

After a few seconds, Max said, "Understood."

He hung up and heard the shower turn on in the bathroom as he set down his phone. He had received Carmichael's message loud and clear, he knew exactly what he needed to do, and he would get started immediately.

Right after his shower.

CHAPTER FORTY-TWO

Dinner the next night was similar, but the portions were smaller, and Kelly took this as a sign that the food supply was running low. They still had a few liters of rice wine, however, and after most of the camp had gone to bed, Kelly and Chewy Chakri sat by the fire and shared most of a bottle. They were left alone except for an older man who came by every thirty minutes or so to tend the fire.

When he'd gone, she asked, "How does a file clerk become the leader of a rebel army?"

"I'm not much of a leader, I'm afraid. My revolution is going to end in a whimper, beaten by the one enemy no army has ever defeated, lack of funding."

"I don't think you're done yet," she said. "These people really believe in you."

"They are, what is the American expression, salt of the earth. The soul of the country. I do not relish the idea of letting them down."

"Why do they follow you with such devotion?"

"It's simple. I tell them the truth."

"Which is?"

"That they have dignity. And that they deserve to be happy, and to control their own destiny."

The wine was warming her; she felt a glow slowly spreading throughout her body. She didn't trust herself tipsy, not since that disastrous night in Chiang Mai, so she thought she had better set some ground rules.

"I'm not going to sleep with you, Chewy. That's not what this is."

He laughed. "I am not trying to seduce you, Officer Riggs. No chance of that."

"That's a pretty strong proclamation. Why, what's wrong with me?"

"Nothing at all, you are beautiful and intriguing. But I don't sleep with colonizers."

Kelly was taken aback. She had been called a lot of things, but never that. However, when she thought back over her career in the agency, and the way she and others had manipulated the politics of this country, she understood that it was the right word. She briefly considered apologizing, but the words would mean nothing, and they both knew it. What was was, and Kelly knew all too well that you couldn't change the past.

Instead she said, "You haven't answered my question. File clerk to rebel leader?"

He nodded and looked at the fire for long enough that she began to think he had no intention of answering. But then he spoke, softly.

"When I was a boy, my father was a bus driver. He drove a tuk-tuk bus, a maximum of sixteen passengers. I had five brothers and sisters, and we were able to get by on what he earned. We were poor, no question about it, but we survived. My father's work ethic was impeccable. He loved Suryaka and was a devout Buddhist. He told me that the most patriotic thing you could do for your country was to be productive. The engine of a nation isn't its army, or its leaders, it is the honest sweat of its people."

"That sounds vaguely communistic."

"Just the opposite, he despised communism. He meant that working for a living, being educated and involved in the health of your local community, and voting every time you had the chance, these are the most patriotic acts possible. He instilled this belief in me."

"So what happened to him?"

"When I was thirteen the Golden Elephants seized power. Our lives didn't change much, until the day some students left a stack of opposition flyers on his bus, under the seat. He was arrested, charged with distributing anti-government propaganda, 'tried'"—here Chakri used air quotes—"convicted, and executed all before he was meant to be home for dinner. We only learned what happened to him when the regime sent my mother a bill for the bullet that killed him."

"It radicalized you?"

"No." He poured them each another glass of wine. "I honored him by continuing to live by his principles. I studied hard. I worked after school. Over the next few years, governments came and went, but I stayed focused on my productivity. Head down and all that. I got a simple but honorable job, working as a supply clerk. Then Chavarat Vinthu began to rise, with all his divisive rhetoric, pitting ethnic groups against each other, and Buddhists against Muslims, and things became dark very quickly. Curfews were imposed. People began to disappear off the streets. And then one day I was at my desk, processing forms, when his thugs raided the depot and slaughtered most of my co-workers. You remember that day."

"Are you saying we radicalized you? That I did?"

"No, because your premise is faulty. I am not radicalized. I do not believe that there are inherently evil people among us, or that some of our citizens worship the wrong God. My revolution is a practical one. If Ruchuphan seizes power, it will be devastating, worse than life under Vinthu, who was merely greedy, and petty. Ruchuphan is ruthless, in ways Vinthu never could have imagined. All I want is to stop him, so that our people get their country back, and so men like my father can work and live and raise their families."

"Only men?"

"You know what I mean."

She nodded. "The media portrays you as a power-hungry, egomaniacal butcher."

He raised his glass. "To the media."

She smiled and they drank. Over the next few hours they talked about all kinds of things, including why she and Max had broken up, and how she wound up married to Derek. She told him what she had been running from when she crashed the chopper, but not why they had been at the palace in the first place. She even told him a little bit about her childhood, but she didn't go into detail. She did tell him that she had started training in secret and became a fighter in order to protect herself from her own father. She probably told him too much and blamed the wine.

Still, she held back the most important thing he should have known, that Vinthu was already dead. She wasn't sure why, but she wanted that in her hip pocket. She wanted to know something he didn't.

They laughed, and he even told some jokes. It was nearly dawn when she walked back to the field hospital, moving very slowly because she was intoxicated and didn't want to re-injure her ankle by falling over, or something equally stupid. She thought about all the things they had talked about, but mostly she thought about how the media portrayed him, as a butcher and a maniac, and the fact that she had so easily accepted it as gospel. Her cynical brain knew she was drunk and that she shouldn't change her mind about him while she could barely stand, so she drank water and went to sleep.

When she woke, she had a clarity that had been missing for the last few years. She had a sense of all the wrong she had done, to strangers, to people who loved her, and even to herself. But mostly to the country she was in the middle of, where she had been, in his word, a colonizer. She had realized overnight that it didn't matter which Chewy was the real Chewy, the maniacal butcher or the nice guy he had been selling her for the last few days. Bottom line, it was his country, not hers, and he was trying to save it the best way he knew how.

She gave herself a whore's bath at the basin, then went to the outdoor kitchen for a cup of strong coffee, building her resolve to find her redemption. She had to do what she could to set things right before it was too late, and if it solved her Derek Moss problem at the same time, well, that was just a bonus.

She walked up to the command tent, where Chakri was meeting with his all-male group of advisors. She lifted the flap and walked in, and they all stopped and stared at her.

"We're in the middle of something important," Chakri said, a little too sternly for her liking. She just stood there, until he finally said, "Well? What is it?"

"Finances are your biggest obstacle, is that the case?"

"You know they are."

"Then it's lucky," she said, "that I know where you can get your hands on four thousand pounds of gold."

CHAPTER FORTY-THREE

Giuliana bought a map of Suryaka at the airport when General Ruchuphan's men put her on a commercial flight to Bangkok. She spread it out as best she could on the tray table and marked various routes north from the border, half of them leading to the same place.

She was met at Suvarnabhumi by AD Lin, who drove her to Deputy Director June Martinson's temporary offices at the American Embassy for a debrief. State Department Karen joined them, and Giuliana spread out her map and explained her theory.

"I know exactly where they're headed."

Lin tried to interrupt, "Agent Abara . . ."

"Look, they went north here, and they have to get to the border in this area, to the northeast. There are several routes, but most of them bottleneck here, at Phaya Nok Ravine . . ."

"The border has been slammed shut on us."

"I know, but please listen. They spread the gold out onto a number of trucks, now, the only reason to do that is for weight. There's a decommissioned suspension bridge at the ravine; they'd want to keep the trucks as light as possible. That has to be where they're headed . . ."

"Agent Abara." This time it was Deputy Director Martinson talking. "We tried this your way. You were ejected from the country and explicitly told not to return by the acting president. To go back would be a violation of their sovereign borders, not to mention international law."

She couldn't give up this easily. "Derek Moss and Kelly Riggs are straight-up criminals, I get it. But Max Starkey was a damn good case officer, he was respected and well liked. It was a tangible loss to the American intelligence community when he decided to retire."

"It's a nonstarter."

And that had been the end of that.

Now she, Lin, Martinson, and Frick and Frack were all at the airport, waiting to board a commercial flight back to DC. State Department Karen had come to see them off. As they watched a mother dose her toddlers with Children's Motrin for the long-haul flight, she casually said to Giuliana, "You were right about where they're heading."

"What do you mean?"

Karen looked to Martinson. "Can I show her?"

Martinson shrugged, why not? Karen keyed in her passcode on her iPad and swiped open some satellite photos.

"These were taken an hour ago in the Phukhao Saksid Mountains."

There were several shots from directly above of four M809 trucks traversing a narrow passage between two karst towers, the tall, pointy limestone mountains specific to the region. Everything looked flat from straight above, but Giuliana knew that on the ground they would look like they were in a painting on a Chinese silk screen.

"You were right about where they're headed," Karen continued. "This is about a hundred and seventy miles southeast of Phaya Nok Ravine. In that terrain we figure it will take them another two and a half days to get there."

Giuliana swiped back and forth through the photos. "Only four trucks. That leaves three unaccounted for." She pinched in on a couple of the photos. She could see a few mercenaries riding in the beds, but no Max. No Derek or Kelly either, for that matter. "Think they could have lost the other trucks along the way?"

"Could be. Or maybe like you said, they only had four to begin with and the other three are somewhere else, unrelated. There's one more thing."

She showed her another set of satellite photos. Even from the air Giuliana recognized the palace. Karen swiped through the photos, which showed the army on the move.

"Ruchuphan has mobilized an entire army division. They are headed directly north; we assume they are going after the gold."

"That tracks. Will they be able to catch up?"

"Starkey and the others took a circuitous, treacherous route, in order to avoid the rebels in the north and army checkpoints in the east. Ruchuphan doesn't have those same concerns, he can take highways. They'll either be waiting for Max at the ravine or arrive around the same time."

Giuliana turned to her bosses. "He has an army coming down on him. This has to mean that we go in."

Martinson shook her head. "I'm sorry. Official policy is still non-engagement."

Frustrated, Giuliana opened her laptop and googled the bridge at Phaya Nok Ravine for the sixth time that day. The gorge was twelve hundred feet deep, and the bridge was a suspension bridge that had been closed to traffic for three years. This was to the Golden Gate Bridge as a rowboat is to a Carnival cruise ship. Jury-rigged or not, it was four hundred yards across, almost a quarter of a mile, and twenty feet wide, with steel mesh laid over enormous wooden planks. She studied the photos of the bridge, and of people crossing it. There was even an old one of three elephants walking across, which someone, presumably Suryaka's version of P. T. Barnum, had marched across to showcase the bridge's strength. She zoomed in on the picture. The mahouts riding the beasts looked terrified.

The trucks wouldn't make it across; she was certain of it. Giuliana rarely dwelt on the cruelty of life, it was just part of being human, but the unfairness of this was hard for her to swallow. She had spent her entire adult life convincing herself that her career was the whole point of her, and that love was a prize she would never win. Then along came Max. She had no idea if they were meant to be together or not, or even whether they would truly fall in love, but she hadn't stopped thinking about him since she woke up in the hospital. That had to mean something. Now even the mere possibility of love was being yanked out from under her. She was supposed to just sit on a plane and let him die, because of regulations?

The PA system announced that their flight would be boarding in five minutes. Giuliana set her laptop on top of her carry-on and excused herself to go to the restroom, needing to splash some water on her face. Five minutes later, as they got in line to board, Lin asked Martinson, "Should I grab her laptop? It has sensitive intel on it."

Martinson sighed. "She's not coming back, is she?"

He shook his head. "I doubt it."

CHAPTER FORTY-FOUR

Cintha could not sleep, no matter how hard she tried. The tiger had been stalking her for three days now, probing the edges of the bamboo, looking for a way to get to her, but luckily, he still could not find one. She continued to hope that he would lose interest, but that was clearly not going to happen. She didn't know if tigers could be obsessed, but this one sure seemed fixated on her. Wherever she moved, he was there, just on the other side of the barrier, a constant oppressive presence. Maybe he was like most of the people she knew and only wanted the things he couldn't have. Whatever it was, he wasn't giving up.

Which is why she had been stalking him right back. She studied him, watching his patterns, learning his rhythms. She knew when he slept at various times of the day, and for how long. She knew how long after he ate before he pooped. She knew the time of day he was the most tired and the times he was most energetic. She knew that every afternoon when the sun was three quarters of the way across the clearing, his frustration would get the better of him and he would bash into the bamboo for fifteen or twenty minutes, roaring, until he tired out and curled up for a nap.

But most importantly, she knew when he got thirsty. Three times a day he would walk out of the clearing to the north or west or southeast or whatever, the way she had first come, and be gone anywhere from five to seven minutes, going by the one-Crocodile, two-Crocodiles in her head. She figured there must be a watering hole a couple of minutes away, maybe even the one she muddied herself up at the first day, while her family was being killed. She could think about them now without bursting into tears every time, but it still made her chest ache.

The tiger's first trip to water in the morning, right when the sun was coming up, seemed to be the longest one, lasting a couple of minutes more than the others. Whether this was because he was still sleepy, or thirstier than usual, or she was just half asleep and counting wrong, she didn't know, but that was the one to use. If she was going to go get the gun, she would have to do it early in the morning when he went to get a drink.

She couldn't sleep because she was nervous, but also because her mind was busy. Over the last couple of days, while she was studying the tiger's routine, she had been thinking a lot about her life as the daughter of a president, and whether she had been naive to think her father was a good dude. All the signs were there. She thought everybody at school liked her, even the bitches, but when she looked at it now, she could see that they were afraid of her. They liked all her instas, they invited her to every party, and they never, ever said a single mean or rude thing to her, not even Kayli with an *i*. She had made the track team, but she was the slowest one on the squad and was starting to wonder if she had even earned her spot. When she did have her very few dates with boys they would never try anything, like they were scared to touch her. She saw a lot of girls pairing up, but she didn't have a bestie. In fact, she was starting to wonder if she had any friends at all.

As for her dad, the more she thought about it, the easier it was to believe that he was what everyone thought he was. When he first became the president, she was a little girl, and she remembered protests all over the place. But there hadn't been any protests in years, the roads were always lined with cheering people wherever they went. Was it more likely that everyone suddenly started liking him, or that the protesters had been swept violently off the streets? Even the genocide thing started seeming pretty likely the more she thought about it. His enemies had a way of disappearing, and he won his last election by 98.5 percent.

How stupid had she been?

If she did survive this fight with the tiger, what would happen to her when she got back to the city? Would they blame her for the fucked-up shit her father did? Would they execute her on sight, or throw her in jail? She would fight back, that's all she knew. She had almost been killed about a bajillion times in the last few days, but she was still alive. She was being hunted by a five-hundred-pound Bengal tiger, and he was wounded and she was still here. Their battle had been physical, but it was mental, too, and when she got back, she would start the mental part of her next fight right away. She would read everything she could about her father, her real father, and when she was educated, she would figure out how to help fix the things he did.

But first she had to kill this fucking tiger.

She turned over on her other side, clutching the bamboo spear she had made to replace the one she stuck him with, and tried to get comfortable. She was tired of sleeping outside, wearing almost nothing and exposed to the elements. Her leg was constantly throbbing, and she worried that it was infected. She was sick of eating handfuls of worms, although she had gotten pretty used to it and it didn't make her gag anymore. She was probably way more thirsty than the tiger was, since she had had only been able to drink whatever she could catch in her mouth when it rained, which it did a lot, which was a mixed blessing because she also had no shelter. She had had enough; it was time to go home.

Please let me sleep, she thought, *Please God, just for two hours or even one, I need sleep.*

At dawn, I run.

CHAPTER FORTY-FIVE

After they crested the switchback, Max had insisted they take a couple of hours for everyone to rest and refresh. Along with the fuel they had unloaded most of the food and water, so they had plenty to stay hydrated. There were mangoes growing all around them and they had a feast on the fruit's tangy flesh. Max slowly started to feel human again.

Derek, on the other hand, seemed to be losing his mind. He'd been getting worse over the last few hours, as Kelly's disappearance weighed on him. He was convinced now that it was no accident, that she had deliberately run out on him. While they were recuperating on top of the ridge, Derek had gotten brief cell service and had checked their joint bank accounts, which were completely drained. Balance, zero. He had been in a spiral of rage and frustration ever since.

They had forged another river, this one shallow and slow moving, without incident. Now they were in the most mountainous region of Suryaka, the narrow dirt road winding around peaks and up and down valleys, all of it blanketed in thick jungle. They had come around a sharp bend two hours ago and found a family of elephants blocking their way, eating bark from the trees that lined the road. The animals had glanced at the trucks, then continued to eat, undisturbed. Honking didn't even rate a glance. Derek jumped out of the second truck and came forward, chambering a round in his Glock.

"We don't have time for this."

"Sure we do," Max answered. "We're still a minimum of two days from the ravine, so let's just get some sleep and wait them out. We'll get to the bridge in forty or fifty hours either way."

"We don't have time for all that shit. Let's just shoot them and get on with it."

"We can't shoot them, Derek."

"Why the hell not?"

"Two reasons. First, just, no. Second, and more importantly, if we do shoot them, we will have dead elephants blocking the road, instead of live elephants that will eventually move out of the way."

Derek simply grunted. He wasn't happy about it, but he couldn't argue the logic, so they waited. Most of the mercenaries had used the down time to get some sleep, but two of them had gone off into the bush and come back with a wild boar, which they were roasting on a spit. They cut it into smaller pieces so it would cook faster and were basting it with juice squeezed out of wild mangoes directly onto the meat. The aroma was literally making Max salivate, and elephants or not, he wasn't going anywhere until that pig was nothing but clean bones.

Derek had spent the time pacing up and down the road, still clutching his Glock, muttering about his whore bitch traitor of a wife, and debating with himself about the pros and cons of the different ways he could kill her. As nearly as Max could tell from his incoherent ramblings, he was leaning toward a combination of garroting her and setting her on fire. Max just hoped Derek wouldn't lose it completely and try to kill him before they reached the bridge. To be on the safe side he loaded his Desert Eagle to capacity and made sure there was a round in the chamber.

As a rule Max avoided killing, but if it came down to it, he would take Derek out with no hesitation. He had learned the hard way that when it was time, you pulled the trigger. When he was a young officer on one of his first assignments, stationed in Cairo, he had the chance to kill a man who needed killing and he hadn't gone through with it. It was the biggest mistake of his career, and in the years since a lot of innocent people had paid the price for his decision. He wouldn't make the same mistake with Derek.

Max was relieved to hear that the bank accounts were drained, since it meant Kelly was probably alive. Even after everything, he didn't wish her dead. He walked to the back of the caravan and found Veronica sitting under a tree, looking at photos on her phone of her wife, Olivia, and their four-year-old daughter, Carmen. He looked over her shoulder at a pic of them in the pool.

"She's getting so big."

She nodded. "She's a holy terror, just like her bio-dad, who is a total maniac."

Max sat beside her but didn't say anything more. She flipped through a few more photos, then tucked the phone in her pocket.

"I almost went over with the truck."

"But you didn't."

"My mother died when I was a year older than Carmen is now, and I don't remember her at all. I'd hate for Carm to grow up not knowing me."

"Maybe you should find another line of work."

"Way ahead of you. This is my last time out, for obvious reasons. If I survive it."

"You ask me, that was your chance to die back there on the switchbacks. You dodged it, so now you'll be okay."

She nodded. After a few moments, she looked at him sideways. "Are we going to pull this off?"

"We are. Although Derek thinks Kelly fled the country, in which case she won't be there to enjoy it."

"Why does he think that?"

"Apparently, before she flew off in the chopper she drained all of their joint accounts."

"Ha!" Veronica grinned. "I didn't think she had it in her."

"I did." It came out with more bitterness than he intended, and Veronica smiled, a little sadly. One of the mercs yelled "Lunch," and they went to eat. The wild boar was as good as it smelled. Derek grabbed a piece and ate it while he continued to pace, still muttering threats against his absent wife between bites.

While they were eating, the elephant family finally moved on, lumbering off into the jungle. As they started up the trucks, Max suggested to Derek that he let someone else drive. Derek turned on him, angry, and for a moment Max thought they were going to shoot it out right there. But Derek just glared at him, climbed into the cab, and took the wheel. As he walked back to the lead truck, Max thought, *Another fifty hours, Derek; just hold on to your sanity for another fifty hours.*

Then I'll give you something to lose your mind over.

SEVEN YEARS AGO

FOUR MONTHS AFTER THE RAID

It had taken Max nearly a month to figure out how to get to Louis Moreau, the name Carmichael had given him as the man who had purchased their codes and sent them on the unsanctioned raid that almost got them killed. He was a large figure in international finance, a few bucks shy of a billionaire, and he always traveled with bodyguards. Max was determined to get the information he needed without killing anyone who didn't deserve it, so the bodyguards were an issue.

Moreau spent most of his time in Hanoi, where he kept a suite of rooms on the top floor of the Sofitel Legend Metropole hotel, where Max could have afforded a third of a room for half an hour. Max had cased the entire hotel. There was no way to scale the place from the outside without being seen, and even if he could get to the top floor from the inside undetected, the two beefy bodyguards would be in the hall. He was going to have to find a crack not in the physical, but in behavior.

He tailed Moreau for two weeks before he saw the pattern. Every few evenings, Moreau would have a girl sent up to the room, never the same girl twice. One of the bodyguards would meet her in the lobby and show her up, and while she was in the room both bodyguards would go down to the lobby bar and have a couple of drinks until they saw her leave. Max figured Moreau was up to some kinky shit up there and didn't want the boys overhearing her screams, or his pleas for her to spank him harder, or whatever his particular bent was. It seemed a little dick shy for a Frenchman, to be honest.

He sat in the lobby until the next girl showed up six days later. She was a beautiful working girl, Max guessed Czech or Romanian because of her long torso and shorter legs. She could have been waiting in the lobby for anyone, but the bodyguard came down and led her to the elevator, so Max put his plan in motion. He paid the bartender his prearranged bribe, took his red vest and his place behind the bar. When the two bodyguards sat down at the bar and ordered, he slipped a Mickey into each of their drinks.

"Where's Joe tonight?" one of them asked.

"His wife had the baby." A simple lie, but it had the effect Max expected, ending the conversation. No one wanted to admit they were the asshole who had been talking to a bartender every night for months and had no idea his wife was pregnant.

He watched their eyelids get heavier, and when he decided they were far enough gone he handed the bar back over to Joe and headed upstairs. The elevator required a key card, but he had that covered, having lifted a passkey off a maid earlier. Once on the top floor, he found the room and listened at the door for a few moments. He could hear voices, and some strange murmuring, but he couldn't make it out.

He opened the door with the passkey and slipped in quietly, closing the door behind him with the handle down, then easing it up into position to avoid the click. Fortunately Moreau hadn't put on the chain lock, or he would have had to go in hot. He slipped out of his shoes, pulled his gun, and walked quietly across the living room in his socks to the bedroom door, where he laughed out loud.

Moreau was on his back, a pacifier in his mouth, lying on an adult-sized diaper with his feet in the air, and the girl was powdering his ass. They both heard him laugh and looked over. The girl saw his gun and started screaming.

"Relax," Max said, "I'm not going to shoot anyone."

She stopped screaming and started cursing at him in Czech, so he'd guessed her ethnicity right. She was determined to be a problem, so Max put her in a chair and had Moreau secure her with the duct tape he had brought along. Then he stuck the pacifier in her mouth and had Moreau tape that in place too. Max waved him back to the bed with the gun.

"I gotta say, I didn't peg you as the baby type."

Moreau pouted. "Don't kink shame."

"I don't give a shit how you get off. I just want to ask you a few questions and you can get back to your playdate. Do you know who I am?"

"I have a pretty good idea."

Moreau kept glancing at the girl. Max said, "She'll be fine."

"It's not that. I'm concerned she will overhear something that will put her life in danger."

Max was impressed; he hadn't expected Moreau to be thinking of her welfare while he sat on the bed in a diaper with a gun in his face. He looked at her and said, in French, "*If I let you go will you keep your mouth shut?*" She just glared at him, with no idea what he had just said. "*Let's speak French, then.*"

Moreau looked surprised at his fluency and nodded. "Ask your questions."

"Someone at Langley sold you our confidential activation codes. Give me a name."

"I don't know who it was."

Max chambered a round. The girl in the chair squealed as best she could with a My Little Pony pacifier in her mouth. Moreau spread his hands.

"I honestly don't know. I hired someone to do a job for me, and they used a contact at Langley to get the codes. He arranged everything."

"Who did you hire?"

Moreau looked at him, confused. "You really don't know?"

"Don't play games. Who arranged the raid?"

Moreau shrugged. "It was Derek Moss."

At first, Max didn't buy it. "No way. He was on the raid with us, he was almost killed. He was in prison the same time I was, and he was tortured for weeks." Or was he? Max hadn't seen any signs of torture on him the day they escaped. "Plus, an American asset was killed."

"The death of the asset was the whole point. The raid was entirely Moss's idea. I hired him to find and terminate the spy in General Vong's household, I didn't care how he did it."

"You're saying Derek Moss was willing to kill an American operative, for . . . ?"

"Half a million dollars. Yes, that is what I am saying. He used you and Kelly Riggs to stage the raid and get him inside, close enough to the asset to kill him."

Max was reeling. He knew Moss was a bad dude, and that he frequently used his position in the CIA to line his pockets. But would he really kill an asset, and risk Max and Kelly's lives as well, for a payday?

"Why did you want the asset dead?"

"Business. I am trying to make inroads into Laos but I'm meeting resistance from certain other entities that control the drug trade there."

"The Ghosts street gang."

Moreau nodded. "General Vong is my strategic partner, and the American was causing me problems, feeding intel about our project to his government, who passed it on to the Ghosts."

Max didn't speak for several minutes, and to his credit, Moreau waited. For better or worse, Max had what he came for. He glanced over at the girl, and her eyes went wide. "Calm down," he said. "I told you; I'm not going to shoot anyone." He used his knife to cut her loose and told her in Czech that he'd give her five minutes to clear the property before he followed her down. She called him a čurák one last time and ran out, clothes in hand.

Max was still in shock on the elevator ride to the lobby. The magnitude of this betrayal was colossal. In a way he should have seen it coming, Derek Moss had always been a bad apple. But this was beyond the pale.

The doors dinged open and almost closed again before he remembered to step out. He glanced into the bar as he walked through the lobby and saw the two bodyguards on their stools where he left them, their heads on the rail, snoring. They would be looking for new jobs soon.

As he walked out the hotel's front door, he heard frantic voices from somewhere on the grounds, and approaching sirens. He'd read about it in tomorrow's edition of the *People's Daily.* Max had kept his promise, he hadn't shot anyone, but apparently some rich weirdo in a diaper had thrown himself off a top floor balcony.

CHAPTER FORTY-SIX

It took Giuliana several tries to locate Iron Sam's house again. She hadn't paid that much attention when they went there the first time, so she paid a tuk-tuk driver to run her up and down the streets of the dodgy neighborhood for two hours until she spotted it. Maybe Sam would know where she could hire mercenaries and maybe he wouldn't, or maybe he had vacated or been arrested and wouldn't be there at all, but he was literally the only person she knew in Bangkok, and she had to start somewhere. She briefly worried that the Ghosts would have someone waiting for her, after all, she had killed one of them. But they had been after Max, not her, and there were none of them left alive that could tell anyone she had even been there.

The tuk-tuk dropped her off on the street and she walked down the alley to the metal gate. She was moving slowly, no longer using the cane at least, but still in tender condition. She hit the buzzer and waited thirty seconds while Sam made up his mind. Finally he buzzed and she went through and crossed the small yard. He opened the back door as she approached.

"I wasn't sure if I should let you in."

"Yet here we are."

He shrugged and she followed him in. Everything was exactly as it was when she last saw it, so apparently the authorities couldn't find it either. The two sex dolls were sleeping cheek to cheek, right where they had been.

"Last time I saw you, I got punched in the face."

“That was Max, not me. Me, I would have shot you.”

Iron Sam laughed, then listened patiently as she described what she needed, which boiled down to five or six good fighters and a pilot to take them into Suryaka.

“I don’t know any people like that.”

“Come on,” she said. “You must supply half the mercenaries in Southeast Asia.”

“These people are obsessive about privacy. I don’t know names or phone numbers. The best I could do is let you wait here until one of them shows up, but that could be days, or weeks.”

They went back and forth a couple of times before Giuliana gave up. She bought a .45 automatic and a Swiss APC9K compact machine gun, which he put in a violin case like in an old-time gangster movie. She felt like James Cagney. She was almost out the door when he said, “Let me make some calls.”

She took her new guns apart and cleaned and loaded them while he made several calls, speaking low and in Thai. They were brand new and didn’t need cleaning, but she did it anyway, for peace of mind. She finished just about the same time he did.

“Okay,” he said, “I couldn’t find any fighters, but I have someone that will fly you to the bridge in a chopper, for three grand American.” He jotted something down on a small piece of paper, folded it, and handed it to Giuliana. “That’s an airfield, ten miles north of the city. When you get there, ask for Gus, he’s expecting you at first light tomorrow.”

She memorized the airfield’s name and tore the paper into small pieces. “Anything else?”

“Yes. Forget my address.”

She smiled. “I never knew it.”

Giuliana got three grand in US currency out of a local bank, paying almost 20 percent in fees for the privilege, checked into a hotel, and got some sleep. Just before dawn, she took a hotel taxi and got to the airfield in twenty minutes. Calling it an airfield was generous; it was more a patch of broken tarmac with weeds growing through it.

The only building was a rusty Quonset hut, and the sole aircraft in sight was an antique Bell Huey chopper that was definitely left over from the Vietnam War. Giuliana looked back over her shoulder as the taxi drove off, realizing too late that she probably should have had it wait.

A man in his sixties, in overalls, with long white hair and a beard, came out of the Quonset hut, wiping grease off his hands on a towel which he tossed on the ground as he approached.

"You must be Iron Sam's friend." He had a thick German accent.

"Giuliana, my friends call me Jules. Gus?"

"Short for Gustav. So, Jules." Giuliana thought, *I guess we're friends already.* "Phaya Nok Ravine?"

"If possible."

"Everything is possible." He smiled, then turned and walked toward the ancient helicopter. He looked back at her. "Coming?"

She realized he meant right now. She followed him, and they strapped into the seats. The chopper looked worse on the inside than it had from the outside, like it had been completely rebuilt with a child's erector set. As the engine warmed up, she asked, "Are you sure this thing will get us there?"

"Of course."

"And back again?"

He smiled. "You Americans want the world."

Before she could protest, he lifted off and they flew north.

CHAPTER FORTY-SEVEN

At first Cintha thought she had overslept. Diffuse light was seeping through the bamboo, and she worried she must have missed the tiger's first water run, but she hadn't. When she got to the edge of the clearing, he was there, still in his nightly sleeping spot beside her brothers' corpses, almost as if he were guarding the gun. She went to the closest mud hole, left over from the rain, and touched up the parts of her skin that had become exposed. Two days ago she had started to do her face as well, so she was caked head to toe in black mud, except for her halter top, her underwear, her torn, floppy shoes, and the miniskirt tied around her leg wound. She quickly downed a couple of handfuls of bamboo worms.

She walked back to the clearing as she chewed, leaning on her sharp bamboo spear. The floppy sole of her Dunk Low made walking awkward and would make running even harder. But she couldn't risk stepping on a stone or a thorn and falling down, she wouldn't have the seconds to spare. She would have to make her limping run with the shoe on. She watched the tiger until he woke up, right on schedule. He stretched out and roared softly. Cintha took a few steps back into the thicket as he came over and sniffed around the edge of the bamboo. So far so good, now all that was left was for him to walk off to the watering hole.

But he didn't go. Every other morning, right at this moment, he would trot off into the jungle. But today he walked in circles, sniffed the air, and writhed around on the ground to scratch his back. Three times he came over to the edge of the bamboo and pushed at it with his head. It was almost as though he knew today was different somehow, that there was a plan afoot, but that was impossible.

Cintha stood absolutely still, watching him, for almost four hours. A few times she lifted each leg by the ankle to stretch it out. When he was looking away, she did a couple of squats, which made the wound on her leg feel like it was on fire, but a muscle spasm as she tried to run would definitely make her his lunch.

Finally, when they were both about to die of thirst, he walked a wide circle around the clearing and headed for the path. Cintha gripped her spear and moved slowly forward to the edge of the bamboo. He left the clearing, and she counted thirty Crocodiles in her head to be sure he was gone.

She broke into the open, half running and half limping as fast as she could. There was no sign of him, and she could see the gun on the ground. The combo of the gash in her leg and the floppy shoe was slowing her down, but not as much as she had feared. A sudden panic hit her; what if the gun was out of bullets? She pushed the fear away and kept running.

She was ten feet from the gun when the tiger charged back into the clearing. He looked like he was going a hundred miles an hour, straight at her. She ran, then dove, dropping her spear on the ground. She grabbed the gun and rolled onto her back, checking with her thumb that the safety was still off, and started firing. She fired shot after shot, until the magazine was empty.

The tiger slammed into her at full speed. She was knocked backward several feet by the bulk of his skull and put her arms up over her face to ward off the death blows she knew were coming. Nothing happened.

She opened her eyes. The tiger's face was less than six inches from her own. His eyes were closed; his face riddled with bullet holes. He wasn't breathing. An enormous wave of relief washed over her, but instead of breaking down in tears, she jumped to her feet and ran to grab her bamboo spear. She plunged the spear into the dead tiger, again and again. She was filled with a rage she had never even dreamt of, screaming at the top of her lungs.

"Fuck you, motherfucker! I win! I fucking win, you fucking motherfucker!"

She kept going, spearing him over and over again, until she exhausted herself and made herself hoarse. She pulled the spear out and staggered back a few steps, looked at the tiger for a long time, then spoke more quietly this time.

"I win."

She heard a twig snap and turned, her bamboo spear at the ready. She froze, not sure what her next move should be. There was a small band of rebels, at first glance she counted five of them, standing at the edge of the clearing, watching her with their jaws hanging open.

CHAPTER FORTY-EIGHT

Kelly had only asked for two things from Chakri in return. "Once you have the gold I walk away, and so does Max Starkey. Alive."

They were in the command tent, with all his advisors. A map of the country was pinned to the canvas wall. Chakri gently shook his head.

"You know how it is in the heat of battle," he said. "Bullets fly, it's confusing, my men will be trying not to die themselves. I can't guarantee anyone's survival, not even my own."

"Then no gold. You know damn well you can torture me for a month and I won't break. The gold will be out of the country in two days. You want it, Starkey lives."

He was conflicted. Starkey was with her at the fuel depot massacre, and Kelly knew Chakri would love to put a bullet in his head. She tried to make the decision easier for him.

"It won't be much of a fight, really, you'll have them outnumbered. And the gold will feed your army for months and buy enough arms to finish your war. I don't really see how this is even a debate."

His advisors agreed and told him so. Starkey was one man in the scheme of a revolution, and really no more of an enemy of the people than any other Westerner, Kelly included. Chakri heard them out and finally agreed.

"Okay."

"I need to hear you say it," Kelly insisted. "Max lives."

"I give you my word. Starkey will not be killed."

Satisfied, Kelly went to the map.

"They are coming up through this region. Max may adjust the route a little bit on the way, depending on what they run into, but eventually they will wind up here, at the bridge at Phaya Nok."

There was a murmur of disbelief. One of Chakri's advisors snorted. "They are going to cross that rickety old bridge with four thousand pounds of gold?"

"They've spread the load out pretty thin over several trucks. Max is confident the bridge will hold."

The men in the tent with her were much less confident, but there was nothing they could do about it. From their position in the foot-hills, they could only approach the ravine from the north. It was therefore decided that they would lie in wait, and strike once Starkey and Moss had brought the gold across. It would save them the trouble of doing it themselves.

They were two days' walk from the bridge, so Chakri decided they would make the journey on foot and horseback. Once they took the gold, they would bring the trucks back with them and add them to their motor pool. Kelly told him there were sixteen of the enemy, fourteen mercenaries plus Max and Derek, so Chakri decided to take forty fighters, roughly three times their number. As she watched them gear up, she realized they were taking water but no food. She asked him why.

"No need to burden our horses. There is a village we will reach around nightfall, they will happily feed us."

They were ready within the hour, and Chakri mounted up and rode to the head of the unit, trotting through camp like Napoleon. Despite his slight stature, he looked more like John Wayne in the saddle because the Thai ponies were so short, most of them not even reaching four and a half feet, or thirteen hands. A soldier brought her a horse of her own and she mounted up.

As they rode out of camp she saw Sarai Makok, the journalist's widow, watching her, her children gathered around her skirts. It reinforced her belief that she was doing the right thing.

For the first time in her life she was thinking beyond herself, past her own needs.

Granted, implicit in the promise that Starkey would live was the concession that Derek would most likely not, and his death solved a major problem for her, to be sure. But it was a beneficial byproduct, not the point of the thing. The revolution was right for the country, and the gold would facilitate it. It would do a lot more good in Chakri's hands than it would in hers, or Max's, or especially Derek's. The gold was her atonement for her sins against nations.

Her atonement to Max would be more personal. She had already decided to split the twenty million in the Cayman account with him. She knew that he dreamt of a simpler life, of owning a bar on a beach somewhere, and of raising a family with a woman he could love, a life he had hoped to have with her. He had talked about the dream often, in bed after they made love, and she had listened, her head on his chest, and internally mocked him for his romantic notions. She would never, could never, share the beach bar dream with him, but she could help him find it with his new wife, Giuliana. It was the least she could do.

And it wasn't nearly enough. Max used to laugh all the time, but she hadn't seen him laugh once since they met in Bangkok. He seemed more hurt than angry with her, although if the tables had been turned, Kelly would have carried her rage to the grave. For all his tough exterior, she knew Max lived in his heart. He needed love the way the rest of us need oxygen, or money, or sex. She would do what she could to atone, by giving him ten million dollars, and by saving his life. But she knew she could never do enough to make up for what she did to him.

SEVEN YEARS AGO

FOUR MONTHS AFTER THE RAID

Getting to Derek would be a lot easier than it had been getting to the Frenchman with the powdery ass. He was staying in a rented town house in Nimman, the closest thing Chiang Mai has to a Brooklyn hipster neighborhood. There were no bodyguards to deal with, nor any practical, physical obstacles to overcome. This time, the challenge would be Derek himself.

The longer he had thought about what Moreau had told him, the more he believed it. He had debated with himself about what to do with the information and had decided that there was only one course of action. Reporting Derek's betrayal wouldn't do any good, since he had no proof. Confronting him would be a waste of time, and dangerous. The only logical move was to kill him. He had no qualms about the act itself; the CIA had sent him to kill men for less than this. But Derek Moss would not be easy to kill. He was lethal, as well trained as Max if not better, and Max was coming off weeks of torture that Derek had avoided. He would be at a physical disadvantage, so he would stack the odds in his favor.

He would wait until 3:00 A.M., when Derek would likely be asleep, go in barefoot, and use a silencer, in case there was anyone else in the house unexpectedly. He had wanted Derek to know why he was dying, but killing him in his sleep was the smarter move. Then he would go home to Kelly, tell her about it, and ask her to spend the rest of her life with him.

He killed the evening hours in a coffee shop situated directly next to a temple, and called, horrifyingly, Sacred Grounds. After two cups he switched to decaf so he wouldn't be jittery going in. To pass the time, he took out the ring and looked at it. He had stayed behind in Hanoi an extra day to buy it and had visited seven shops before he found one that he was sure she would like. It had an elegant array of diamonds that added up to nearly three carats, but it wasn't ostentatious. He knew her taste and knew she would like it.

He had been away in Hanoi for almost a month, and although they had talked every night, he missed her badly. He had almost gone to her first but had forced himself to finish his business with Derek before anything else. He didn't want to drag her into it, so that they could start fresh. Killing Derek would be the last bit of ugliness in their life together, and he'd handle it alone.

At 2:50 A.M., he left five hundred baht on the table and set out for the ten-minute walk to Derek's town house. He had gone about half a block when two Thai men stepped out of the dark, the bigger one wielding a knife.

"What's this, fellas?"

"Hand over the ring, farang."

Of course. It had been stupid to pull the ring out and admire it in an all-night coffee shop, but his mind had been on other things. The bigger man thrust the knife at him. It was nice, with a leather handle and a carbon steel blade.

"Quit stalling, hand it over!"

He left them alive and kept the knife.

He stood under a tree across the street from Derek's three-story town house for about ten minutes, watching for movement. There was none, and there were no lights on. He waited for some foot traffic to pass, crossed the street, and went around the side of the house. The windows and doors on the first floor were locked, but there was a window slightly open on the second floor. He took his shoes and socks off and climbed the drainpipe, pushed the window open—it stuck a bit, but he got it to move without too much noise—and slid into a bedroom that was being used as a lounge, with a pool table and a full bar. He drew his gun and screwed on the silencer, then slipped into the hall.

He checked all the rooms on the second floor and found them empty, so he headed up the stairs. Halfway up a stair creaked under his foot, so he waited, gun pointed at the third-floor landing. Nobody came, so he continued up.

He went to clear the first room but then he heard Derek's voice, murmuring quietly, from behind the ajar door at the end of the hall. So he was awake. That made it more challenging, but he still had the element of surprise on his side. He started down the hallway, and the sounds from the room became clearer. There were two voices, and they weren't talking; they were fucking.

Derek had a woman in bed with him.

He sighed. He wasn't going to kill some innocent woman, so Derek's execution would have to wait for another night. As he turned to go, the woman started to orgasm, her moans rising in volume and rhythm. Max stood frozen, as the earth fell away under his feet.

He knew the thing to do was to leave, but he had to see it with his own eyes. He moved quietly to the door, stepping over their clothes, which were strewn in the hallway, looked through the narrow gap, and the world as he knew it ceased to exist.

The woman in bed with Derek was Kelly.

CHAPTER FORTY-NINE

Gustav landed the chopper on a small patch of dirt outside of a village whose name Giuliana couldn't pronounce but which meant "beautiful island," an odd choice considering the nearest ocean was at least three hundred miles away. Technically it was a refueling and maintenance stop, but the people knew Gustav well and provided them with overwhelming hospitality, laying out a feast and giving them beds for the night. Giuliana wanted to refuel and keep going, but Gustav didn't want to fly over the jungle at night, which may have been more about one villager in particular, a beautiful, sturdy widow in her fifties called Sawan, who was especially happy to see Gustav.

After dinner Gustav and Sawan retired to her hut, and Giuliana was shown to one of her own. A couple of the male villagers offered her their companionship, but she demurred. She lay down in the porch hammock and watched the stars. They were so bright here, in the middle of the jungle, like a blanket of white lights thrown over a glass bowl. She had never seen so many stars in her life. She was near to drifting off when one of the men returned. She thought she would have to rebuff him again, but he was just there with some advice.

"Don't sleep outside," he said, "or the tigers will eat you."

She laughed, but he shook his head seriously, and repeated, "Don't sleep outside or the tigers will eat you."

She still thought he was messing with her, pretty sure that man-eating tigers were not a real thing, but she moved inside just in case. She had a fitful night's sleep, imagining snuffles and growls in the dark, spurred on by the fact that if a tiger was determined to eat her, the bamboo door and thatch walls wouldn't stop him. She kept her pistol under her pillow.

In the morning, after a breakfast of fresh fruit and a delicious jerky that turned out to be Siamese crocodile harvested from a local river, she walked to the chopper only to find half of the engine laid out on the grass. Gustav and two local men were staring into what was left. He spotted her and walked over.

"Good morning," he said. "Small problem. We will be back in the air in no time."

"What's the issue?"

"Broken cotter pin. I don't have a replacement, so we are improvising."

"I can help chew gum," Giuliana said, "if you need it to hold the thing together."

Gustav laughed. "Give me an hour. Maybe two."

While he worked on whatever it was he planned to improvise, which she figured she was better off not knowing, Giuliana took a walk down a well-marked path to a stream. She noticed a couple of the village men were shadowing her, thirty feet behind or so. She assumed it was for her safety and was actually grateful to have them there.

The stream wasn't very big, but it was moving fast and the water was clear. She would have loved to strip down and wash herself in the cool water, but her sutures weren't completely healed, and she didn't want to risk bacteria, plus she wasn't a hundred percent certain they couldn't have gotten the crocodile they had for breakfast out of a stream this size. So instead she sat on a rock, watched the water bubble past, and thought about what lay ahead.

She had, by necessity, changed her objective. Her original plan was to arrest Derek Moss and Kelly Riggs, and Max as well if she had to. But she had no support from the brass, no jurisdiction, and no tactical support except for Gustav, a blue-eyed, blond-haired semi-crazy German pilot, whom—she had learned during their flight—had been born and raised in Argentina, which brought his family history into somewhat startling focus. In light of all of that, she had pivoted to a straight-up rescue mission.

She knew the army was after the trucks, so she had to get to Max before they did and extract him. Her hope was to catch him before he crossed the bridge, since the army would catch up to them on the other side. The rest of them could all get killed as far as she was concerned, and the gold was going to the general either way. All she cared about was getting Max out alive.

Which still seemed odd, since the truth was that she barely knew him. Sure, they had shared a lot during those six weeks in the cabin, but they had both held a lot back too. She didn't share that she was FBI, for obvious reasons, and he didn't tell her about his CIA past. They had played chess and hidden a large part of themselves from the other, even while they grew close. One night of passion and some quick revelations later, she was going alone into the middle of a hostile, unstable country, risking her life for him. She couldn't decide if it was romantic, desperate, or just plain stupid, but she knew she had to go.

She slid off the rock to head back to the village and found the two men who had followed her down with their shirts off and their grins on. They hadn't been there to protect her after all.

One of them actually had his hand on his junk. She sighed and tried to pass, but they grabbed at her, speaking over each other. "What's your hurry?" "Let's mess around a little."

She didn't have time for this shit. The first one who laid hands on her got a broken finger and knee to the balls. The second one threw a punch, which she easily ducked, and got a rabbit punch of his own to the throat. She pushed them both into the stream and said in her best Suryakan, "I don't mess around."

She winced as she touched her abdomen and realized she had ripped one of her sutures. No big deal, she would sew it closed again herself, with the first aid kit in the chopper. She left the men in the stream, trying to keep their heads above water and gasping for breath. Maybe the crocodiles would get them.

She went back to the landing pad and told Gustav, "*Wir müssen uns beeilen.*" Twenty minutes later they were back in the air.

CHAPTER FIFTY

It was during a driver swap that Derek finally snapped. He had been fuming for days, working himself into a frenzy over Kelly's betrayal. Everyone in the caravan was wary, watching him like a boiling pot with the lid screwed on too tight. He had hired Veronica, who had brought them all in, so he was the boss, but they could clearly see that his seams were unraveling. His jaw was clenched, and he never stopped muttering to himself. No one wanted to ride shotgun with him. There was nowhere for all that fury to go, until there was.

Max sent the signal out that it was time to change drivers, and the caravan pulled into a banana grove just after midnight. Derek wasn't paying attention, and he bumped the parked truck in front of him. It was a minor tap, but Derek leapt out of the cab and started yelling at the driver of the other truck, a merc named Murphy, that it was his fault, because he had stopped short with no warning.

"I stopped in formation," Murphy said. "You weren't paying attention."

"Bullshit! You stopped short, I couldn't have avoided you if I tried."

"All due respect, boss, that's horseshit."

"Are you calling me a liar?"

"Whoa, hold on, guys." Max had walked back and had taken a look at the trucks. "It was a minor tap, there's not even any damage, it's nobody's fault."

The rest of the crew was gathering, watching.

"That's not the point," Derek said, practically frothing at the mouth. "He's calling me a liar."

"I stopped in formation and you ran into me," Murphy said, "Be a man for Christ's sake and own it."

Derek sucker punched him. It was a massive roundhouse right, and Max swore he heard Murphy's jaw snap before he went down. Another merc, a close friend of Murphy's, spun Derek around and punched him just as hard, but Derek had a jaw of steel. He staggered back a few feet, then pulled his Glock and put two bullets into the man.

Every member of the company except for Max and Veronica had their guns trained on Derek before the dead man hit the ground. Derek waved his Glock around, as if he thought he could take them all on. Max got in front of him.

"Whoa, whoa!" he said. "Everyone calm down. Let's not do anything stupid."

"He killed one of us," a female merc said. "That's a frag."

Milo chimed in, "Technically, a frag is done with a grenade. A fragmentation grenade, or fragger, hence the name." A "Shut up, Milo" came from somewhere in the pack. Milo nodded.

The female merc continued, "We can't exactly court-martial him, so he has to pay another way."

"Any suggestions?" Max asked.

"Yeah," one of the others said, "Get out of the way and let us shoot him."

"No more killing," Max said. He turned to Derek and spoke quietly. "Let me have your gun."

"No fucking way."

"I'll give it back when you've calmed down. There are seven highly trained people aiming automatic weapons at you right now. De-escalate."

Derek looked around, and the red veil lifted just a bit. For the first time he seemed to understand the position he was in. After a few moments he spoke to the group.

"I'm sorry I shot him. I overreacted in the heat of the moment." Max nodded, and cocked his head, what else? Derek continued, "I'll double everyone's pay."

The crew seemed to like the idea, but they didn't lower their guns. Veronica stepped into the half circle with Max and Derek.

"Come on, guys," she said, "Put them down. Be practical. The job's almost done, a few more hours. You kill him now, it's over, and we did all this for nothing. Take the extra pay, let this go, and do your jobs."

She had brought them all in and was essentially their commanding officer, so they all lowered their weapons and peeled off. Max looked at Veronica and nodded, thanks. She said quietly to Derek, "If you have phone reception, pay them now." She walked away, leaving Max and Derek alone.

"Jesus, Derek."

"These motherfuckers better figure out who's boss."

Max grabbed him by the lapels and slammed him against the side of the truck so forcefully that Derek was too surprised to react. Max spoke quietly, but intensely.

"Get your act together. I get that you're an asshole, but now you're acting like a lunatic."

"Who do you think you're talking to?"

"You're jeopardizing everything," Max continued. "All of our hard work. There's nothing you can do about Kelly out here. Nothing. Stop letting it drive you crazy. I need you present, so put her out of your mind and deal with it later. You can hunt her down later . . ."

"And I will."

". . . but first we get this goddam gold across the border. Okay?"

Derek looked at him for a long few moments, then nodded. "Okay." He paused. "Am I really acting that crazy?"

"Yes."

"Then I'll pull it together. I don't like being out of control. It's my shift to sleep; I just need some rack time."

"And forget about Kelly for now."

Derek smiled. "Who?"

Max shook his head, Jesus. Derek laughed as he went to the cab to sleep, as if the whole thing had been a lark. Max walked to the back of the caravan and found Veronica tending to Murphy.

"Did he break your jaw?"

"No."

"You going to be able to move on from this?"

Murphy stood and tucked his shirt in, looked Max in the eye. "I'm a professional." He walked off and Max looked to Veronica, who shook her head.

"Maybe we should have let them kill him."

"Someone once told me, killing's too good for him," Max answered.

"And if he goes off again?"

"I'll deal with Derek; you just keep the company in line."

"Aye aye, skipper."

Max walked forward the length of the caravan to his own truck, so he could get some sleep too. He had never told Derek or Kelly that he knew it was Derek that almost got them all killed at Vong's villa. He wasn't even sure if Kelly knew it, even after all these years. Max had also never mentioned, at least verbally, that he had been in the town house that night and seen them together. Kelly knew, but not because of anything he said.

He had stood there in the hallway for a few minutes, doing his best to shut out the sounds coming from the bedroom, and contemplating his next move. His first impulse was to walk in and shoot them both, but he forced himself to stop and think it through. The fact was, he loved Kelly and could never live with himself if he killed her, even if she deserved it, which she didn't. Causing the death of an asset, betraying your coworkers and almost getting them murdered, those are killing offenses. Cheating on your boyfriend is not and never would be. He might have stood there debating with himself all night, but the sex ended and was replaced by the soft voices and gentle laughter of the afterglow. It somehow hurt worse than the sex itself, so he left.

Over the next couple of years he did a lot more digging, but he could never find anything to tie Kelly to Derek's plot at General Vong's villa. He never asked her, because she would have lied, but he was convinced that she didn't know about it. He also never heard whether they had identified Derek's accomplice at Langley, and he stopped caring about it. In fact, he had all but moved on from the whole thing, when word got around to him that Kelly and Derek had gotten married and all the rage and anguish came back as viscerally as if it had happened yesterday.

As the caravan pulled back out onto the road, Max drifted off to sleep thinking, *I just have to hold this thing together for another two days*. He had thought the bridge would be the most challenging part of the journey, but he knew now that he had been dead wrong.

CHAPTER FIFTY-ONE

Kelly, Chewy Chakri, and the band of forty rebels reached the village just after sunset. They had passed acres of rice paddies coming in, but they were empty, the workers already home for supper. Kelly had been in a hundred villages like it before, nestled beside a river, compact dirt streets lined by houses on low stilts to avoid flooding, barefoot children playing among the chickens and livestock. She estimated it had a population of four to five hundred, making it on the smaller end of average. Some of the villages in the region had septic tanks and fresh running water, courtesy of various NGOs. This one didn't. It was remote, and they still got their water from the river.

When they rode and marched into the village, the children scattered like frightened bunnies, running to their various houses. Kelly knew that for these people, a group of armed strangers could mean a lot of things, none of them good. Some of the scattering kids had already seen their older sisters sold off to intruders like this for ten million kip, or a little under five hundred American dollars. Doors stayed closed, and no one emerged.

"Not a very friendly welcome," Kelly said to Chakri.

"They don't know it's me yet. When they hear my name, they will feed us."

He walked to an open area at what could roughly be considered the center of the village and spoke in a loud voice. "I am Chewy Chakri, liberator of the people. My men and I require food, beds, and comfort." Kelly didn't want to think about what comfort might mean.

A tiny old man wearing a knit cap and smoking a pipe, his trousers held up by a frayed rope through the belt loops, emerged from one of the huts and made a slow journey down the stairs. Kelly could hear Chakri sigh with impatience at his slow descent. He finally reached Chakri and pressed his hands together in greeting, and they began to talk. Kelly was too far away to hear them, but from Chakri's increasingly annoyed tone and the old man's gentle head shakes, she understood that it wasn't going the way the rebel leader wanted.

Kelly was startled when Chakri slapped the old man, hard across the face. He staggered and almost fell, then kept his head down as Chakri leaned over him, yelling and pointing back at his army. Finally he shoved the old man down to the dirt and walked back to the others.

"What the hell was that?" Kelly asked him.

"Ah, he claims they had a bad season, that their supplies are low. He says if they feed us, they will starve."

"So what are we going to do?"

He looked at her like she was an imbecile. "We're going to eat." He turned to his second in command, a nasty piece of work named Minh. "Search the huts, bring whatever food you find. Look for storehouses. If they don't have enough, kill one of their buffalo."

Minh nodded and started barking orders at the men.

"Chewy," Kelly said, "you said they would happily feed us."

"I gave them the chance."

"But they claim they don't have enough."

He waved his hand dismissively and walked off to deal with other logistics. Kelly walked through the village, watching the men ransack the huts. At first, they were merely aggressive, waving their guns and shouting, taking whatever food they could find. But a few of the villagers resisted, and the atmosphere began to intensify. She saw men and women thrown down the front steps of their huts. Soon after that she heard a gunshot, followed by two more.

She went back to the village center to find Chakri, but he wasn't there. The men were bringing sacks of rice and freshly killed chickens back and throwing them in a pile, then returning to find more. Kelly heard a scream, looked toward the sound, and saw a hut in flames.

Before long the sacking of the village had taken on a life of its own, it was a living thing, growing and impossible to stop. Several huts were ablaze, the air thick with smoke. Kelly saw men dragging women and girls into the trees or into huts. Men were being beaten and shot all around her.

She finally spotted Chakri, walking back toward the village center with Minh and two others. She ran to meet him beside the pile of food.

"You have to stop this!"

He appeared genuinely baffled. "Stop what?"

"They're raping them!"

He laughed. "Don't be hysterical. They've been in the jungle a long time. Men have needs."

Kelly was floored. Her voice hardened. "Stop them. Stop them now."

He turned to Minh. "Shut her up. But don't kill her."

Minh went to grab her, and Kelly laid him out with a jab to the kidney and an elbow to the head. Chakri watched, amused, as she used her one good arm to beat down the next two rebels who tried to grab her. Eventually a bunch of them swarmed her all at once, and even though she poked an eye or two and crushed at least one testicle, they finally overwhelmed her and dragged her down.

They gagged her with a bandana and tied her to a tree, where she had a head-on view of the burning village. It was a nightmare, villagers running and being shot in the back, women being raped right in her line of sight, and terrified children huddling together under any structure or porch that was not on fire.

Minh walked over, his face bleeding where she elbowed him. "He said not to kill you." So instead, he kicked her with his steel-toed boot, hard enough that she couldn't catch her breath, breaking a rib.

The old man started pleading with Chakri. Chakri knocked him down again, but this time he pulled his machete and fell on him and began hacking him to pieces. Kelly watched the machete rise and fall, blood arcing off the blade against the background of flames. She tried to look into his eyes but couldn't. Or maybe she did, but there was nothing there to see.

She had wanted to believe in the version of himself he had sold her at the camp, but deep down she always knew the truth, that everything she had heard about him was true. Chakri the maniac. Chewy the butcher. Worst of all, Chewy Chakri the psychopath, able to present himself to her as sane, rational, even noble and caring. It was a sickeningly familiar feeling, the shame covering her like a familiar blanket. Her father, telling her he loved her and then splitting her in half in the night. Derek calling her his partner, then controlling every breath she took. What was wrong with her? Why did she always want so badly to believe the lies men told?

Chakri walked back to their circle, wiping the blood from his eyes. He saw the horrified look on her face and stopped for a moment.

"They had their chance."

She watched him strut away. He was exactly what everyone said he was, an amoral, violent, power-hungry thug. And she had pointed him straight toward the only two men she had ever cared about.

SEVEN YEARS AGO

FOUR MONTHS AFTER THE RAID

Max sat up all night at Kelly's Lanna house after he left Derek's, thinking about what to do. Derek needed to be punished, but if he killed him now it would always feel dirty, like he did it because he caught him in bed with Kelly. Even though he knew that wasn't the case, it would always gnaw at his conscience and make him feel small. Maybe the thing to do was to report him to Langley after all and let them sort it out, for better or worse. All he knew was he needed to put this behind him. The three of them were in a business built on deceit. Everyone lied to everyone, all the time. But when you started lying to each other, your fellow officers, the only people on earth you should be able to trust, the game was over. Forget "Ye shall know the truth and the truth shall make you free," the CIA motto ought to be "Trust no one and everyone is an asshole."

As for Kelly, he had made his decision. He wouldn't say anything about what he had just seen. He'd take the high road, propose to her as planned, and if she said yes, he would never mention it, ever. They would get married, move on with their lives, and leave Laos, Thailand, and Derek Moss in the past. He could pretend it never happened, if she could.

Kelly woke up with a throbbing headache, and it took her a minute to remember where she was, and who was lying next to her. Derek Moss, Christ. Oh well. She didn't feel particularly bad about it; it was a one-off and had just kind of happened. What was the old joke, I tripped and landed on his dick? This situation wasn't that far off. Max had been away for a month on some assignment she wasn't read in on, and she had been drinking alone at My Bar, an overly touristy place inside the walls of Chiang Mai's Old City. She had never cheated on Max before, but she was horny, had half a buzz on, and was already thinking about maybe picking up some anonymous workhorse when Derek walked in and sat down beside her. He was arrogant and boorish and a little homely. A few more drinks and she wound up in his bed.

Now she slipped out of it as quietly as she could, not wanting to wake him. She had no illusions that he would invite her to breakfast or anything, she simply didn't want to deal with talking to him at all. Plus she wanted to be there when Max called, as he had done every day since he left. She missed him.

She picked up her clothes, following a trail of them out into the hall. She couldn't find her underwear. She looked under his clothes, and briefly felt around in the sheets, but she couldn't remember where they had come off, or even which of them had taken them off. Oh well, they were nothing special, just some green cotton Victoria's Secret briefs that came three for thirty-nine bucks. She got dressed without them, figuring Derek would find a nice souvenir one day. She let herself out, walked to the main road, and flagged down a tuk-tuk.

Max was waiting in her living room when she got home. She didn't have to fake her surprise.

"Max!"

He took her in his arms and kissed her. She might have been worried about him smelling another man on her, but men didn't have that sensor. A woman can smell another woman's pussy from the driveway, but men are oblivious. He smiled and brushed the hair away from her face and asked, "Where were you?"

"I went out drinking with some mercs. Had a little too much, stayed on a friend's sofa."

He nodded and headed for the kitchen. "I made coffee."

"Just let me shower first."

"No, coffee first," he said. "I want to ask you something."

She followed him into the kitchen, and he poured them each a cup of rich Thai coffee, with ground cardamom and condensed milk. Typical Max, it was exactly what she needed at that moment. He let her savor a few sips, then got down on one knee.

"Max? What the fuck?"

"It's no secret that I love you, Kel." He took out a ring box. She said, "Oh, shit," but wasn't sure if she said it out loud or in her head. The latter, she guessed, because he kept going. "I want to spend the rest of my life with you. Marry me."

He opened the box. The ring was dazzling, and she stared at it, mesmerized, until he asked, "What do you say?"

"What if we get separate assignments? Suppose I'm running guns in Myanmar and you're, I don't know, burning poppy fields in Afghanistan?"

"I'm going to resign."

"What?" She was genuinely shocked.

"I'll resign, and if you don't want to, you can take a desk at Langley, or run a station, anything that doesn't involve getting tortured in foreign prisons."

"I've never been tortured in a foreign prison."

"You know what I mean. What do you say?"

She paused, playing for time to think. "The ring is beautiful."

"I already knew that."

"I love you; you know that I do. But I can't walk away from this."

"Why not?"

"Because I don't want to. I love the job."

She was lying. At that moment she would give anything to say yes, to walk away with him and never look back. But she knew they'd be divorced in a year, because of her, not him. He was strong, sensitive, loyal, and would be a great husband. She was selfish, greedy, and a liar, and she knew it. He was literally proposing to her while another man's sperm was dying inside of her. The answer had to be no, for everyone's sake.

"Stand up, Max." He did. "I'm sorry."

"Nothing I can do to change your mind?"

She shook her head, afraid she would cry if she tried to speak. He took her in his arms and held her.

"I'll always love you."

"No, you won't," she whispered. "But it's sweet that you think you will."

They held each other a little longer, then he kissed her lightly on the lips and headed for the door. He hesitated with his hand on the knob.

"Will you tell me something honestly?"

"Of course."

"Did you ever cheat on me?"

It would have been easy to lie to him, but for some reason she couldn't. Not completely, anyway.

"Just once."

"With who?"

"It doesn't matter. Just some guy I picked up in a bar. I was drunk; you were out of town. Not an excuse, but it happened. I'm sorry."

"When was this?"

"A long time ago, Max. Ages ago."

He looked into her eyes for a few moments, nodded, and then he was gone.

Kelly had never felt so awful in her life, although in four minutes she would feel worse. She finished her coffee, went upstairs, and started to draw a bath. As she got undressed in front of her full-length mirror, a flash of color caught her eye. She turned to look and saw her green cotton Victoria's Secret panties laid out on the bed.

It took her a few seconds to realize what that meant.

CHAPTER FIFTY-TWO

It was seven P.M., and they had been driving for eleven straight days and nights when a driver fell asleep and drove into a tree. They were only going ten miles an hour, so there was no real damage, and the gold bricks shifted only a little and were quickly put back in place. But it made them all aware that they were pushing too hard, that even driving in shifts the rivers and switchbacks and mud and generally nasty terrain had them all exhausted. Even Derek, who had managed to calm himself down since the debacle at the banana grove, knew they needed rest. He had gotten a brief signal and had wired double the money into the account Veronica was using to pay the mercs, but Max wasn't impressed since he figured Derek had held back most of what Vinthu had given him for expenses in the first place.

As the driver backed the truck onto the road, Max, Derek, and Veronica met at the back of Max's truck. "The bridge is going to be especially difficult," Max said. "I don't think we should go at it in a state of exhaustion."

Derek nodded. "For once I agree with you, Starkey."

"There's a turnout ten or fifteen miles up the road, and from there it's a ten-minute drive to the bridge. I suggest we stop there and let everyone sleep for a few hours."

The others both agreed, and the caravan drove on. It turned out to be closer to twenty miles, so Max had a little time to think. His plan was coming together, but the next twelve hours had to go like clockwork, so he was grateful for the chance to get some rack time as well.

They finally reached the turnout, and he eased the M809 to the side. They were on a high ridge looking out over a valley. He parked his truck and walked over to the edge to take in the view, which was spectacular in the light of a full moon. After he parked his own truck, Derek came over and joined him on the precipice.

"What are you looking at?"

"That."

Derek looked where he was pointing and drew in a sharp breath. The ravine snaked through their entire view, twisty and deep, which explained its name, Phaya Nok, which translated to Snake of Fortune. The bridge was almost directly below them, and the narrower pedestrian bridge a hundred yards beyond it. It was foreboding even though it looked small from here, like a child's toy if the child had also done the engineering.

The ravine was twelve hundred feet deep and almost a quarter mile across, sheer drop-offs on each side, varying between seventy and ninety degrees. Because of the different faces they showed to the weather, the two sides were different. On the near side, tree ferns and orchids grew through the cracks in the limestone and schist, a lush blanket of green splashed with bright colors, creating the disorienting illusion of a garden growing sideways out of the rock. The far side was more barren, a few rugged hemp palms clawing out an existence on the cliff face, which was mostly smooth stone. Two different ecosystems, less than 1,500 feet apart.

Max knew that in the daytime the water in the stream below was almost the same color as the rock, causing the strange sensation of a bottomless gorge. Now, at night, the moonlight only reached the top third of the ravine, and you couldn't see the bottom at all. It was a black abyss.

"Pretty, isn't she?" Veronica said as she joined them.

"Pretty terrifying," Derek answered. They stood there looking at it a little longer, each of them contemplating the idea of a twelve-hundred-foot drop to certain death.

"I've been thinking about this," Max said. "I should drive all four trucks across."

"Why?" Veronica asked, before Derek could.

"Because the reward is ours, mine and Derek's, so the risk should be too. You and the rest of these guys are hired hands. Falling into a ravine was not in the job description."

"You're right," Derek said. "I'll ride with you."

"No, we want the trucks as light as possible. I'll just keep one merc on this side with me in case anything comes up."

"I can do that," Veronica offered.

"Good. Derek, you and the others cross on foot and wait for me on the other side."

Derek scoffed. "You want me to leave you across a gorge with all the gold?"

"Leave me the keys for the first truck and take the other three sets with you. I'll drive the truck across, get the next set of keys, walk back and drive that one across, and so on. That way the worst I could do is run off with one truck, in which case you'd have three, so what the hell's the point? One truck isn't even my agreed-upon split."

Derek looked to Veronica. He trusted her opinion, because he had hired her and figured that bought her loyalty. "What do you think?"

"It makes sense to me. Seems like the simplest way to do it, and I don't have to risk my men's lives."

"Unless you want to drive and I'll wait with the keys," Max said.

Derek looked at the bridge for a moment. "No, it's fine, you drive."

Max allowed himself the slightest smile. You could never lose betting on an egomaniac's cowardice. He knew there was no way in hell that Derek would want to drive even one truck across the bridge, let alone four.

He said, "You guys get some sleep, I'm going to walk down and take a look at what we're facing."

"Alone?" Derek asked.

"Yeah, why?"

Derek looked at him, then back at the trucks. Max knew he was trying to decide which was the bigger gamble, leaving the gold for an hour or letting Max go off alone to do God knows what. He chose correctly.

"I'll go with you."

Max nodded and the two of them headed straight down the hillside rather than following the road the longer way around. Max was taking a risk being alone with Derek, but as certain as he was that Derek planned to kill him, he was equally sure that he wouldn't do it until the gold was safely across the bridge. After they had been walking awhile, Derek took a swig from a pocket flask and held it out to Max. Max took it and wiped it with his sleeve before drinking.

"Really?" Derek asked. "Should I be offended?"

"Hey, I know where your mouth has been."

Derek looked at him sharply, then laughed. "I guess you do. Next, you're going to tell me I should have seen this betrayal coming."

"When it comes to Kelly Riggs, I'm the last person you should listen to."

"She is unpredictable." He swigged and passed the flask to Max again. This time Max drank without wiping. "When she first took off, I thought maybe the two of you were working something together. But no, she was just fucking me over, the same way she did you."

"Not quite the same way."

"Fair enough. I didn't know you were a couple at the time, Starkey."

What the fuck was this?

"I knew you worked together a lot," Derek continued, "but I didn't know you were, you know, a thing, until she told me after we were married. I guess our one-night stand was right before you broke up anyway, so maybe she had one foot out the door, but we didn't actually get together until over a year later."

"What makes you think I knew about that night?"

"She told me about the little trick you pulled with the panties. Pretty funny, I never would have thought of that."

"Why are you telling me this?"

"It's no secret I never liked you. You were so gung ho, Mr. All American Patriot, it kind of made me sick. I might have shot you, but I would never snake your woman."

"Are you seriously quoting the bro code to me right now?"

Derek laughed. "I guess I am."

Max shook his head, then asked, "When will it be enough, Derek?"

"Enough what?"

"Money, what else? Everything you scammed while you were an active-duty officer, all you and Kel have made since you resigned . . ."

"I'm afraid that's gone."

"Now you'll get her share and walk away from this heist with eighty-eight million."

"Sixty-six."

"What?"

"She's gone. The three-way split is now fifty-fifty."

Sure, Max thought. It's easy to be generous with percentages when you plan to kill the guy you're splitting it with as soon as he crosses the bridge. "I agreed to a third," he said. "I'm taking a third. What you do with the rest is your business."

"I may have planned this, but you pulled it off. I never would have gotten the gold this far without you. That's a bet."

"Still." They each took another swig. "You never answered my question. When will it be enough?"

"When I get there, I'll let you know."

When they reached the bridge Max had a momentary panic attack. It was in terrible shape. Derek whistled.

"It looks like the rust is the only thing holding it together."

Max spent about an hour examining the cables and ropes that he could reach and shined a flashlight out along the deck as far as he could. It was not reassuring. He also examined the gate that was locked in place to keep people from stupidly risking their lives doing the very thing he intended to do in a few hours.

He took his time, and when he was done, they walked back along the road. It was a little longer route, but much easier than climbing back up the steep hill. Altogether they were gone about three hours. Max laid down and stretched out a few feet from Veronica, who was already out and snoring. He found the familiar sound comforting. He put his wadded-up jacket under his head and was asleep in thirty seconds.

SEVEN YEARS AGO

FOUR AND A HALF MONTHS AFTER THE RAID

Since the night Kelly delivered the one thousandth cut, Max had been drinking for two weeks straight in the rooftop bar of the Akara Hotel, a midlevel, sixty-dollar-a-night place in the heart of Bangkok but away from the tourists and the sex trade, and which had quickly become popular with people in his line of work who were lying low. Max liked it for three simple reasons: It was almost brand new at the time, meaning it was clean; the bar had both a good view of the city and a passable middle shelf; and despite being less than a year old, the Akara already had a reputation for being haunted. He hadn't seen a ghost yet, but he hadn't lost hope either.

A woman approached him and said, "Hey, I know you."

She looked familiar but he couldn't quite place her, either because he was too drunk or because nothing outside of the sphere of his rage and heartbreak mattered at the moment. She was blond and obviously physically strong, with the muscular, compact body of an MMA fighter that her casual jeans and Hawaiian shirt couldn't conceal. She continued, "I don't know your name, but I do know you. I was there the night you broke out of Phonthong."

He took a closer look. "You led us to the car and drove us out."

"You were a mess. Still are, it looks like."

He raised his glass. "This time it's self-inflicted."

She sat down at the barstool next to him and extended her hand. "Veronica Usher."

"As in, the house of?" he asked as he shook.

"Hah, I never heard that one before." She signaled the bartender, *Bring two of whatever he's drinking.* Max hadn't spoken to anyone other than to say "I need a room" or "I'll have another" in two weeks, so he decided what the hell, a little human interaction wouldn't kill him.

"Max Starkey. You with the Company?"

"Nah, independent contractor, former US Marine. Whoever wanted you out paid the Ghosts, the Ghosts hired me. Based on your last question, I assume that was the CIA."

He said wryly, "I can neither confirm nor deny."

"So Max Starkey, why are you drinking yourself into a coma?"

"I'm plotting the demise of my mortal enemy."

"Always a fun activity. What did he or she do to deserve killing?"

"It's a long story."

She waved a hand at the shelves behind the bar. "They don't look like they're gonna run out of booze any time soon."

So he told her. He didn't leave anything out, although they kept drinking as he talked, so it wasn't in strict chronological order. He told her about Derek arranging the deliberate murder of an American asset. He told her about Kelly, and the ring, and his plans for their life together, and how Derek's plot at the villa almost got them killed and led to weeks of brutal torture for Max.

He told her about catching them in bed together, and about leaving her underwear for her to find, which made Veronica lean back and say, "damn." When he was done, she just shook her head.

"Derek fucking Moss."

Surprised, he asked, "You know him?"

"I wanted to shoot him when I realized it was him outside the prison. But I did my job."

"Why, what did he do to you?"

"Not me personally. My girlfriend." So she was gay. Through his alcohol-induced haze, Max was oddly relieved. He enjoyed her company and liked talking to her, but he wasn't ready for anything else. She continued, "Screwed her out of a lot of money on a gig."

"She's a mercenary too?"

She shook her head. "She works transpo. She laid out her own cash to get the vehicles he needed, and he stiffed her. She never got her fee either. Altogether he took her for about three hundred grand."

"That hardly seems like enough reason to kill someone."

Veronica grinned. "You haven't seen my girlfriend."

He saw her the next night. Her name was Olivia, and she lived up to the hype. Half Thai, half Spanish, tall and thin, with jet-black hair down to the top of her ass, she could have been a countess. Max thought, *Hell, I'd kill a stranger if this woman asked me to.*

She had tickets for a Muay Thai bout at Rajadamnern Stadium between the legendary Saenchai and a young contender. Their third, a business associate of Olivia's, had a conflict and Veronica convinced Max to use his seat. The match was great, but the contender's raw power was ultimately no match for Saenchai's focused strength and experience, and he went down in the fourth round after a deviously deceptive switch kick to the head. As much fun as it was watching the match, Max had just as good a time watching Olivia completely lose her shit over it, standing and screaming, urging the combatants on, cursing the referee. Veronica almost never looked at the match; she adored Olivia.

Afterward they went out to dinner, and a friendship was kindled that would last the rest of their lives. On the day Veronica and Olivia were scheduled to fly back to the States, Max was accosted by a group of Ghosts who not so gently reminded him of his contract and urged him to fulfill it posthaste. He bought a ticket and flew back with the women four hours later.

He had been in various hotspots overseas for years and had nowhere to go, so V & O put him up in their guest house behind their Craftsman bungalow in Pasadena. He stayed two years, while he figured out his life post-CIA. The three of them had dinner together almost every night, and the women got a lot of amusement out of his various attempts at a straight job. He would keep one company while the other was away for work, and they grew close. Max was the best man at their wedding, and when they decided to have a child, a few months after Max had moved out, he was the logical choice and had been touched when they asked him. He became the biological father to their daughter, Carmen, and had agreed that she would never know. Olivia carried her to term, and Max saw her only occasionally. She was their daughter, not his, but it tugged at his paternal instincts and for the first time he started seriously thinking about having kids of his own.

On the day he found out that Kelly had married Derek, he showed up at their door and reminded Veronica of their first conversation in the Akara bar. “It’s time to finally kill him.”

She surprised him. “I don’t think so.”

“What?”

“We kill him and his punishment is over. We need to come up with something worse.”

“What’s worse than death?”

“For Derek? Embarrassment. Knowing he’s been beat. Loss of money. I’ve thought about this a lot. We should lie low and wait for an opportunity to fuck him all the way over but leave him alive to experience the humiliation.”

Olivia piped in. “I agree,” she said. “Killing is too good for him.”

CHAPTER FIFTY-THREE

Cintha had been riding in the Jeep with the five rebels who saw her kill the tiger for several days. In all that time, she had never once let go of her bamboo spear, and they only tried to take it from her once. She had reacted so violently that they shrugged and let her hold on to it. It wasn't much use as a practical weapon, but it made her feel safe, like her childhood blanket, Mr. Pinkie. She had no idea where they were headed, and assumed she was a captive even though they hadn't said anything to that effect and hadn't tried to tie her up or, God forbid, tried to take any liberties. They had let her clean her leg wound with a first aid kit and put on some actual bandages, but she could tell she was going to need a hospital.

One of the men had found her a pair of fatigues that were too big for her and given her his belt to cinch around the waist, so she rolled up the cuffs and made do, relieved that her legs were no longer exposed. Her Nikes had finally fallen completely apart, so she had chucked them and was making the ride in her ankle socks.

She was dead certain the men didn't know who she was, because if they did know they would not be treating her so casually. To keep it that way, every time they stopped, she put more mud on her face, arms, and torso. She told them it was to keep the bugs off, but really it was to hide. They offered her some bottled mosquito repellant and had a good laugh when she said she preferred her method. They thought she was a feral, half-crazed jungle girl, raised by monkeys or something, which suited her fine. She didn't know why, but she figured it would be very bad for her if they learned her identity, and she would be proven right when they ran into the others.

Kelly was no longer bound or gagged, and was back on her horse riding south, but with forty men armed to the teeth around her and no weapon of her own, she might as well have been in chains. She was in an emotional fog, unable to process her life up to this point, or what would happen when they reached the bridge. *I might be going catatonic,* she thought, and then reminded herself that catatonic people can't think that. She roused from her stupor and pulled her horse up short when she heard Chakri bark out a command for the company to halt. She could hear an engine coming, and all the rebels raised their weapons and took defensive positions until they saw who it was. Then they lowered their weapons and there were exuberant greetings all around.

The new arrivals were five rebels in a Jeep, but Kelly was more fascinated by their captive. She was a young woman, thin, around five feet two inches. She was wearing oversized fatigues and covered head to waist in thick black mud like an Asaro Mudman and was gripping a four-foot-long bamboo spear so tightly that her knuckles were white. She climbed out of the Jeep with some difficulty and stretched. Kelly listened to the men but kept her eyes on the strange girl.

"Welcome, Minti," Chakri said to the newcomer. "How did you find us?"

"We came north the long way around. When we reached the outskirts of camp, they told us you were headed to kill some farangs, so we hurried to catch up."

Chakri nodded at the girl. "What's the story there?"

"We found her in the jungle. She killed a male tiger, a massive one, right in front of us."

"With that?" He pointed to her bamboo stick.

"She brought him down with this," he handed Chakri the pistol she had used, "and finished him off with that. Commander, I've never seen anything like it."

As Kelly studied the girl, fascinated, Cintha met her eyes, and Kelly nearly fell off her horse. She hid her shock as best she could and looked around at the others, but for now, no one else had clocked her identity.

"The tiger clawed the back of her leg," Minti continued, "she needs medical attention."

Chakri nodded and waved for Dr. Pham to help Cintha, but when he stepped toward her, she raised her spear and jabbed at him, keeping him back. The other rebels broke out in laughter. The girl wasn't laughing, though, and Kelly believed she would die before she let one of them touch her.

She called out, "Let me do it. It will be easier for her. Woman to woman."

"Fine, whatever," Chakri said. He nodded at a man who took Kelly's horse as she dismounted. She walked over to the girl, who raised her spear. Kelly held up a hand.

"I just want to help you. From what I can tell you've survived a lot. Don't die of an infection after all that."

The girl nodded and lowered her weapon. Kelly took her by the shoulders and led her toward Dr. Pham's horse with the medical supplies. As they walked, she whispered urgently, "Whatever you do, don't let them find out who you are. You'll be dead in under a minute, or worse. These men are animals; I've seen it firsthand. Tell me you understand, they cannot find out who you are." Cintha nodded.

Kelly cleaned and dressed her wound as best she could and gave her a shot of antibiotics. Dr. Pham stayed away and let her work alone. She could tell that Cintha didn't like accepting help from her, but she didn't put up a fuss. To her credit, the girl was doing her best to stay anonymous.

"I'm sorry to ask this," Kelly said gently, "but I have to treat all your wounds. Did they violate you?" Cintha shook her head. "Are you sure? There's no shame if they did, and it's better I know."

"No, Officer Riggs. They did not."

The way she said it startled Kelly. This didn't sound like the whiny little brat that had climbed into Max's bed to piss off her mother, she seemed ten years older. When the medical supplies were put away, Kelly put Cintha on her horse and walked alongside her for the rest of the day. She pointed out to one of the men that she was in nothing but socks, and he found an ill-fitting pair of boots for her. Cintha slipped them on without stopping the horse.

"They're too big," she said to Kelly. "If I walk in these, I'll get blisters."

"It's the best I can do for now."

They stopped for the night about three hours shy of the bridge. Chakri's plan was to get there at daybreak and stay hidden in the trees until the gold showed up. It could be hours or days, they had no idea where Max and Derek were in their journey. Chewy Chakri told Cintha to get a good night's rest, because over breakfast he wanted to hear all about her and the slaying of the tiger. Then he ordered two men to watch the women overnight, guarding them in a small tent.

As they bedded down, Kelly told her, "Be cool. Don't stab anyone with that stick. When they're all asleep, we'll escape." Cintha looked at her but didn't say anything, then curled herself around her bamboo spear and went to sleep.

Kelly stayed awake, planning it out. She was determined to get Cintha out of here, but not because of any of the nonsense she'd deluded herself with over the last few days. Atonement, being a better person, doing something positive for the world, it had all added up to nothing. She was over trying to achieve any kind of redemption, she just wanted to get Cintha out of there because she knew what would happen to her if she didn't, and she was just plain tired of watching men treat women like shit.

She had paid attention when Chakri posted perimeter guards for the night. They were sparse, since they didn't expect to encounter anyone out here. Their only enemy was the army, which didn't travel with stealth, they'd hear them coming from five miles away. The real problem was the two men sitting watch over them in the tent, who both had machine guns, and tactical knives strapped to their thighs. Step one would be getting one of the knives.

Thinking both women were asleep, one of the men tapped the other and gestured toward them, should we? The second man considered it, then shook his head. The first man slapped his arm, why not? The second man whispered, "We'll get Chakri's permission tomorrow, our reward for keeping guard." *You're going to get a reward all right,* Kelly thought, *but it's not what you're thinking.*

After about an hour, the man who had kept the other one in check nodded off. The first man waited a few minutes until he was really out, then set down his machine gun and slowly started crawling toward Cintha. He reached out for her, and Kelly wrapped her cast around his neck and jerked him forward, pulling his knife from his sheath and plunging it into his stomach. She quickly stabbed him five more times and rolled him onto the floor.

The commotion woke the second man, who grabbed his machine gun and swung it around. Kelly jammed her finger under the trigger so he couldn't fire. It hurt like hell as he kept squeezing it, trying to get a shot off. They wrestled over the gun, and he twisted it, breaking her finger, but she didn't cry out. She lost leverage though, and he got on top of her and pushed the machine gun down across her throat. She fought as hard as she could, but with one arm in a cast he had too much leverage over her, and she started to feel her windpipe give.

Cintha drove her bamboo spear into him from behind, with so much thrust that it almost went through him and into Kelly. She pulled it back out, Kelly looked up at her, shocked, and Cintha put her fingers over her lips, shhh. What the fuck happened to this kid?

Kelly stuck the knife into one of her RAT boots, took a machine gun and offered one to Cintha, who demurred, holding up her spear. Kelly gestured for Cintha to follow her, and they slipped out of the tent and crept through camp, holding still periodically when a man shifted in his sleep. Kelly grabbed Dr. Pham's medical backpack, and they made for the trees. There was one guard posted the direction they went, but he was focused away from camp and Kelly grabbed him from behind and slit his throat before he heard them coming.

Kelly headed into the trees at a quick jog, but Cintha was lagging behind.

"Can you go any faster?"

"Not in these shoes. I told you, they're too big."

"Okay. You set the pace."

As they walked, Kelly snapped her broken finger into place and wrapped it in medical tape. After twenty minutes or so, Cintha asked, "Will he send men after us?"

"I doubt it," Kelly answered. "He's got bigger fish to fry. I don't think he'll waste resources chasing a couple of women around the bush. There's no upside. No, I think we're free of him."

"Okay."

Great, Cintha thought. *I'm free, and right back in the fucking jungle.*

CHAPTER FIFTY-FOUR

THE BRIDGE

The jungle had been cleared for a hundred yards or so on both sides of the bridge. On each side, there were small clusters of huts near the pedestrian bridge, not villages really, just random collections of people who made trinkets or cooked food on open-air carts to sell to the travelers who crossed on foot. There were also two or three men on each side whose life work was to battle the jungle and keep it from taking back over.

When Max drove into the clearing in the first truck, heads turned, and kids came out to see. When the other three trucks pulled in behind him, nearly everyone in the area came to look. Derek walked alongside Max as he collected the truck keys from the other three drivers.

"We're drawing a crowd."

"No one has driven across this thing in years, it's an event. Besides, who wouldn't want to see a big-ass truck fall into that giant crevice? Everyone is hoping to see a disaster."

"Like NASCAR. You really think it will hold?"

"I sure as hell hope so, since I'm the one driving." He was 90 percent certain it would hold as long as he needed it to. Maybe 80 percent.

First, they used bolt cutters to cut the chains blocking access to the bridge, then they spent two hours stripping the trucks down.

They took off the fenders, the extra fuel tanks, the front grills, and even the side mirrors. Veronica double-checked that the loads were secure, and they removed the slats around the cargo bed. Anything that wasn't directly tied to making the truck move or securing the load was stripped off. If Max could have, he would have removed four of the eight rear tires on each truck, but that would have created a balance problem and possibly caused the loads to shift, which could be fatal on a swinging bridge. They also ditched the cargo, taking out the water tanks, extra fuel, and the gasoline they had salvaged from the Jeeps. They drained the fuel tanks into barrels, leaving just enough diesel in them to make it across the bridge, plus a small reserve. By the time they finished, Max figured they had stripped at least fifteen hundred pounds from each truck.

"Think it's enough?" Veronica asked.

"It'll have to be."

He gave the keys to the other three trucks to Derek, good lucks were shared all around, and Veronica stayed with Max as the seven remaining mercenaries, each carrying as much weaponry as they could, followed Derek out onto the bridge. Veronica stood beside Max as they watched them go and looked around at the thickening crowd of spectators.

"It's good that we have a crowd. It will provide cover."

"Yes." He didn't say any more. Veronica could see that he was laser focused on the task ahead and shut up to let him concentrate.

Derek was halfway across the bridge and was feeling a little nauseous. With every step he took, the bridge creaked and gave a little, swayed a little. He looked down and he could see through two of the slats directly into the chasm beneath his feet. It wasn't quite Tu San, which was almost 2,500 feet deep, but because of the optical illusion of the bottomless gorge it seemed deeper, and he felt his head spinning. It was as if the stream bed was moving, getting farther away. He grabbed onto a rope as the bridge swayed in the wind, and said, "He's batshit crazy."

None of the mercs had to ask who he meant.

Max got behind the wheel of the first truck. Veronica stood nearby, an AK-47 slung over her shoulder. "Hey," he called to her. "If I don't make it . . ."

She cut him off. "Don't be an asshole."

He nodded and put the truck in gear. As he started moving down the embankment there was a smattering of applause from the spectators gathered. They had been waiting all morning for this and were ready for blood.

He eased the front tires onto the bridge and instantly felt it give, sinking slightly. He said to himself, out loud, "Breathe."

He kept going and soon all eight rear tires were on the bridge. He drove forward at five miles an hour. He could hear the bridge creaking and moaning under the weight, but he had expected that. What he hadn't anticipated was how much the truck would affect the pitch. He was going down at a much steeper angle than Derek and the mercs had on foot, the weight of the truck stretching the bridge like a yo-yo on a string. He mopped his brow and kept going.

At the middle of the bridge, he came to a spot where a circular section about five feet in diameter had been repaired. He stopped the truck and got out to inspect it. To his chagrin, the section of bridge had been repaired in a slipshod way. Max could see several layers of plywood under the metal patch that had been laid and riveted to the original metal on both ends. He didn't trust it and could only hope that he had room to go around it.

He got back into the truck and backed up a little bit. He could see Derek and the mercs on the far side, watching him intently. He couldn't see Veronica, because he had no side mirrors, but he was sure that she was doing the same.

He turned the truck to the right and started to ease around the patched section. Driving mostly on one side, rather than in the center, caused the bridge to start swinging, but he didn't panic and didn't rush. Once he was safely around the patch, he aligned the truck back to the center of the bridge and let the swaying settle before he continued. In a couple of extremely long minutes, he pulled up onto the embankment. The crowds on both ends broke into applause.

When he was sure he was on solid bedrock, he pulled the truck to the side, shut it off, and got out, fighting the urge to throw up.

Derek was waiting for him. “So far so good.”

“One down, three to go.”

He gave Derek the truck keys and took the second set in return, then walked back across the bridge. He stopped for a few minutes in the middle to examine the patch more closely. While he was standing there, he felt the wind intensifying, which would not be helpful. As for the patch, he didn’t like the looks of it.

The second truck proved him right. He was maneuvering around the patch but misjudged slightly. He heard metal tearing and wood splintering, and the left front tire dropped a foot and a half into the gap. He knew he had to get it out quickly, because if the hole opened all the way and the tire fell in, the truck would be stuck there forever. Going quickly on this bridge went against every instinct he had, but he hit the accelerator as he shifted gears. The front tire came up and out, and the patch fell away as the four left rear tires were crossing it, leaving a wide-open hole. The rear tires’ combined length was longer than the hole, and he got across okay, but he would need to maneuver the next truck around an open gap.

Derek was silent this time as they switched keys, and all the other mercs averted their eyes. Max figured he was like a pitcher in the middle of throwing a no-hitter, and no one wanted to talk to him or even look at him for fear of jinxing it. As he made his way back across, the wind was really picking up, and the bridge was swinging slightly. On top of that, there was no way to quantify it, but he was certain the middle of the bridge was at least ten feet lower than it had been when he first came across. The weight of the trucks was stretching the cables.

When he reached the embankment, he realized he was shaking, his heart racing. He had to take a few minutes to calm down.

Veronica handed him a canteen of water but didn't speak to him. He drank a long, cool draft, handed it back to her, nodded, and got back behind the wheel.

Getting the third truck across was more difficult than the first two combined. The wind was really up now, gusting down the canyon, and rather than the truck stabilizing the bridge with its weight, it provided a large flat surface for the wind to push against. The bridge was seesawing violently side to side, and Max had to get the truck around the hole while fighting the sway.

To make matters worse, between the weight of the trucks and the wind, the bridge was taking a beating. He could see cables and ropes snapping and coming loose as he drove and knew the whole thing could go at any time. When he finally drove up onto the far embankment he could have wept, but of course he didn't.

They exchanged keys again and he started the walk back. It rained a little bit, but it was a tropical rain, and it was gone by the time he was halfway across, and thank God, it took the wind with it. As he was passing the hole he saw an old Bell Huey helicopter land in the clearing where the fourth truck was waiting.

Derek saw it, too, and his suspicions immediately came up again. He thought about heading over there via the pedestrian bridge, but he didn't want to leave the gold. Instead, he snarled, "Who the fuck is that?"

CHAPTER FIFTY-FIVE

Giuliana and Gustav had been in the air all morning. They had faced rain and some heavy winds, but Gustav turned out to be a damn good pilot, and they made it to Phaya Nok Ravine by early afternoon. As they came over the hill, she could see that three of the trucks were already across, and one was still on this side.

Gustav asked, "Where do you want it?"

She searched, until she spotted a figure crossing the bridge in this direction on foot. It was Max, she would know that white marble anywhere.

"This side, please."

She was unbuckled and out the door before the runners were on the ground. She ran as best she could with her wounded abdomen, straight for the bridge, and she saw the surprise and—she was certain of it—delight on his face when he realized it was her. Not a big leap, since there probably weren't that many nearly six-foot-tall Black women running around this part of the jungle. He started toward her.

On the far side of the ravine, Derek was perplexed. "It's his wife, June. What the hell is she doing here?"

Max took Giuliana in his arms and kissed her, briefly. "You came all the way out here?"

"Of course I did," she answered.

"But why? Are you here to arrest me?"

"What?" She looked at him, perplexed. "No, I came to take you out. I mean, out of here, not—"

"We've established that you're not an assassin."

"I'm off the clock and probably fired. The idea was to rescue you."

He looked at her for a moment, then his eyes softened. "I think you just did."

In her peripheral vision, Giuliana could see a female mercenary, with blond hair and an AK-47, watching them with a lopsided, amused grin on her face.

"Who's this then?" the merc asked.

"This is Giuliana," Max answered. "I haven't had a chance to tell you about her."

"No shit."

"Jules, this is Veronica, one of my closest friends." The two women exchanged nods.

"Max," Giuliana said, "you need to come with me, both of you if you like, but we need to go now."

"What are you talking about?"

"General Ruchuphan is leading an entire army division here, on the north side of the ravine. He wants the gold, and they'll kill you as soon as they have it."

Max and Veronica exchanged a glance, then Max took Giuliana by the shoulders. "Jules, listen to me. You have to get back in the bird and leave, right now."

"Didn't you hear me? He's coming!"

"Please, listen. I love that you came here for me. I love that you cared enough to risk everything. I lo . . ." He almost said it. "But the best way you can help me is to get back on the helo and leave, now."

She searched his eyes, but he wouldn't say anymore.

She said, "I can't lose you before I even have you."

"Then listen to me and go."

He walked her back to the chopper. She was completely lost. "I don't understand."

"You will soon," he said. "I promise." He kissed her again. "Hear this if nothing else. You will see me again. Trust me."

She got into the helo and Max nodded to the pilot, whom he recognized from a few jobs in the region. As he ran back to the truck, Gustav lifted off and started flying back the way they came. They were almost over the hill when Giuliana said, "Wait! Can we hover for a minute?"

Gustav turned the helo, so they were facing back to the ravine, and hovered there, just in time for Giuliana to see the truck drive onto the bridge. It was only ten feet out when there was a low, almost inaudible cracking sound. It seemed to Giuliana that everything went into slow motion as a massive dust cloud billowed out from under the abutment on the near side. Even over the chopper's rotors, she could hear the grinding of metal, a deep, mournful groan followed by a deafening snap. For a moment, the world was frozen.

Then everything snapped back into motion, as the near end of the bridge came loose and fell, dropping into the abyss. She saw the truck, but only for an instant, as it fell out of the dust cloud and plummeted out of sight.

"Take me back! Take me back!"

"No can do. Look."

She looked where he was pointing and saw rebel soldiers pouring out of the trees on the far side. Gustav said, "We're leaving."

He turned the chopper and headed back to Thailand.

CHAPTER FIFTY-SIX

Derek watched Max and Veronica get into the last truck and drive onto the bridge. His mind was already on the next task, which was killing Max. He'd have to get him away from the group, he couldn't shoot another member of their expedition in front of these men or they'd kill him. If possible, he'd—

He heard a noise, like a giant cracking its neck. He saw a dust cloud, then the bridge came loose from the far end and dropped away. He ran closer to the edge and watched the truck fall, violently careening off the carpet-like layer of ferns on the sheer cliff face. Two of the tires were knocked loose and bounced down the side. It seemed to take forever before the mangled truck finally hit the bottom and came to a crashing stop. He could barely see it from up here, but it looked to him like it was upside down, wheels in the air.

He yelled to no one in particular, "What the hell happened?"

Milo was nearby. "It appears the abutment on the far embankment failed and simply broke apart. Of all the possible ways for the bridge to collapse, that was one of the longer odds."

"Is there a way down there?"

"Why?"

"That's twenty-five percent of my gold in that ditch!"

"Actually, you come out ahead. Your share, together with your wife's, was two thirds, eighty-eight million dollars. Now there is less gold overall, but your partner is also dead, so you wind up with the total seventy-five percent that's left, closer to a hundred. You just made twelve million dollars in eight and a half seconds."

"For fuck's sake, who asked you?"

Before Milo could answer, there was a war whoop and over three dozen heavily armed rebels charged from the trees, surrounding them. Derek began shouting orders to the mercenaries, pointing to defensive positions, but they ignored him and simply put their weapons down and raised their hands in the air, giving up without a fight. They were all looking at him, and he understood. They were not going to fight for the man who had shot one of them.

Before he could figure out an exit strategy, the rebels were on them. They gathered the mercenaries together, and Derek was held at gunpoint twelve feet away. He picked up fragments of their conversation, "Just hired hands," "No stake in the gold," "We don't give a fuck who winds up with it." After a short discussion the rebel leader waved a hand, and they let them go. They filed off into the jungle and were gone, just like that. Derek was dragged before the leader, whom he recognized instantly as Chewy Chakri. He struggled against the men holding him.

"The gold is mine, Chakri! I fought for it! I brought it over the mountains and across that bridge! It's mine, goddam it!"

Chakri smiled. "It's mine now."

"Wait," Derek said. "How did you even know about it?"

Chakri grinned. "Your wife told me."

Derek thought he would literally explode. He was bright red with rage and could hear the blood pumping in his head. From behind his red veil he distantly heard a rebel soldier say, "Sir, you're going to want to see this."

Derek was held where he was as Chakri went and looked in the back of the truck. He looked at his soldier, shocked. He went quickly to the other two trucks as his men removed the tarps, his expression growing angrier with each of them. Whatever was wrong, it was wrong with all three trucks. He gestured and Derek was dragged to the back of the truck.

"What are you pulling?" He jammed his gun against Derek's head. "What the fuck is this?"

Derek couldn't speak. Under the tarps, the trucks were loaded with lead bars. There wasn't a single ounce of gold anywhere.

BIG BEAR, CALIFORNIA

THREE WEEKS BEFORE BANGKOK

Max was enjoying the company of the woman Rocket had sent to stay with him, Jules, even if she was three moves away from checkmating him again for the second time today. She had opened with her own variation of the Nakhmanson Gambit but had quickly started improvising. She was one of the most beautiful women he had ever seen, and smelled faintly of almond butter, so maybe he was just distracted, but to be honest, he hadn't expected her to be so creative at chess. He was used to being five moves ahead of every opponent he played, and for the first couple of matches, nearly three weeks ago, he had gone easy on her and she had won.

Then he started giving her his A game, and she still beat him more than half the time.

She said, "You gonna move soon, baby, or should I order in supplies?" He sighed and tipped over his king, then waved at the shelves of board games left by the owners for short-term renters.

"Next time we're playing Candy Land."

"Oh, I'm a bad bitch at Candy Land. I'll be at Lollipop Woods before you get through the Peppermint Forest."

"I don't doubt it." His phone rang. He didn't recognize the number, but most people in his line of work used burners anyway. "Hello?"

A voice said, "Please hold for the president." Max scoffed and hung up.

"Wrong number?"

"Prankster. Some kid fucking around." She was resetting her side of the board, so he did the same, thinking he must be a glutton for punishment. The phone rang again, same number. He poked at the button and held it to his ear. "Look asshole, go bother someone else."

"Starkey? Max Starkey? Is that you?"

He knew the voice but couldn't place it. "Who's asking?"

"It's Vinthu. President Chavarat Vinthu, in Suryaka. Do you remember me?"

Max was more than surprised. "Of course I do. Hold on one second." He covered the mouthpiece and spoke to Jules, who was setting up her pawns and trying not to appear curious. "Can you do me a favor? We're out of beer; would you mind running to the market? There's money in my wallet, next to the car keys, take whatever you need."

She nodded, knowing he was asking for privacy, and was out the door in less than twenty seconds. "Mr. President, how can I be of assistance?"

"I have a big problem. A four-thousand-pound problem, to be exact. I need your help."

He explained everything to Max, about the impending coup, his frozen assets, the gold in the basement, and how the CIA had abandoned him.

"You're the best I've ever worked with," he said. "I need you to do this. I'll pay you ten percent to get the gold out of the country."

"Twenty."

"Fifteen. But time is of the essence. It will take about three weeks to make arrangements for my family and myself to find sanctuary and secure our exit. Can you do it that quickly?"

"For twenty percent I can, Mr. President. Do you mind calling me tomorrow to finalize the details?"

"But you're in? At twenty?"

"I'm in." He hung up and speed-dialed Veronica. Jules came back while they were on the phone, so he went for a walk in the dirty California snow while they talked.

"This is what we've been waiting for. Our chance to fuck Derek in the ass."

"Why is it," Veronica asked, "that when straight men get worked up, they go right for the gay imagery?"

Max just grunted.

They talked for three hours, roughing out the idea, making adjustments and discussing logistics. They knew, without a doubt, that if Derek signed on, he would try to steal the gold, so they needed to slip it away from him while he thought he was making off with it. By the time Vinthu called the next day, they had a solid plan in place.

"To make this work, Mr. President," Max said, "I need you to do a little subterfuge for me. I cannot possibly do this job without the help of Derek Moss, but if I ask him, he won't get near it. I need you to pretend we never spoke, call him as if he's your first call, and hire him, but tell him that you want me on the job, take it or leave it. That way he'll think bringing me in was his move, and that he's in charge."

"If you do that, he'll want to hire the crew."

"That's fine. I'm sure he'll pick the best available people." Which meant Veronica.

"He's a double act, you know. That crazy-ass wife of his."

"Tell him you don't need her, just him. Be adamant, his wife doesn't come."

"Understood." That part hadn't worked out, obviously, and she had come along anyway. Max had hoped to get through this without seeing her, and his shock when she walked into his hotel room in Patpong was genuine.

There was nothing for Max to do now but wait and see how Derek reached out. Would he call him directly or set up some scam to get him to Southeast Asia to recruit him in person? For the first time in months he felt energized, filled with purpose. He didn't lose another chess match the entire weekend.

The first thing Veronica did was put out the word that she was available and looking for a gig. Then she called around so that she'd have her crew ready to assemble when Derek reached out to her. They were confident he would pick her, as she was not only the best operator in the game right now, but she knew the region. Also, Derek would remember the night she helped them escape from Phonthong Prison and would feel comfortable with her. It wasn't hard for her to find a dozen mercenaries willing to help fuck over Derek Moss, he left a trail of enemies everywhere he went.

The next morning she and Olivia dropped Carmen off at O's mother's house in Altadena and boarded a plane to Bangkok. There was a lot of prep to do, and they had a little under three weeks to get it done.

Once on the ground, Olivia secured the trucks they would need to move the gold, two panel trucks with fortified suspension and hidden cargo bays behind false walls, specifically outfitted for smuggling. They were marked as produce vans and the visible part of the bays would be filled with bananas on the day. She also bought a Ford Ranger pickup truck that would be hidden near the bridge at Phaya Nok, for Max and Veronica to make their getaway. Olivia spent two days artificially distressing it to add the appearance of age and rust, but under the hood it was a beast.

Olivia followed in a rental car as Veronica drove the Ford Ranger up to Phaya Nok, where they met a civil engineer Veronica had hired out of Phnom Penh. He spent two days examining the abandoned bridge and declared it safe to drive across but strongly recommended they not try it with anything exceeding twenty thousand pounds. She thanked him, paid him, and sent him home. Olivia was familiar with the trucks they would be using, M809s, and told her that they weighed that much on their own. Veronica called to discuss it with Max, and they decided that they would carry a thousand pounds on each truck, then strip them down before the crossing to get as close to the weight limit as possible.

The last thing Veronica did before she left Phaya Nok was set the explosives. It was a treacherous job, principally because she needed to do it in the dark of night, when the local merchants were asleep in their huts near the pedestrian bridge, a hundred yards away. She had to climb down under the bridge to set the charges along the abutment, a single carabiner the only thing between her and the canyon floor twelve hundred feet below. The charges needed to be precise, big enough to bring it down but small enough for the percussion to pass for the cracking of distressed concrete. Once she set the remote detonators, she climbed back up and she and Olivia returned to Bangkok in the rental car.

There were a few other things to iron out. Max would have to change the route along the way, in case Derek had arranged an ambush somewhere, but he could improvise that. Just when he was beginning to think it wasn't going to happen, Max was called into LA to Rocket's office, where he was given the fake assignment in Bangkok, which was the cover Derek was using to get him to the region.

The actual swapping of the gold on the night was a relatively low-tech affair. In the week before showing up at the palace, the mercs had practiced it two dozen times, until they had it down to an hour and fifty-two minutes. It wasn't going to get any faster than that, especially now that they were down six men. Max was sure that Derek would walk down to the bridge with him that night, but if he had chosen to stay with the gold, they had a contingency plan in place involving heavy sedatives.

When Max and Derek were halfway down the hill, Veronica signaled Olivia, and she and a driver she knew and trusted brought the two produce trucks up the road and around the bend, the second one pulling a winch on a trailer. Veronica and Olivia hadn't seen each other since before the palace, but there was no time for any reunion more than a quick, chaste kiss hello. They went to work immediately, swapping the gold for the lead bars that she brought in the produce vans. With six fewer men they got it done in an hour and fifty-seven minutes, only five minutes over their best rehearsal. Max had promised to keep Derek at the bridge for three hours, so they made it with plenty of time.

Olivia and her driver headed south, the way the caravan had just come. She would dump the winch and make her way east to the border to meet up with Max and Veronica later. It was very unlikely they would encounter any issues; no one was looking to hijack bananas in the middle of a jungle with a million banana trees in it. By the time

Max and Derek walked back up the road from the bridge, the gold was long gone.

When asked about it later, neither Max nor Veronica had any idea where the other two M809s had gone. Wherever they were, it had nothing to do with them.

Once he was on the bridge in the first truck, Max had been genuinely afraid that the civil engineer from Cambodia was a charlatan, and that he wouldn't make it across once, let alone three times. The bridge was creaking and snapping and swaying and generally felt like a death trap. But he had made it, and finally it was time to close the deal.

After Jules showed up and almost sent everything sideways, Max and Veronica got into the last truck. The overnight stay on the hill served another purpose too. If they had driven straight through, they were in danger of arriving too early, but now the timing was perfect, and the afternoon sun was shining directly into Derek's eyes on the other rim of the ravine. He would have to squint, and that combined with ten days of filth on the windshield would provide the cover they needed. Max put the truck in gear and eased out onto the bridge. Veronica handed him a lead bar from the back, which he used to weigh the gas pedal down. Then they both went through the back window, across the bed, and out the back of the truck.

As soon as they reached solid ground, Veronica pressed the detonator and the bridge snapped loose with a cracking sound. They knew everyone's eyes would follow the falling truck, giving them a few seconds of cover to blend into the crowd. They started for the pickup truck, stashed nearby, but stopped when they heard whooping and saw rebels pouring out of the jungle and surrounding Derek. They stayed, hidden by the crowd, long enough to see the rebels let the mercenaries go. They got to enjoy the moment when Derek realized he had been, as Max so eloquently put it, fucked in the ass. Both of them thought the moment was worth all the effort they put in. They stayed a few more minutes, just long enough to see Derek fly.

CHAPTER FIFTY-SEVEN

Derek stared at the lead bars in disbelief. He couldn't comprehend how this was done, but he knew Max Starkey was behind it. He also knew there was no way in hell that Max was in that truck at the bottom of the ravine. He had been very insistent that they come this way and cross this goddam bridge, so the collapse of it had to be part of his plan. He intended to leave Derek here with the lead, thinking he was dead, and go live a life of luxury on Derek's gold. He was sure of one more thing: He would eventually find Starkey and kill him, but first he had to get away from these foul-smelling rebels.

He was on the ground with a rebel's boot on his neck, and Chewy Chakri was shouting questions at him. He knew he could talk his way out of this, he had talked his way out of worse situations before, and if he couldn't, well, there were plenty of guns around, he just had to get his hands on one of them.

He was yanked to his feet and slammed against the side of one of the trucks. Chakri shouted directly into his face.

"Where is it? Where's the gold?"

"Honestly, I have no idea." He was punched in the face, hard, three times.

"Tell me where the gold is!"

"Okay, okay, fine." He nodded at one of the rebels. "It's in that guy's asshole."

He was punched in the kidney this time and tried to double over in pain, but they held him up. He laughed.

"Something's funny?"

"You and I want the same thing, and unless you stop beating on me, neither one of us is going to get it."

"Will you tell me where it is or not?"

"Sure," Derek said. "Let me go and I'll track it down. As soon as I find it, I'll call you."

Chakri glared at him for a few seconds, then jerked his head toward the ravine. Two of his men dragged Derek toward the edge, and when he realized what they were going to do, two wasn't enough. He laid them both out, broke loose, and ran full speed for the jungle. A shot rang out and he felt a searing pain as the bullet went through his thigh. He had been shot many times before, but for some reason this one hurt more. Maybe because he knew it was the last one.

The two men picked him up again, dragged him kicking and screaming to the edge of the ravine, and threw him off.

It took him ten seconds to fall the twelve hundred feet. For the first three he was terrified. For the next five he was angry again, at Max, at Kelly, at himself, at the whole world. For the last two he was distracted by the sound of a massive gunfight erupting above him.

And then he was dead, his broken body splayed out on a pile of lead bars.

Almost at the same moment that his men threw Moss over the edge, Chewy Chakri heard a massive rumble of engines. An entire division of the Suryakan army was coming down the road from the north. They saw the rebels and started shooting, and his men started firing back.

They were vastly outnumbered and pinned against the edge of the ravine, so Chakri did what any rebel leader would do in his situation; he ran.

As most of his men engaged the army, five of them surrounded Chakri and rushed him along behind the trucks, using them as cover. By the time they reached the trees three of them had fallen. As he ran into the jungle, Chakri looked back and saw that the commander of the unit was General Ruchuphan himself.

Ruchuphan sent men after him, but Chakri had been living in this jungle for years now and knew every stone and branch. He would lose them. He had only gone about a hundred yards when the gunfire stopped, meaning that all his men were either dead or had surrendered. He hoped they had fought to the death and not taken the coward's way out.

He easily lost the patrol chasing him, and he and his two remaining men looped around and headed north again. This was not the end. He would rebuild his army, recruiting from the villages in the mountains. He would add them to the fighters that were left behind at camp, and in a matter of weeks he would strike back and rise to glory.

CHAPTER FIFTY-EIGHT

Kelly and Cintha had been walking through the jungle all night. The girl was still clutching her bamboo spear and hadn't said a word, and Kelly hadn't pushed her, letting her decide when to communicate. Kelly navigated by the stars first, and then the rising sun, keeping them moving in a generally southeast direction toward the border. It would take them weeks to get there on foot, but she knew there were roads and at least one highway this way, so with any luck they would find one and be able to flag down a ride. There were scattered villages in the area, too, where they could find a meal. If they didn't get to food soon, they'd have to forage.

They had been walking in silence for so long that she almost jumped when the girl finally spoke. "Why did you come here?"

"Your father hired us to move his gold."

"No," Cintha said. "Why did you come here in the first place? To our country?"

"Oh. Well, it was my job."

"To interfere in our elections?"

"Yes. But I was just following orders."

She knew immediately how lame that sounded, but it was the truth. She tried to make it sound a little better but only made it worse. "I don't make the policy; I just carry it out. The tip of the spear, as they say."

"Did you know what my father was, before you helped put him in power?"

"I don't understand, what was he?"

"You know what I mean," Cintha said. "Don't treat me like a child. Did you know he was such an evil man? That he would kill all those people?"

"Honestly? I had an idea. I didn't know he would be as . . . ruthless as he was, but I knew he would be bad."

"But you did it anyway."

"Yes."

"All that death, all the destruction. My whole family dead. It will take Suryaka years to recover. But it's okay, because you were just following orders."

Kelly didn't answer, after all, what could she say? They walked in silence for a few minutes, until Cintha said, "I'm getting blisters."

"Do you want to stop for a while?"

"No." Her voice got quieter. "That man at the camp was the first person I ever killed."

"I assumed as much," Kelly said. "We can talk about it if you want. I know it's hard."

"It wasn't hard."

"It wasn't?"

"No," Cintha said. "It was easy."

Kelly didn't even see her spin, and the bamboo spear was all the way through her before she realized what was happening. Cintha had scored a direct hit, through her navel and out her back. Cintha's face was inches from her own, and Kelly looked into her angry eyes, shocked, but somehow not surprised.

Cintha pulled the spear out, and Kelly fell to her knees and then onto her back. She looked up at the girl, and as her life drained into the mud, she thought, *This makes perfect sense.*

CHAPTER FIFTY-NINE

They were taking the most direct route they could, southeast toward the border, where Olivia would be waiting with the gold. Veronica had insisted on driving, so Max relaxed in the cab of the Ford Ranger and thought about the last few days.

It had been their intention to leave Derek alive; Veronica and Olivia had insisted on it.

Max ultimately relented, but what they didn't understand was that Max and Derek were inevitable; eventually one of them would kill the other. Now Derek had been thrown to his death by rebels, saving Max the trouble, so he supposed things had a way of working out for the best. He had no idea where Kelly was or what had happened to her. He'd try to find out eventually, but right now all he could think about was getting to Jules.

He fervently hoped she had understood his message, that she absolutely would see him again, but if she hadn't then she was mourning him. If that were the case, she might be so angry to find out that he was still alive that she would never forgive him, but he had to let her know he wasn't dead, to ease that pain at least.

There were a few things he needed to wrap up in Asia before he went back and threw a dart at the map to determine where to open his bar. The mercenaries were splitting 20 percent of the profits, rounded up to twenty-eight million, two million dollars each. It would still be split fourteen ways, with the families of those who died getting their share. That left nearly 80 percent for Max and Veronica to split, giving each of them about fifty-two million.

"What are you going to do with your share?" he asked her.

"First, a college fund for Carm. Then I'm hanging up my spurs and just living."

"No more paid ops?"

"I'm done with this shit. Unless you need me for something."

"Same here."

"And you? What's your first move?"

He shouted, "Look out!" Veronica slammed on the brakes and slid to a stop.

There was a young Suryakan woman standing in the road. She was wearing fatigues and a halter top, her upper body and face caked in mud, and she was holding a four-foot-long bamboo spear with dried blood on it. Max's first thought was that she looked like a heroine from a graphic novel, or something out of a Frank Frazetta painting, minus the freakishly large boobs.

His second thought, he said out loud. "Holy shit. That's Cintha Vinthu."

Veronica scoffed. "No fucking way."

"I'm telling you. Look at the eyes."

Veronica looked at the girl, then let out a whistle. "Jesus. What happened to her?"

"Only one way to find out." He started to get out of the truck, then noticed something else. "Am I crazy," he asked Veronica, "or is she wearing Kelly's boots?"

Cintha found the pedestrian bridge and walked across it while some commotion was going on at another bridge, then started down this road. When he first stopped for her, she thought about killing Max Starkey with her spear too. Instead, she threw it aside and left it on the road. She was tired of all the death, and to be honest, killing Kelly Riggs hadn't given her the satisfaction she hoped it would. She was exhausted from all the blood, the fighting, the hatred.

Plus, she needed the ride.

CHAPTER SIXTY

Giuliana couldn't get a flight out of Bangkok until the next day, so against her better judgment she checked back into the dive hotel in Patpong where she and Max had stayed when they first arrived. She even got the same room, which seemed like a good idea at the time, but which wound up depressing her more. She washed herself in the shower where they first made love, then sat on the bed where they had done it three more times. She had seen the truck fall with her own eyes, yet she simply could not accept that he was dead. She was clinging to a flimsy strand of hope, the last thing he had said to her, that she would definitely see him again and that she should trust him. It wasn't much, but it was all she had.

She couldn't sit there any longer, so she made sure her phone was fully charged, pulled it from the wall, and took a walk. She strolled through the neon canyon of Patpong, watching middle-aged foreign men purchase the flesh of young Thai women. Even that depressing spectacle made her think about Max. What would it be like to grow up as the child of one of these women? She hadn't known him that long, but she believed that he loved her, and he obviously had loved Kelly Riggs intensely. Why didn't he hate them? Why didn't he hate all women, or all men, or all something? How did his childhood spent in a brothel not leave him a basket case?

She went into a club creatively called Thigh Bar and had a drink while she watched a woman smoke a cigarette with her vagina. She could make smoke rings; Giuliana was actually quite impressed.

She had a second drink and stayed for the next act, which involved another girl and some ping-pong balls, and she managed to forget about Max for several seconds at a time. The only problem was, when she did forget him, her own troubles rushed in to take his place.

She had no idea what was waiting for her back at J. Edgar. The promotion she had been so confident about was clearly gone; in light of her recent actions it was far more likely she would be disciplined or even fired along with the hundreds of others caught up in the new administration's purge. All she knew for sure was that she was finished with honey trapping. She had sold herself the lie that it was no different than finding casual hookups on the apps, but there was an emotional toll she couldn't ignore any longer. Besides, if Max were miraculously somehow still alive, she didn't intend to sleep with anyone else again, ever.

Whatever act was coming onstage next involved canaries, and she would rather not know how, so she paid her bill and walked back to the hotel. As she crossed the lobby the front desk clerk called to her, holding out a hotel envelope.

"Miss Abara? I have a message for you."

"Thank you." As she took it, she asked, "Do you know who it's from?"

"They didn't leave a name. Anonymous phone call. Not much of a message though."

Giuliana nodded and walked a few feet away from the desk and tore it open. She read the message, and relief flooded through her. The desk clerk was right, it wasn't much of a message, just two words, but they were enough. It read:

Egress successful.

CHAPTER SIXTY-ONE

LOOSE ENDS

Max still wasn't a hundred percent sure he was going to kill General Vong until he found him. He wasn't certain that it would get the Ghosts off his back after seven years anyway, but he wanted to be able to travel freely without getting shot at every time he set foot in Asia. When he did find him, in the back room of a brothel outside of Ban Houayxay with two eight-year-old boys, he decided he needed killing even if it didn't fix his Ghost problem. He shot him in front of the kids, figuring they were so traumatized already by what Vong was doing to them that he couldn't make it much worse. Hell, maybe seeing him die would actually help them.

He considered killing Iron Sam for setting him up with the Ghosts, but he figured the old man deserved to make a few extra baht where he could.

He flew back to LA to deal with his next loose end, Rocket. He had set Max up, sent him on a fool's errand to Bangkok when for all he knew Max was going there to be executed.

"You sent me to my death without a second thought. For what? Eighty grand?"

"Max, wait," Rocket said. "We can talk about this."

They never did.

His next stop was Dallas, and the brothel he grew up in. His mother, Diane, was thrilled to see him, but he had been away awhile and none of the girls that had been there during his childhood were still around. A couple had married clients, and a handful had died, but most of them had just left the life at some point when it ground them down. He and Diane sat in the bar, which looked like something out of an old Western with its red velvet and gold tassels, and Max told her the story of the last few weeks. She laughed uproariously at most of it and nodded sympathetically when he told her he had confirmed that Kelly died in the jungle.

"The bottom line is, Mom, I can take care of you now, and for the rest of your life. You can leave here and never look back."

"Maxie, I don't want to leave."

"Why not?"

"The girls depend on me. I take care of them. I keep the house drug free; I bring a doctor in once a week. I know which customers are trouble and which girls can handle them. They'd be lost without me; I watch over them."

"Like a mother."

"Well, yes." Diane said. "I can't just walk away."

Max didn't understand exactly, but he accepted it, so instead of taking her away he bought the place and signed the deed over to her, making her the sole proprietor of the best not-so-little whorehouse in Texas.

There was only one thing left to do, the most important thing of all. He took a rideshare to Love Field and bought a first-class ticket to Washington, DC.

CHAPTER SIXTY-TWO

After Max Starkey and the mercenary, Veronica, dropped her off at the hospital, Cintha Vinthu watched them drive away before going in to get patched up. Her leg was in worse shape than she had thought, and she would walk with a limp for the rest of her life. But she wouldn't let it slow her down. Her nation was on the cusp of an army-led coup, and as bad a president as her father had been, she knew that a military dictatorship would be far worse.

So when she was called to testify about the death of her father, she told it to the court exactly how she remembered it. General Ruchuphan had arrived at the palace with a battalion of soldiers, then murdered her father and staged it to look like a suicide, so he could seize power.

She testified to how her mother had escaped into the jungle with her and her brothers, where the three of them were killed by Ruchuphan's men, and how she eluded the soldiers only to be stalked for several days by a man-eating tiger. The entire nation listened, rapt, as she told the story of how she killed the tiger, backed up by eyewitness accounts from captured rebel soldiers who had actually seen her do it. Her testimony was widely believed to be the major reason that the coup was stopped in its tracks. Within two weeks of the inquest General Ruchuphan was executed, and his family was billed for the bullet.

Cintha started a podcast, a TikTok, and an Instagram account, all under the banner Girl Who Killed the Tiger. She discussed and exposed the hypocrisy of her father, the country's sham constitution, and the interference in her country's politics, and its citizens' lives, by the United States, and more specifically, the CIA. She inspired teens and young adults from all walks of life, who became devoted to both her content, and the content of her character. In turn, they told their parents about her, and Cintha coalesced them into a political movement under the GWKT banner.

Over the years the meaning of the Tiger changed, as her legend grew. On the legend side, the gun eventually left the story completely, leaving only the tale of a young girl killing a five-hundred-pound, ten-foot-long rabid beast with a bamboo stick. On the political side, "The Tiger" began to refer to the status quo, the political elite that kept the average person trampled underfoot. "Killing the Tiger" became, for Suryakans, what Americans used to call "Putting it to the Man," any action that pitted the seemingly helpless against the rich and powerful, especially if it resulted in victory.

In Cintha Vinthu's long, happy life, she was the driving force behind real change for the better in Suryaka. She remained a virgin until her marriage, at the age of thirty-two, after she had accomplished many other things.

CHAPTER SIXTY-THREE

Veronica and Olivia bought a house in the country, an hour outside of Manhattan, that had belonged to a famous magician in the 1930s and was variously believed to be haunted, cursed, or harboring a secret speakeasy that had been walled up for ninety years. Veronica never found evidence of any of them. She buried her weapons in the basement and poured concrete over them, which she had seen in a movie and thought was pretty cool. That way she could get to them again if she needed to, but not easily. She devoted herself to her family, caring for Carmen, being a good wife to Olivia, and taking care of the house. She even made cookies for the PTA bake sale.

Her new lifestyle lasted six weeks before she was ready to shoot herself out of boredom. Olivia, on the other hand, didn't miss her transpo work at all and thrived as a stay-at-home mom, so she took over, her only nod to her former life being that she did all the mechanical work on their cars, and most of their friends' cars too.

Veronica took a job for a Blackwater-type company, where she signed an NDA and trained private soldiers for them to deploy for the fieldwork she used to do. The job fit her like a glove. She could shoot guns and throw people around on mats all day, and be home in time for dinner, bath, story and bedtime for Carmen, and still have enough energy left to take Olivia to bed and remind them both why life was worth living. She didn't miss the field at all, sticking to her vow not to go back unless Max needed her.

That call came sooner than she expected.

CHAPTER SIXTY-FOUR

Chewy Chakri was captured a few months later by a division of the provisional army, his numbers having dwindled after the events at Phaya Nok Ravine to a few dozen scrawny fighters, half mad with hunger. He was given what was, under the circumstances, a surprisingly fair trial for multiple murders and sedition, and was sentenced to life in prison.

When reforms finally came to the country six years later, he was reclassified as a political prisoner and set free. He went back to his given name, Charles, and took a job in a shoe factory, doing the stitching work on Nike Dunk Lows. Every once in a while, he would catch a co-worker looking at him, slightly befuddled, as if trying to remember if he had met him on the street somewhere.

He returned to the news briefly a few years later, when he was found beaten to death in an alley. No one was ever arrested for his murder, but it happened shortly after a number of young men from a village in the north were hired on at the shoe factory.

That same year the first free elections for the office of president of Suryaka were held. Several people ran, including a general, a well-known journalist, and a visibly corrupt city councilman. Together they only managed 12 percent of the vote, losing in a landslide to a twenty-four-year-old woman with a political pedigree that could have hurt her but which she turned to her advantage, a head full of progressive ideas, and who referred to herself in her election materials as the Girl Who Killed the Tiger.

CHAPTER SIXTY-FIVE

THREE WEEKS AFTER PHAYA NOK RAVINE

To her surprise, Giuliana was not fired and the discipline she was expecting never came. She wasn't sure why exactly, but she wasn't complaining. On the day she got back to the States she was called in to AD Lin's office, only to find Deputy Director June Martinson there as well. After they reminded her of the three dozen ways she had broken protocol and international law, and expecting to be ripped a new asshole, she was surprised when they asked her what she saw as her future in the bureau. She had talked about a lot of different options, but the one thing she was adamant about was that she was done with honey trapping. In the heat of the moment she may have used the phrase, "No more fucking for my country."

She knew she had gone rogue over there, but she also knew that before she did, she had given them intel they never would have had otherwise. Maybe the two washed each other out. Or maybe they were afraid that if they fired her, she would go public with the whole honey trap thing, which she never would have done. Whatever the reason, three weeks later she was at a ceremony, receiving a promotion.

As she left the ceremony that night, she saw that the Arlington Cinema 'N' Drafthouse was showing a restored print of Monty Python's *Life of Brian*. It was her second favorite Python, and she almost never got to see it on the big screen, so she went.

Max found her there in the dark. He simply walked in and sat down beside her after the lights went out and kissed her. They clung to one another, holding each other in a tight embrace through the entire previews and the opening credits, without a word. When she trusted herself to speak without crying, she said, "I knew you weren't dead."

"It took me thirty-five years to find you," he said. "You won't get rid of me that easily."

"I got your message. How did you know I'd be back at that awful hotel?"

"I didn't. I sent the same message to basically every hotel in Bangkok."

She kissed him again, a deep, sensual kiss, lips and tongues and salty tears. When they broke the kiss he whispered, "So who's this Brian guy and why is his life so damned interesting?"

"Just watch," she said, "you'll like it."

They settled back but held onto each other, their hands clasped as if each of them was afraid that if they let go, the other would float away. They shared her popcorn and her mixed blue and red Icee and got lost in the movie.

He laughed his ass off.

ACKNOWLEDGMENTS

I owe a huge debt of gratitude to my editor, Keith Wallman. I've been earning a living as a writer for forty years, but this is a lot different than writing for the screen, and without his guidance, I wouldn't have made it. The same goes for my agent, Michael Signorelli, who wouldn't take no for an answer, and everyone at Aevitas Creative Management.

Thanks to my friend LeVar Burton, who was the first reader of this novel and who encouraged me to develop my voice. LeVar, your love and friendship has gotten me through a lot of tough times.

Thanks to Andrew W. Marlowe, a writer whose talent I can only aspire to, for saying to me over donuts one day at the Original Farmer's Market on Fairfax and Third, "You should be a novelist."

Thanks to my Hollywood team, from Sugar23—Michael Sugar, Josh Kesselman, Katrina Escudero—my lawyer Don Steele; and all the folks at United Talent Agency—Keya Khayatian, Alex Rincon, Becca Cimini, Mickey Berman, and Abby Glusker. In a business that worships youth, you have stuck with this industry vet, which says more about you than it does about me.

I especially want to thank my children, Will, Joe, Vlad, and Orion, whom I love with all my heart even when they don't want me to, and my mother, Gloria, who always encouraged my storytelling.

And last but not least, my wife, Anya, my muse and my inspiration (they are not the same thing), who loves me in spite of everything and who looks at me every morning around 10:00 A.M., glances at the clock, and says, "Get typing, man."

ABOUT THE AUTHOR

Gregory Poirier is an acclaimed screenwriter, director, and producer whose work spans film and television. His credits include *National Treasure: Book of Secrets, Knox Goes Away,* and *Rosewood.* A graduate of the USC School of Theater and the UCLA master's program in screenwriting, he brings a sharp, cinematic eye to fiction. *A Thousand Cuts* is his debut novel. He lives in Los Angeles.